Necessary Fictions

Winner of the
Drue Heinz Literature Prize 1998

Necessary Fictions

Barbara Croft

University of Pittsburgh Press

Published by the University of Pittsburgh Press, Pittsburgh, Pa. 15261
Copyright © 1998, University of Pittsburgh Press
Manufactured in the United States of America
Printed on acid-free paper
10 9 8 7 6 5 4 3 2 1

This book was written, in part, with the support of an Artists Fellowship
Award in 1996 from the Illinois Arts Council. "Bonaparte" first appeared in
Sou'wester in the fall of 1993. Portions of this book were first published in a
short story, "Someday House," published in an earlier collection called *Pri-
mary Colors and Other Stories,* published in 1991 by New Rivers Press.

Library of Congress Cataloging-in-Publication Data will be found
at the end of this book.

A CIP catalog record for this book is available from the British Library.

Contents

Part One

The Woman in the Headlights

In dreams, the headlights make two narrow tunnels through the darkness. The woman appears on the right. The dun-colored grocery bag she carries shields her face, so that all that Chapin sees is a fringe of curly white hair and a white-gloved hand. He lifts his foot to apply the brakes, but something prevents him. He struggles and presses backward and feels the prickle of nylon upholstery on his neck. She starts to cross, and there is that moment that Chapin can't get past.

Then the bag flies upward in slow motion, cartwheels, and spills over the hood, dumping a shower of pickle jars and paper towels and Jell-O pudding boxes. There is no sound while this happens. There is no color, except the pearly pale green of a cabbage, tumbling slowly toward the windshield, casting its shadow over the dashboard, striking noiselessly.

Chapin awakes. The sheets are tangled around his ankles. Marilyn stirs but seems to know what has happened. It is the same dream, and not a dream. She reaches over and rubs his shoulder automatically.

Chapin gets up and walks down the hall to the kitchen. Sunlight is pouring in. He starts the coffee, feeds the cat, brings the paper in. The sea is brilliant. The light makes Chapin dizzy, and only opening the patio doors to the chilly, copper taste of the air clears his head. He goes out on the deck and down the wooden steps to the beach.

It happened two years ago, during a guest semester at Grinnell College. Someone had loaned him a battered white Toyota. He drove to Iowa City; he did that often. The woman must have been deaf, senile, something. The coroner said that she never knew what hit her. The verdict was that Chapin had not been at fault. The woman was eighty-one, had a history of erratic behavior, one of those reclusive types that lives in a crumbling house with a zillion cats. Chapin had, for once, not been drinking.

He stops at the little coffee shop on the beach. The girl behind the counter is wearing cut-off jeans that barely cover her ass and the sort of tight knit top they call a "sports bra." She is lean and tan. Her hair is, of course, blond. And when she hands Chapin the coffee cup, she lets her fingertips slide over his so lightly that he's not completely sure he feels anything. A faint disturbance of air, perhaps, that's all.

"Have a good one."

Chapin was not invited back to Grinnell. The department chair denied there was any connection. "Fresh faces," he said, "new points of view." And maybe, in fact, there wasn't any connection. Maybe they liked his work. Chapin remembers standing in the flat wash of late afternoon sunlight, he and the chair, on the walkway to Old Main. The chair's voice was like the hum of insects. Staring down, Chapin saw the bricks of the sidewalk begin to separate. They lifted and floated apart, but very slowly, the way dye spreads in water, the way clouds move.

❦

Two children are playing on the beach. A golden retriever chases between them. They are six or seven, a boy and a girl. The sunlight striking the reds and blues of their clothing is almost painful against the pale sand.

His first impulse had been to just keep going. Independent of his will, his right foot pressed down hard. The pedal went clear to the floor, and the car surged forward. Then, again of its own will, his foot jumped off the gas and hit the brake. The car swung to the left. Chapin remembers revolving on the wet pavement, the car spinning slowly like a tired carnival ride. When it stopped he was facing the way he had come.

❦

"It was two years ago," Chapin told his therapist. Seeing her was Marilyn's idea.

"And?"

Chapin bowed his head slightly toward her, raised his eyebrows. This was back in New York, three months ago.

"Have you been able to put it behind you?" she said.

Chapin surveyed the cluttered landscape of her desk: pictures of children—a boy and a girl—in various poses, in ornate frames, "Daddy" leaning into some of the shots; papers, folders, desktop toys, the kind of thing you give a professional person in order to show you are not intimidated. Underneath the gild of our educations, these things insisted, aren't we all just simply human beings?

"It's not really the kind of thing you 'put behind you,'" Chapin said dryly.

"Still having the dreams?"

"Dream. Yes."

She glanced at her watch, pulled a pad of paper from a desk drawer. "I'm going to give you something to help you sleep."

She scribbled quickly, folded the paper, and handed it over.

Chapin stood, extending his hand.

"The directions will be on the bottle."

He nodded.

"Take them," she said, looking into his eyes with professional concern. "Promise me?"

He nodded again.

He walked out, closing the door on the tasteful mauve carpet, the well-groomed plants. Smiling at the receptionist, Chapin crumpled the prescription in his pocket.

༄

"Have a good walk?"

Chapin nods.

Marilyn is puttering with petunias in a cedar windowbox. Dirt streaks her long, freckled forearms. "Have Kit and Harry opened up their place?"

Chapin appraises her bones. Her lankiness delights him, the functionality of her frame. "I didn't notice," he says.

She smiles, for no reason. Why does she do that?

Chapin has decided to leave his wife, or, better yet, to make his wife leave him. It's too much trouble now, keeping it up. The daily exercise of marriage exhausts him, the effort of slogging through the little things: shopping and holidays, laundry, and brief and boring vacations to all the predictable places; her family and his family and their mutual friends. And, he thinks, any kind of change . . .

"I'm driving into town later," she says. "Want to come along?"

He shakes his head.

"You could drive."

He says nothing.

"You know, you should get back to it," she says. "Start driving again, let go of the past."

"Why?"

"Oh, David." She tilts her head to the left. "Come with me."

"I just don't want to," he says.

⁜

The moment she goes, he feels a sense of relief. Not happiness, but the freedom to be depressed. He feels almost lighthearted. He changes into swim trunks, selects a paperback book he's been meaning to read, finds a beach chair on the deck, and goes down to the sand.

The sea is a flat gray-blue. No breakers today. The waves uncurl in creamy ruffles and pull back with a sigh. Other than the scuff marks left by the children, there is not a footprint anywhere, not yet.

How to do it. Quickly. How to make it easy and all right. She has this loyalty thing, and so domestic. A good soldier, Marilyn. He doesn't want to hurt her.

When they met, she was seventeen. He was two years older. It seems impossible to ever have been that young. His parents and her parents belonged to the same club. They met at the pool. He remembers showing off, pulling funny stunts on the low board; he almost feels it physically: the cannonball, the fake fall, his arms and legs cocked at odd angles, dropping through sunlight, falling, falling; then the cold explosion of the water. In the silence he almost hears her laughter.

The girl from the coffee shop walks by, smiles at him. He gets the feeling she does this to every man. It amuses her to turn them on, gives her a sense of power. Chapin on the beach, the grizzled hair on his sagging chest, the blue-veined legs, the twisted toes with their horny, yellow nails, is no longer the man young women yearn for. He knows this. He feels satirized.

She sets up near him, makes a show of spreading her yellow towel, bending at the waist to give him ideas. Then the meditation: standing, left knee bent. She must have seen this on a postcard somewhere. Her left hand fanned on her left hipbone, she puts the right demurely to her brow, shades her eyes, and looks out on the sea, pensive. Ah, my dear, Chapin thinks. Such an amateur.

Chapin opens his book and tries the first paragraph. Individual words make sense, but not the whole thing. He tries it again. He reads the first two pages. Nothing grabs him. He flips to the middle and reads a passage or two, goes back and starts at the beginning. Three pages in, he is still not connecting. He turns to the back cover and finds out what the book is about.

"Good?"

Chapin looks up.

The girl nods toward the book.

"Not very."

"Those bestsellers are always a disappointment."

Like she would know, Chapin thinks. On the other hand, . . .

An airplane goes over, a prop plane, pulling a gaudy banner. The drone of the engine sounds like a giant insect. They ought to ban those things, Chapin thinks. An Airedale trots by, yards ahead of his owner. No leash, Chapin notes. And the rule is, always has been, all dogs must be leashed.

"Would you like to get a drink?" This comes out so predictably Chapin would have felt negligent not to have said it. Of course, it was inevitable. So much is.

She smiles. "Love to."

She has that kind of downturned smile that Marilyn always makes fun of, the kind that says, Ain't I cute? Well, why not? She is.

They walk to The Cove, an ersatz pirates' lair, and order daiquiris, which, Chapin thinks, is just about perfect.

❦

"You had an affair."
"I had a fling." He told Marilyn right away.
"With a woman who drinks daiquiris." Marilyn is a scotch drinker. Glenfiddich, no ice. "Were these banana daiquiris?" she says.
Chapin says nothing.
"I'm more hurt than angry. You know that." She lights a cigarette. "Now you've got me smoking again," she says.
The hard part is that it would be so easy. Just the one word—"Sorry."—would probably do it. Marilyn loves him. As though he were worth it. Amazing.

❦

Chapin sees the girl again, more daiquiris, and, yes, as a matter of fact, they are banana. She is a comfort, someone that he can't hurt. Ironically, the tacky nautical setting of The Cove, all fishing nets and lobster traps, the overripe appearance of the girl, make the thing look a little like cartoon lust: an aging intellectual with a faithful, classy wife making a fool of himself with a nubile gum-popper half his age. He can imagine his therapist shaking her head.
But with such insight.

❦

Hurricane lamps on the glass-top table, white linen, a small crystal bowl full of unassuming, pastel flowers. The table is set by the patio doors, which are closed against the wind. Dusk. The glass reflects them at their dinner—ghost marrieds, keeping it under control.
"'Through a glass darkly,'" Chapin says, nodding toward the glass doors in which an echoing Chapin is nodding back. "I feel watched."
"I'll open them," Marilyn says
"No, don't."
Chapin's wife is an excellent cook. She does simple things, but in

such a way that the essence of the dish—in this case, chicken simmered in a light wine and tarragon sauce—presents itself. Chapin eats quietly, slowly, savoring a glass of chilled Chablis.

"Why don't you say something?" she says.

"Me?"

She looks around the room pointedly. "Do you see anyone else?"

Chapin nods discreetly toward the patio doors. "Mon frère." Marilyn smiles.

"It wouldn't take much," she says, "to save it."

"I know."

Sand drifts across the patio floor. The darkness deepens. Chapin puts down his fork and stares out to sea.

⁕

Once you have killed, it is easy to kill again. Crossed the line, something like that.

But how?

He and the bimbo discovered in bed? Tacky. Chapin rejects it. Suicide attempt? Too predictable. The silent treatment takes too long, and uncontrollable lapses into happiness intrude, set you back for months. Something quicker.

Marilyn is sleeping in a canvas deck chair, an old *New Yorker* open in her lap. The sun bleaches her out. She seems transparent, no more substantial than her magazine. She has pushed her glasses up on her forehead, and Chapin watches her eyes. REM beneath the eyelids. Does she dream? Her hair is down. Chapin lifts a lock and tickles her ear. She tosses her head like a colt but doesn't wake. He slicks it into a thin red strand and holds it under her nose—a Fu Manchu, drooping, comic, Yosemite Sam.

Which came first, the chicken or the egg? Chapin makes a low, cluck-clucking sound. The fact is, he is not a very good writer. Or, maybe he is, and his style is just not in fashion. In an age of memoirs, Chapin avoids first person, strives for a clean narrative line, shaped by character. Character is the heart of fiction, Chapin tells—used to tell—his students. Plot is just revelation. But which came first?

Her hair is a paintbrush. He trails it down her neck, dusts the hollow at the base of her throat. She stretches as though responding to a caress, and Chapin notes how fine her hair is, how the color reminds him of strawberry jam. The midday sunlight ignites it, and just as he is about to kiss her, Marilyn awakes and smiles at him.

⁘

Chapin's wife believes he is suicidal. No, he just wants his life to fit. The mismatch of their spirits causes her pain. So, this is a love story after all.

"I called for reservations," she says.

She is dressed for dinner in beige silk and stands before the hallway mirror, primping. Chapin watches. Thinking, thinking, he cannot find a way out. Guilt would be easy, but Chapin, in fact, is not guilty. So much for a ritualized release.

"Want to drive?"

Chapin shakes his head.

"Do you good."

How can he tell her he doesn't want good done?

She tilts her head, fastening an earring. Light falls on the delicate curve of her neck, a simple thing that almost breaks his heart.

"There won't be any traffic," she says.

"I don't know."

She puts her arms around his waist. "Do it for me," she says.

They take the dark blue Crown Victoria, purchased with money from Marilyn's father's estate. It's four years old, but looks brand new, and Chapin delights in the feel of the wheel in his hand, the way the engine responds to the slightest pressure on the gas. They take the narrow two-lane road to the restaurant, the one that winds southwest through the forest preserve. The night is damp, the road like satin; the smell of the pine trees hits them like a jolt of pure oxygen.

"I'm glad to see you doing this," she says.

Chapin doesn't take his eyes from the road. "Like riding a bicycle," he says. "I thought I'd forgotten."

"Feels all right?"

Chapin nods.

Marilyn settles back and closes her eyes. "Things are getting better," she says. "I know it."

Chapin's eyes are riveted on the road. He senses the depth of darkness to his left but dares not look into it.

"Were you working this morning?" Marilyn says.

"Sort of. Looking over some old starts."

"That's great."

"What's so great about it?"

She smiles. It's an indulgent smile. Chapin hates the triumph he sees in her face. Doesn't she know that the question is still open? The ancient, cosmic question of chicken and egg. Was Chapin's character the causal egg, the "accident" a revelation of sorts? In that case, the sour downward spiral that brought him here was, in classical terms, inevitable.

"What about the novel?"

"I've got pieces," Chapin says. "Some of them pretty good, but . . ."

On the other hand: wasn't he just like everyone else until then? Promising, compromised, flawed. In that case, killing an old woman, lugging pudding boxes back to her flat, was impersonal, circumstantial, truly an accident, and in that case, . . .

"So?"

"I can't sort it out, I guess."

Unjust.

"Not true," Marilyn says. "You 'sorted out' that magazine piece in—what was it?—three days?"

"How I spent my summer vacation."

"You made some very clever observations."

"Dreck," he says.

"Why do you insist . . ."

"What?"

Marilyn says nothing.

"You think everything can be fixed," he says.

"If you want it fixed, yes, I do."

The road has modulated into a series of tricky curves, poorly banked so that Chapin has to fight the wheel for control. They seem to come up faster than he expects.

"Slow down," she says.

The woods close in. Only six o'clock, and yet a smoky blue-green darkness hovers around them.

"I'm thinking omelet," Chapin says.

The curves get tighter. They're like a puzzle with no clues. You have to guess the way the road wants to go.

Marilyn shifts in her seat. "Want me to drive?"

Chapin feels he is getting the hang of it. The trick is to accelerate through the curves.

"There's a great one-liner," Chapin says. "Groucho Marx, I think."

"Watch the road."

"'She criticized my apartment, so I knocked her flat.'"

"Let me drive." Marilyn says. "Really."

"Get it? 'Knocked her flat.'"

"Oh, for God's sake, David, let it go."

Chapin rounds a corner, and the landscape opens out. The pine trees fall away on either side, and the road runs straight, perhaps forever, toward the sun. Chapin is lost in the brilliance. It is finally too much. Chapin throws his hands up, lets go of the wheel.

Suddenly the windshield is spattered with shadows. Someone screams as the car jolts down an embankment, through a tangle of weeds. The engine quits. The wheels sink in mud, and the car stops.

Chapin is out and, oddly gleeful, circles the car, dancing. The crash has started a scatter of birds that whispers up from the grass. They lift and fan out across the sky, released.

Marilyn is still facing forward, but when Chapin arrives at the passenger window, she turns. And, finally, the look on her face is one he has never seen before.

"Are you all right?" she says.

Chapin leans in close and whispers: "You said, 'Let go.'"

❧

Marilyn's car is a practical white Ford Escort. It stands at the gate with the doors open. A small blue train case and a matching Pullman lay on the back seat.

"Well, that's everything," she says.

He says nothing.

"Unless . . ."

Chapin can't meet her eyes, won't meet her eyes. He has to hold out just a little bit longer.

"I hadn't realized," she says. "I'm sorry."

Seconds pass. Chapin, half-turned away from her, his hands in his pockets, feels her holding her breath. There is a perfectly round bruise over her right eyebrow, like a shadow, oddly beautiful. Chapin feels her shift her weight and pretends to notice something on the horizon. Of course, there is nothing there, but it kills any impulse she might have had to make some sort of gesture, to reach out and touch him.

"We don't have to do this," she says.

He turns. He faces her. He looks her in the eye and says, as though in casual conversation, "Do what?"

❧

"So. Things are improving."

The therapist has cut her hair. She looks younger, happier somehow. Chapin wants to support her in the illusion that he has been "helped."

"Definitely."

"I'm so glad."

They stare at one another. Does she like daiquiris?

"I know you haven't been taking your medication." There is no accusation in her voice. "Any particular reason?" she says.

Chapin shrugs. There are a thousand reasons. And, there is, finally, no reason at all.

"I killed someone."

He thinks she may want to argue about the verb. Usually she corrects him: "I was responsible for someone's death." But this time she merely nods her head. "An old woman, you told me."

"Her, too."

❧

The beach house is empty, filled with Marilyn's things. Chapin can barely endure it. Daiquiri is still available. She telephones now, now that Chapin's alone, and one day he invites her over, a first. She arrives with all the eagerness of a college girl out on a blind date and carries a grocery bag with a loaf of French bread and a stalk of celery sticking out of the top.

"I thought we'd cook."

"Fine."

She stands there. "So? Where's the kitchen?"

Chapin shakes his head like a man awaking from a long, convoluted dream. "Sorry. It's this way."

He leads her back through the narrow hallway, takes the bag from her hands, and puts it on the countertop.

"Drink?" he says.

"Sure."

He opens the freezer for ice, fills two glasses.

"Scotch?" she says, already resisting.

"Just try it."

"I don't know."

She takes a sip and wrinkles her nose. "Ugh," she says. "It's bitter."

"Yes, a little. You get used to it."

Bonaparte

The death mask of Napoleon Bonaparte was nearly lost forever, cast into the trashman's cart around the turn of the century by some tidy bureaucrat. It was retrieved only by chance when someone noticed, amid the papers and rags and broken bottles, that delicate bronze face floating.

But that's history. What attracted my mother when we saw it six years ago in New Orleans was the way the head was tilted back, the lips parted, different but the same, she said, as the head of John the Baptist at the Hirschhorn. An "almost sexual ecstasy" is how she liked to describe it, even to me. My mother does not shy from explicit statement. The skull is fine and oddly fragile. "This man was no soldier," my mother said. I saw it, too. That wantonness. A sly knowing seeps out beneath the eyelids. Sunk in luxury, the mask sighs.

My mother should know, for she herself is an artifact, although for a while she considered herself an artist. To prove the point, she left my father when I was twelve years old and dragged me with her down to New Orleans, where, she said, a woman could be free.

She rented a seedy upstairs flat in the quarter and bought a dozen tubes of oil and an easel, a few yards of rough, cream-colored canvas. Of course, we were cramped in those two tiny rooms after the spaciousness of our house in Chicago, but it was nothing, my mother said, compared to how our souls had been cramped up north. Now, certainly, in the warmth of New Orleans, something would emerge. Now that she was free—she trilled the word in the back of her throat—art would flow from her like a song from a bird.

Which is not exactly what happened. Instead, she met Mr. Conroy, a silver-gray kind of man who owned a trucking company—I think it was trucking. He took her around to the galleries; he had some connections, power, like my father. He tried to make her into something and, in an odd way, I suppose, he succeeded.

My mother was an art major at the University of Iowa and had advanced to the spring term of her sophomore year when she met my father, a windy young man from Chicago. Of course, at the time, she didn't think of him as windy, and domineering, which he is. She fell in love with him.

He persuaded her to drop art and major in business instead, a field that would mesh more neatly with his own plans for law. My mother's business career, he told her, would help the team get started—he referred to them as a team. They could gain some yardage if my mother ran interference. She could always pick up art again later on, he said, when he was making two hundred thousand dollars a year.

It is, I suppose, some sort of testimony to my mother's tragic faith in men that she accepted this plan. She did graduate in business and worked for several years as an administrative assistant in order to help the team, and my father did go on to law school. But it was a long time before he was making two hundred thousand dollars a year. In fact, he was making considerably less than that when my mother and I left him. She was, by that time, well into her thirties, aging fast, and her soul had been badly damaged. I think she knew, even while she was planning her escape, that it was too late for any kind of real change. Saddled with me—an accident, I understand—and without money, she had very little chance of redeeming her life.

"This is crazy," my father said. I remember the scene particularly well because my mother was giving herself a facial, wearing a white mask of some sort of face cream that hardened as it dried and, in the process, supposedly pulled all the impurities from the skin. Her eyes seemed unnaturally dark and secretive in contrast, but so alive. They glittered with a fierce will that thrilled me and must have alarmed my father.

She was packing a pale blue suitcase, rolling up my jeans and T-shirts navy style to save space and taking an eccentric mix of jeans and party clothes from her own wardrobe—clothing for extremes.

"Where do you think you're going?" my father said.

My mother didn't bother to answer him. Perhaps she didn't know.

At Union Station we got on board "The City of New Orleans" for no better reason than that it left at 6:25, and it happened to be 6:25, and it was a bleak and hopeless November Tuesday night in Chicago, and my mother knew the Arlo Guthrie song.

꧁꧂

"The thing I can't understand," my mother said, "is how they didn't see it." We were strolling through the Louisiana State Museum in New Orleans—or we seemed to be strolling—and a gauzy light was floating through the windows. In fact, we were moving deliberately if slowly toward the death mask of Napoleon Bonaparte.

"It's unmistakable," my mother said.

She brought her face so close to the glass case that her dark red hair and huge round eyes, reflected, superimposed themselves on the mask. A museum guard, alarmed, started toward us. "How could they not see it?" my mother said.

My mother found it literally incredible that even a bureaucrat would not notice the fragile hallmark of art on the Bonaparte death mask, but I told her things of value are thrown away every day. My friend, Stephanie, found a silver ring in the ladies room at the Pizza Hut, and Jeffrey Hample found a twenty-dollar bill in the weeds of a vacant lot. My mother then was deliberate and thoughtful and did not understand the relentless randomness of life. Until she met Mr. Conroy she believed that beauty was obvious and true and that one had only to look in order to see it.

In her own work, I'm sorry to say, beauty was not obvious, and I looked as hard as I could to try to find it. Influenced by Georgia O'Keeffe, my mother attempted a series of large, vibrant canvases filled with huge hot-colored flowers, opening into what in O'Keeffe is a shameless, natural sexuality, but was, in my mother's work, a kind of naive obscenity, which is to say, a vulnerability.

"I think they're just wonderful," Mr. Conroy said. "Very promising, indeed." You could tell he didn't mean a word he said.

Mr. Conroy, incidentally, predictably, could not see anything special in the mask of Bonaparte.

"It must be very valuable," he said.

When she insisted on the mystery in that face, Mr. Conroy told my mother a number of stories about the man he called "the real Napoleon Bonaparte," instructing her in the details of his career. He showed her pictures, notably the one in which Napoleon seizes the crown from the hands of the pope. He then went on to explain physiology, intending by this two-pronged lecture to convince her that the delicacy, the art she saw in Bonaparte's face was merely an illusion brought on by death.

"The muscles relax," Mr. Conroy said. "What you think you see is simply that slackening of tone. First and foremost," Mr. Conroy concluded, "the man was a soldier."

One very crisp day in March, Mr. Conroy took my mother and me to brunch at The Court of Two Sisters and, during coffee, presented her with a small velvet box. Of course, it was a diamond, and, of course, it was large, well over two carats.

"Let me think about it," my mother said. "I feel a bit rushed."

Mr. Conroy took the ring from the box and held it up to the light, rotating it slowly so that color flashed from the stone. "If I let you think," he told her, "there's a chance that you'll say no. And, like your friend Napoleon, I leave nothing to chance."

He slipped the ring on her finger. "There," he said, smiling. "I've conquered you."

My mother did her makeup seated at a low antique vanity with a triptych mirror that reflected her head and shoulders from three angles. In the right-hand mirror, she looked her age, thirty-seven, but in the left, the wry arch of her left eyebrow and the sweep of her hair made her look younger and a little dangerous. She never compared these opposing viewpoints, however, but confronted herself head on, her back straight and her chin lifted.

She began with white Erase under each eye, which she patted on with her index finger, then applied an ivory base, smoothing it to her hairline and down her neck halfway to her collarbone. The base needed time to "set," my mother said. In fact, after each phase of the makeup process my mother would stop and place her hands flat on the scarred vanity surface and wait, staring into the mirror, unblinking.

She had an assortment of sable brushes, one for eyebrows, several for eyelids, several for lips, and brushes could not be mixed. A brush used for violet shadow, for example, could not be used for blue. She also had a brush for loose powder and a jar of small white sponges that she dampened and used to set the base and powder.

In those days my mother preferred the old-fashioned mascara that comes in a small rectangular cake, and perhaps the most vivid memory I have of this elaborate makeup ritual—which I must have witnessed dozens of times in New Orleans—is my mother spitting demurely onto the little cake of mascara and rubbing it with a brush to produce a fine, chocolatey liquid. Squinting into the mirror, her mouth slightly open in a shallow, sideways oval, she applied this with yet another brush, stroking her lashes until they formed a stiff surprised and surprising crescent of spikes above each eye.

Then lipstick—she outlined her lips first with a lighter shade, using a sharp-pointed brush to draw an artificial Joan Crawford bow, then filled in the lines with Revlon red from the tube.

Finally, perfume. In five places: behind each ear—she eyed herself slyly, sidelong, as she placed each drop—inside each wrist and deep in the vee between her breasts. When she raised her head, finished, complete, she would look at me, seated behind her on the bed and reflected in the center mirror, and smile the dazzling smile she only smiled in full makeup, a smile of secret triumph.

"Well?" she would say.

"Perfect," I would reply.

She was deep in this makeup ritual on the morning when my father stormed up the stairs and into our French Quarter flat bent on confrontation. He had spent some time and effort tracking my mother down and, he emphasized, considerable money. He felt that he was owed an explanation.

My mother sat with her hands flat on the vanity top, staring into the mirror. She was wearing a peach-colored slip and a Chinese wrapper, and her hair was pinned up at the nape of her long neck. "I don't see how what I do is any concern of yours," she said finally, as though her refusal to see would somehow end the matter.

"Oh, you don't," he said. "You don't? I'll tell you how it concerns me. Val," he said, pointing at me. "Valerie 'concerns' me."

It was a new experience for me to be a concern to my father, and I was savoring the moment when Mr. Conroy pressed the buzzer downstairs. We knew it was he, my mother and I, because he always rang one long and two short, like an impatient driver urging traffic to clear.

"I can't discuss it now," my mother said. She still had not moved from the mirror.

The buzzer sounded again.

"Val, see who that is," my father said, taking charge.

"We know who it is," my mother said.

To make a long story short, Mr. Conroy came up, and he and my father blustered and feinted at one another for ten or fifteen minutes, during which my mother finished her makeup. She was, as usual, perfect, and I told her so, and just as she had flashed me her special smile, my father turned away from Mr. Conroy, as though he had just remembered her as the source of the argument. Without any warning his hand swept backward and slapped her hard across the face.

She fell against the vanity, spilling her jars and bottles and brushes, and in the commotion, Mr. Conroy came forward, to no effect, and my father halfway threatened to hit him, too. I don't know where I was, still on the bed, I suppose, and watching in the mirror.

No one knew what to do next. They seemed embarrassed. Finally Mr. Conroy said, "I think we all need to cool off a little," and walked out of the room and down the stairs, and after a minute or so of awkward silence, my father followed.

The irony of all this fuss—and I'm sure my mother saw it—was that there was essentially no difference between my father and Mr. Conroy. Both were rich, or rich enough. And both saw Mother as an asset. Mr. Conroy didn't refer to "the team," but it was clear to my mother and me what her role would be if she divorced my father and married him. He was a businessman and entertained often. He needed a competent, ornamental woman.

❀

On the train going back north my mother sat by the window, watching the bayous seem to burn in the setting sun, seeing the way they were slashed in twilight by the broken black limbs of trees. The air conditioning was on, full blast, the way my father liked it, and she had the wide soft collar of her beige cashmere jacket pulled tight around her throat.

Night came on. Just outside of Jackson my father went to the bar car alone. My mother settled back and closed her eyes, ignoring her perfect face, reflected in profile, still in the flat black window of the train.

My mother's new beauty was ghostly and seemed to lie entirely on the surface. She had aged, and when she closed her eyes, it frightened me. There were then just the perfect cheekbones, the fragile angular jaw.

❀

My mother had knelt and picked up her cosmetics one at a time, inspecting each jar and bottle for damage and wiping up any spills with wadded Kleenex.

"Val, honey, get my dress," she said.

She intended to wear a short beaded chemise that showed off her long legs. It was carnival in New Orleans, and she had a sequined mask that matched the dress, and she intended to wear the dress and the mask to dinner with Mr. Conroy. As it turned out, she dined at Galatoire's with both Mr. Conroy and my father, and there was, I understand, a controlled and lengthy conversation, the result of which was that my mother agreed, for my sake and for other reasons, to return to Chicago with my father.

I carried the dress from the wardrobe in outstretched arms, a servant obedient to the altar of beauty.

"Thank you, baby," she said.

We could hear my father and Mr. Conroy talking in the foyer down below. Their low voices and their cigarette smoke filtered up to us. Once my father—or perhaps it was Mr. Conroy—said something in a fast, staccato rhythm, and both of them laughed.

A bruise was spreading under my mother's left eye, bronze, like the green-gold shimmer of a peacock's tail. Her mask concealed it, and it was not discussed, and I don't know whether my father or Mr. Conroy ever mentioned or even noticed it, but that, of course, is not really the point.

The point is art. In the swift and sudden sweep of my father's hand, my mother crossed over from artist to work of art and froze into the stillness I now sense in her. The face slipped away behind the makeup, wandering in its own perfect isolation, and surface became everything.

It's like carnival. The trinkets thrown from the floats are cheap and gaudy, literally trash, nor are they especially meant for you.

Yet you want them. That is art.

My mother knows this, not in theory, that the appearance is the reality, and making yourself wanted is all that counts. Beauty is an illusion, and my mother is beautiful. Which is why you have to believe her when my mother talks about masks.

Martha's Eye

In the late 1890s, a farm boy living near Sargents, Ohio, shot and killed a passenger pigeon, the last of this species believed to exist in the wild. Others lived on in captivity, however, notably Martha, an attraction at the Cincinnati Zoo and, officially, the last American passenger pigeon.

Imagine a flock of birds so large it takes two days to pass your vantage point; imagine the whole sky in soft twilight and the rush of wings lifting. Imagine how beautiful they were.

James Fenimore Cooper saw them, and John James Audubon, who remembered the earth shadowed by thousands of birds and called the species "inexhaustible." Imagine the little boy.

Let's call him Cal. Let's say he's ten years old, born and bred in Ohio. Let's make his father a strong man, a blacksmith, perhaps, and his mother what mothers have always been in fiction: patient and stout. Let's say she reads the Bible, wears her hair in a twisted, steel-gray bun at the back of her neck.

Now we send Cal out of the little cabin where they live and into the woods with a rifle on his shoulder. Let's imagine Martha's sharp dark eye is watching him.

He runs through a blaze of color—it is fall: gold and rusty brown. A shower of yellow maple leaves blesses his shoulders. He sees the bird immediately. It is almost too easy. He shoots.

The recoil pushes him back, twists his body to the right. The whole earth shifts. The crack of the rifle splits time: before and after. This is the moment when there is now no more, when some soft unseen tragedy occurs, and yet the boy goes on as though nothing has happened.

And the bird falls, falls, heavy for such a little thing, falls into golden maple leaves and dies. It is dead before it hits the ground.

"Cal?"

The mother calls from the cabin, her voice breaking the boy's name.

"Cal-vin?"

The sound winds like smoke through the golden woods.

°°°

A young woman works in the Cincinnati Zoo, unusual for the time. It is 1914, and it is spring. She has never been to Sargents, Ohio—no matter. She is one of those pretty, innocent girls we encounter only in fiction, and we realize at once that she stands for something.

The boy, Calvin, now a man, walks down a path one day and sees her, sees she is beautiful.

He tips his hat. He smiles.

To save time, let us project ourselves forward—through the usual walks in the park, the ice cream socials, Cal and the girl holding hands in her mother's parlor—up to the moment he kisses her, in a shadowy spot near the bird house, a quick kiss, yet lingering. She falls, in love with him.

°°°

The sky is bright blue. There are no shadows. James Fenimore Cooper might say that this is a day for adventure. Cal decides to take Amelia hunting. That is the young woman's name.

"Oh, Cal," she says, "I don't know. Hunting?"

"Sure. It isn't like you think."

She agrees to go along, puts on a functional tweed, heavy boots. She takes a pair of cotton gloves and, after debate, decides to wear a canvas hat for the sun, the kind of hat that men wear, but tailored to suit a woman.

"Fetching," he says.

She smiles.

Martha's eye watches them go. He is driving the carriage. Martha notes the reins tight in his hands, the way the horses toss their heads.

°°°

Again, it is fall—for unity. Again, Calvin walks beneath the maples. It is not too late, but it is very late. Amelia walks beside him.

What kind of story can there be in all this?

Cal leads Amelia down a slope, down to a shady ravine where a brook winds idly over flat gray stones. He doesn't know exactly where he is going.

"Cal?"

He seems to be seeking the darkness deliberately.

Suddenly, forty yards away, a beautiful buck steps out of the woods to drink. He is magnificent. He is beyond anything we have ever seen.

Amelia catches her breath. "Oh," she says. "Oh, Cal."

"Aim."

"What?" she whispers.

Cal moves behind her, folds his arms over hers, and raises the rifle. "Aim right for the heart."

"I can't," she says.

The buck stretches toward the water, leans, yearning, so that the clean white underside is open. His front legs are forward, his head down.

Cal puts his right hand over Amelia's hand, threads her index finger through the trigger guard and pulls, and that rifle shot is the sound of now too late.

The buck does not fall but lifts its head, stricken, runs in panic a few yards and stops, swaying. Then its knees buckle; it goes down in slow motion, a great ship foundering, the saddest thing we have ever seen.

Amelia is heartbroken, begins to cry. Cal sweeps his arms around her, twisting her down. They struggle a little, not much. He covers her neck and her breasts with kisses, pins her arms down; she is no match for him, the way he is, determined and exhilarated with blood. It is over before she can even cry out.

❀

The sun pulls a sharp angle of darkness across the brook and the dead buck, which is too heavy to carry. The world is silent and moving into night.

"What are you going to do?"

Cal takes the head with a hunting knife—a fabulous trophy, he says—and leaves the carcass. And blood pours out and seeps through the golden leaves and swirls into the narrow brook, which runs, eventually, to a river and, eventually, to the sea.

"I'm cold," Amelia says.

He takes off his jacket and wraps it around her shoulders.

No one saw Martha die. She simply let go of the tenuous hold she had, fell, lightly; and where is the story in that? Except that it was September 1, just on the eve of World War I, and someone—maybe Amelia—thought to pack the body in dry ice to preserve it, cared enough to ship it to the Smithsonian Institution, where all of our lost things are still remembered. But even that gesture was meaningless; it was now. And, after all, the whole world was at war.

Them

Miriam noticed them standing across the street when she took Caitlin to day care, and they were still there when she came back: a woman, fairly well-dressed, in her late forties, a man, a little older.

"Ignore them," Brian said.

"What do they want?"

"Just ignore them," her husband said. "They're just gawking."

"Do you think they want something?"

"I don't know."

"Well . . ."

"Everyone wants something," he said.

He picked up his briefcase. "I'll be late."

She watched as he walked out through the carport and into the garage—he didn't look back. The leaves were beginning to turn on the yellow maples. The gladiolas along the fence had died. The last days of summer were always so precious, and so brief. After a moment, the garage doors opened silently, and the silver Volvo glided down the drive and curved out into the street, the engine ticking smugly beneath the hood.

They were still there at midmorning, although she couldn't be sure. They might have left and returned. They didn't seem to be vagrants.

"Dee?"

The housekeeper dropped her laundry basket. She hated interruptions.

"Do you see that couple out there?"

"Can't hardly miss 'em."

"What do you think they want?"

Dee put her face to the casement window. It was a Prairie-style house in north Oak Park, not a Frank Lloyd Wright house, but from the same era. Brian was very proud of it and pretended not to be.

"Just lookin', near as I can figure," Dee said.

It made Miriam uneasy. They were used to tours. Every spring and every fall, the village organized architectural tours of the prominent area houses, and their house, the Henry Garvey House, was always included. Brian would not allow anyone inside, but clusters of people dressed in gaudy walking shorts and carrying cameras gathered beyond the gate. Inside she and Brian could hear the tour guide going over the fine points of their house.

"Close the blinds," Miriam said. "Dee?"

—☙—

She worked at her desk until lunch and almost forgot they were there. She was on the guild auxiliary board, among others, and it was almost time for the annual event. Harriet had charged her to come up with something completely different this year, some new fundraising scheme, but everything had been done to death: masquerades and garden walks and silent auctions, all of that.

"Just ask them," Brian had said. "Call everybody up and say, 'We need twenty-five thousand dollars, and what's your share going to be?'"

"We couldn't do that."

"Why not?"

"I don't know. It has to be fun," she'd said. "There has to be some sort of occasion."

Dee had lunch laid out on the patio. The moment she sat down, Miriam saw them again. They seemed to be just walking by, but walking so slowly that it was obvious they were staring.

"I think they're casing us," Miriam said. "Is that the word?"

"I wouldn't know, Ma'am."

"I'm going to speak to them."

"I could call somebody," Dee said.

"No. No, but they just can't *stand* there all day."

Miriam refolded her napkin and stood up. The couple didn't move, although certainly they were aware of her, watching them.

"Hello," she called, walking down the drive. The man whispered something to the woman, and she shook her head.

"Can I help you?" Miriam said.

"No."

The woman was short and pudgy, "peasant stock," Brian called it, that squatty look. They were ruddy, healthy, not homeless people.

"We were just looking," she said. "Admiring your home. It isn't Wright, is it?"

"Actually, no. But it's Prairie School. We've tried to trace the architect, but no luck."

"Stell's a student of architecture," the man told Miriam.

"More an admirer," the woman said. "Must have been built about 1910."

Miriam was surprised. "Exactly."

"I can tell by the roofline, partly. Not as elegant as Wright, of course, but the impulse is the same."

They stood in silence, admiring the house. It had a deep porch and tree-of-life art-glass windows in an iridescent lavender that Miriam always instructed the gardeners to pick up in the lavender impatiens around the base of the oak trees.

"It's beautiful."

Miriam was flattered. She looked herself. Yes, it was. Beautiful. "Thank you," she said.

"I hope you haven't overfurnished it."

"No, I don't think so."

"That would be a mistake."

"Yes, I suppose it would." Miriam wondered if she *had* overdone it just a bit.

"You want the lines—does it have oak wainscoting?"

"Yes, it does."

"Open beams."

"Yes."

"You want those to dominate."

"Would you like to come in?"

Miriam said it so suddenly she surprised herself.

"Thank you, we would."

The man murmured something in the woman's ear. "Just for a minute," she said.

The door was solid oak, heavy. "We keep meaning to replace this," Miriam said, "with something a little easier to manage. It's so hard to open."

"But that's the original door."

"Well, yes, it is. It's just that it's so heavy, so hard to open. Oh, by the way," she said, "I'm Miriam. Miriam Towle."

"Like the silver."

"Yes."

"I'm Estelle Link. This is my husband, Bill."

"Well, . . . welcome," Miriam said.

The foyer was tiled in slate, probably the whole house had been slate originally, but someone had carpeted over the living and dining rooms with a nondescript beige velvet pile. "I'd take that up," Estelle said.

"Stell!" Her husband leaned toward her, hissed her name. "Let's go."

"It's nothing personal."

"You're absolutely right," Miriam said. "I keep telling Brian—that's my husband—I keep saying, 'You know, we should take this carpet up,' but he says, slate is so cold . . ."

Estelle had wandered over to the staircase.

". . . in the winter," Miriam said.

"Stell?" The husband had a worried look that Miriam didn't like. "Stell, honey? We're keeping Mrs. . . ."

"Towle," Miriam said.

"Mrs. Towle. Stell? Honey?"

They caught sight of the woman's running shoes disappearing up the stairs. The man smiled apologetically. "I'll get her," he said. "If you don't mind."

Miriam followed him up the stairs. The woman was in the master bedroom, staring out the window. "Oak Park," she said.

Miriam smiled. "Do you live in the neighborhood?"

"A place of broad lawns and narrow minds."

The woman turned around. "Know who said that?"

"Pardon?"

"Hemingway."

Miriam looked puzzled.

"Hemingway, Hemingway. Ernest Hemingway."

"Oh," Miriam said. "Of course. The writer."

The woman walked toward the bed. "You sleep here?"

"Yes."

"Look, Bill, she sleeps here." She said it as though it were something miraculous. She patted the mattress gently. "Safe and sound. Right here."

The bed was queen-sized, a dark walnut four-poster with a white Battenberg lace coverlet. "Is this old?"

"The duvet? Actually, no, it's . . . it's an import. I got it at Carsons. Quite inexpensive. It's handmade, in China, I believe."

"Carsons has nice things."

The woman started to sit on the bed, then caught herself. "And every morning when you wake up, you can see that lilac bush through the side window," she said. "Think, when it's blooming, Bill, in spring, the fragrance. I'll bet there are birds, too. Are there?"

"I'm afraid . . ."

"We have to go," the husband said. "We're going now."

He ushered the woman down the back staircase, the servants' stairs that led to the big kitchen, where Dee was fixing dinner, then out through the dining room. Miriam had a huge oak china cabinet full of glass.

"You collect Lalique." the woman said.

"Yes."

"You would."

"Stell."

"You don't want glass here. You want pottery. Blue-green, Newcomb, Van Briggle. Not glass."

"I happen to like glass."

The woman smiled with mock sweetness. "In that case, Dearie, don't buy a Prairie School house."

"Now wait just a minute," Miriam said, but the woman had already left the dining room.

"Mrs. Towle, . . ." The man positioned himself in front of Miriam, blocking her way. "See, the thing of it is," he said, "we've had some bad luck."

"Who are you people?"

"Links. We're the Links. We live over there." He pointed west. "I'm sort of retired. Health problems. My wife's a teacher—part-time, college English. But it's hard to get work right now."

"I'm afraid I'm going to have to ask you to leave," Miriam said. "I have to pick up my daughter."

"We are, we are leaving. I'll just get Stell."

In the living room, the woman was examining the fireplace. "Terra-cotta," she said. "This is not original."

"Well, no."

"It should be fieldstone."

"Well, I'm sorry," Miriam said sarcastically. "We happen to like it."

The woman looked slowly around the room. Her eyes filled with tears.

"Honey?"

"This is a Robert Spencer house," she said. "I can tell by the window hardware."

"Is it?" Miriam said.

"Spencer and Powers actually, but it's clearly Spencer's work."

"Spencer, Spencer," Miriam said. "No, I don't think so. I don't remember that name."

"Robert Closson Spencer, Jr."

"I don't *think* so. My husband had the house researched."

"Spencer. Robert Spencer." The woman turned to face her and took a step or two forward. Her eyes were blazing. "Good God! You own this and you don't even know what you have."

"We need to go," Bill said.

The woman was crying silently with her head up. She was crying as though that were the obvious thing to do.

"Mrs. Link . . ." Miriam took a step toward her. "Estelle." She reached out to take the woman's hand.

The woman looked her straight in the eye. "It's beautiful," she said.

The woman's eyes were a strange Icelandic blue, indigo washed pale by tears. They were the eyes of a starved spirit, and Miriam saw that nothing she could say would make any difference.

"Yes. Yes, it is," she said. "Very beautiful."

"Spencer."

"I suppose."

Bill put his arm around his wife and guided her to the door. Miriam trailed them. The lining of the woman's coat hung frayed below the hem; her shoes were worn. "I'll have to tell Brian," Miriam said. "Spencer. He'll be glad to know. Finally."

Miriam struggled with the door. "Oh, this door," she said. "It's so darn heavy."

"It's the original door," the woman said softly.

"Yes, it is."

"It's authentic."

The man and woman passed over the threshold and down the walk. When they were almost out to the street, the woman looked back. She looked at the bedroom window where, ten minutes before, she had looked out. She looked for a long time, and then her husband squeezed her shoulder and whispered something in her ear, and they started to walk south toward Lake Street, slowly—he was rubbing her shoulder—and in a minute or two they were out of sight.

꧁꧂

Brian got home late, and when she told him the house was a Spencer, he shook his head. "Who told you that?"

She told him about the Links, how the woman, Estelle, had identified the house by the casement windows as early Spencer, Spencer and Powers; and he said, again, no, he'd checked that out.

"Who were these people?" he said. "What were they, renters?" There was a string of apartment buildings over on Oak Park Avenue.

"I suppose so," she said.

Then she told him about Estelle and how she had stood in the living room and cried. "It sort of got to me," she said.

"Why did you let them in?"

Dark Matter

My father died of emphysema and left half a carton of Camels on top of the fridge. My brother, Larry, smoked them all while we waited to bury Pop. By the time my sister, Adele, got in from New York, the air in the flat was a dull blue-gray.

"You have no respect," Adele said.

Larry never looked up, just sat at the kitchen table, smoking, the way Pop used to do. His hair was thinning; our father's ironic tonsure was beginning to show itself. The index finger of his right hand was stained tobacco amber, too, but none of us women said, "quit," and every once in a while, my mother would get up and dump the big glass ashtray.

Adele thought everything should stay in place, just the way Pop left it, but it seemed to Larry and me that his death had released the ancient chaos, left everything loose and floating, that there were no rules of allegiance anymore.

"Larry. Girls. Just don't fight, for once," my mother said.

First, we had to wait two days for Adele—she couldn't get a flight right away—and then they don't bury people on Sunday, I guess, so it was Monday, Monday afternoon before we could finish it.

Mom said she felt like she'd lost her best friend.

"You're glad," Adele told Larry. "You're glad he's dead."

In fact, it is harder to lose your enemy.

The four of us spent the mornings drinking coffee, Mom in her housecoat till noon. She dragged out every article my father had ever touched or commented on; she told his life story and cataloged his favorite foods. She settled for us, once and for all, what he was like and what he was not like, as if to literally put him in his place and make him stop being what he had always been for us. Her monologue was broken only when the phone rang or a neighbor stopped by with a casserole.

By Saturday morning Larry had had enough and silently withdrew from the kitchen table to watch cartoons in the living room.

"I don't think that's very respectful," Adele shouted in to him from the kitchen. "If there's some sort of point you're trying to make . . ."

Then there was dinner. Adele glared at Larry and me over the macaroni and cheese, over the ham and scalloped corn, playing at suffering, mostly for Mom's sake, implying with subtle gestures and brief, enigmatic remarks: *You two never loved him. I was always the good one.*

Larry smoked through dessert, which caused Adele to push away her carrot cake and rise dramatically from the kitchen table. She opened every window—it was February—turned on the exhaust fan over the stove, and covered her nose with a yellow paper napkin.

"Kids, please," my mother said.

At the funeral, Adele broke down, and a bevy of women—neighbors, aunts—descended on her like pigeons on spilled popcorn. They offered worn-out bits of philosophy and brought forth various home remedies from the depths of their plastic handbags. Larry slipped outside to smoke, and I followed him.

Larry is an astronomer. I always have to explain that to people, especially the people in our neighborhood.

"Someone who looks at the stars."

Mrs. Winkowski, my mother's friend, nodded uncertainly. Nobody ever believes it's a real occupation, like being a plumber, selling insurance. Looking at stars all day.

"All night, actually," Larry corrected me. "You can't see the stars in the daytime." He pointed up. "There's too much light."

Mrs. Winkowski, midway up the steps of St. Agnes Church, smiled and glanced through the double doors, eager to go on in and see the casket. It was clear she preferred familiar company to these two strange, talkative Norberg children.

"I'll just pop inside and have a word with your mother," she said.

"Actually what I see is what's not there," Larry called after her.

"Don't let us keep you," I said.

"There's quite a bit of it," he yelled. "Emptiness. I'm busy as a beaver all night long."

She glanced around her and smiled uncertainly. "I'm so sorry," she said.

⁘

Larry and Pop used to argue about the Hubble telescope. The "great American boondoggle," Pop called it. "Damned thing doesn't even work," he'd say. "And what did it cost us? Millions? Billions?"

"Billions, Pop. Kazillions. Taxpayers' money. Thrown away on knowledge."

"And what are these questions you say it's gonna answer? What are we gonna learn? I'm only asking."

"Meaning of life, Pop. God, death, immortality, the whole shitload, entire kit and caboodle."

"You don't say."

"I do."

"That'd be something," Pop said.

"Wouldn't it just."

⁘

The casket was closed, a honey oak space capsule. "Aerodynamic," Larry whispered.

Alone in the dark, my father was already hurtling far beyond us, streaking through the dark and timeless time. I heard a cartoon whoosh of air and saw the fringe of his thin gray hair ruffled by cosmic winds.

"*. . . through the valley of the shadow of . . . Amen.*"

⁘

Mrs. Murray and her mother buttonholed us as we left the church. Both were wearing ranch mink coats, full skin, with matching pillbox hats. They looked like a sister act. The Murrays were the wealthy branch of the family: Buick Regal, brocade sofa and matching Queen Anne chairs, custom made "window treatments," shizu, above-ground pool. My father, who was a carpenter, had never been impressed with Murray, who was in plumbing supplies. "Guy can't even make a picture frame."

"Neither can I," Larry would say.

"You I've given up on."

"I'm so sorry," Mrs. Murray said. Her mother smiled.

"I understand it was quite sudden."

"No."

"I mean the actual . . ."

No one knew what to say. For it was, in fact, a deliberate darkening. Years and years of willful, relentless smoking, defiant through the hacking cough, against the doctor's orders, eyeing us each in turn as he lit them up, almost as though he wanted to kill himself and didn't know quite how to go about it.

"Mother got a new hearing aid," Mrs. Murray said finally. She twisted the old lady's head gently and pulled back a tuft of curly white hair to reveal a flesh-colored lump of plastic.

"That's nice."

The old lady made no response.

"I said, THAT'S NICE." I yelled in her ear.

"I don't think so, Dear. It's too warm."

"No, NICE." I pointed to her ear, and she smiled. "WHAT KIND IS IT?" I yelled.

She looked at her tiny gold wristwatch. "It's four-thirty."

My father loved to argue. He and Larry had running feuds about politics, religion, current affairs. It was a game between them, verbal tennis; it kept them sharp. Larry was an egghead, a bleeding heart, all wet on crime, taxes, welfare—what did he know? College education but no sense. And this environment thing. An absolute and total obsession with him, my father said. The snail darter, the manatee. Who gives a damn? Do we eat manatees? Do we wear their fur?

"Manatees don't have fur."

"Fuck 'em," my father said.

❦

The cars pulled out of the parking lot and headed west on Roo-sevelt. It was a raw afternoon. Night was coming on. The sky was bruised with purple, and, underneath, inching along, a black bull snake of funeral cars.

"You know, I never rode in a limo," Mom said. "In all these years."

Nobody said anything.

"It's nice."

I imagined myself in my father's arms—a child again, his little girl—and I had the warmth of his barrel chest and the smell of tobac-co smoke. I imagined myself inside his darkness, my ear against his heart. His heart was enormous. The shiny black lungs, thick with tar, inhaled, exhaled.

"Are you crying?" Adele poked me. "Ma, she's crying."

"It's a funeral, Adele."

❦

Tell what happened to the dinosaurs.

I used to beg for that story. And Larry would summon up an an-cient planet, sunlit, dense with dark green foliage, another world, a world of dinosaurs. The way he told it, I could see them, moving in their slow, regal bulk: not human, more than animal, absurdly shaped yet elegant, wise.

Look out, look out!

Out of the sky, a fiery comet descending—"Look out, Karla," Larry would cry, diving under the dining room table. A cosmic collision; a giant cloud of dust rises slowly from the earth, then falls, coating the plains and the forests and blocking out the sun.

"And the earth grows darker and darker," Larry would say, making his voice go spooky, "and all the plants and all the animals die."

❦

Mom put her arm around me, buddy style, wedged my left shoulder under her right armpit—amazing how well we fit together. "When you kids were little," she said, "you were all afraid of the dark."

"I wasn't," Adele said.

"No, not you so much. But Karla and Larry."

Larry had flashlights stashed all over his room. He must have had five or six of them hidden in dresser drawers, under the bed, in the closet. When Pop called "lights out," Larry would fetch out two or three flashlights and set them up on the floor where they would spray fragile columns of light up to the ceiling; the room looked like a cathedral. And Pop, who could see the faint line of light seeping out from underneath Larry's door, would call up from the bottom of the stairs, "Are you reading up there? Lawrence? Are you reading up there?"

Larry called Pop the Rodney Dangerfield of Cicero. He never thought that he was getting his due. Embattled, who knows why? Life's little betrayals. Insults, mistakes. Not the least of which was that his son was good in school, a science whiz, so good that Mom had decided that Larry should go to college.

"College, schmollege," my father said. "Let him work with his hands."

The more Larry succeeded in school, the more it got Pop's goat. "Out of his league," my father said, "kid's in way over his head." Some very high-class schools were after my brother, offered him money just to go there. Pop couldn't understand it.

"Pay a kid to read books?"

"Sure." Mom had faith.

"There's a catch to it somewhere."

These conversations always took place at bedtime, after a night of brooding in front of the TV set. Pop's voice would filter up to us in the darkness. Adele would stick her fingers in her ears and hum herself to sleep, and I would tiptoe into Larry's room where the flashlights were glowing.

※

At Rest Haven there was still snow on the ground.

"This is such a dreary time of year." Adele pulled her coat collar tight.

"They found a four-thousand-year-old mummy up on a mountain in Austria. Bronze Age," Larry said. "Like our own. The Iceman Cometh."

"I know. I saw it on Dan Rather," Adele said, putting on a fresh coat of purple-pink lipstick. "Ten thousand feet up a mountain. Imagine." She snapped her compact shut. "Nobody should try to climb that high."

The Iceman had the ironic smile of death. His skin was like parchment, his eyes were dried wide open. Scientists think he was caught by an early darkness. Night came on. He lost his way.

"Maybe he stopped to rest," my mother said.

Young and armed, a hunter, and yet he died. Fell asleep in the snow, no flashlight for comfort.

"What was he doing way up there? That's what I'd like to know. Why would anyone go so far?" Adele knew very little about ambition.

"Hunting," Larry said, "escaping domestic life like Rip Van Winkle, on his way to the Seven-Eleven. Who knows? In the midst of life we are in death."

Adele adjusted her earring. "I don't think we should talk about this now."

The cosmic collision, Larry told me, sent a cloud of sulfuric acid skyward. All of this was millions of years ago. The dust from the comet settled back to earth and formed a layer that Alvarez called the K-T boundary, a permanent marker of the disaster, a division between the old life and the new. All the plants and all the animals perished. "Catastrophe," Larry said. "Annihilation."

Mom pulled out a hankie, getting ready. "Do you think there's life on other planets?"

⁘

The cars pulled into the cemetery and wound back in along the narrow roads.

"I always loved this place," my mother said. "Isn't that morbid?"

The graves spread out like a parking lot. I imagined a maze of neat, narrow apartments underground, and roots branching, mirrors of the trees. Death was simply the world inverted, light and darkness reversed, like a photograph negative, or, perhaps, there was nothing at all. Only a small portion of our universe is visible—ten percent, Larry says. The rest is called dark matter.

"So many," my mother said, looking over the graves. "There won't be any room for the rest of us."

Larry tried to kill himself once; he was twelve. Swallowed a bottle of Bufferin and a jelly glass full of vodka that he found in the back of a kitchen cabinet. The doctors pumped his stomach and reassured my mother that the combination probably wouldn't have killed him.

"It's the thought that counts," my father said.

By the time Larry went to college, the suicide attempt had been re-defined as a prank; my father's remark was remembered as a joke, a witty retort. Was it then that the game began in earnest?

The procession stopped beside the open grave. It was six, sixteen, sixty feet deep. It had no depth, a hole into which you just kept falling. It's not so much what's down there, out there—*that* we can handle with flashlights. It's what's inside.

"I just wish the sun would come out," Mom said.

Something holds us together—love, hate. Until the Hubble, scientists thought the universe was a mass of small red stars—red dwarfs, they call them—dim, ordinary matter, not visible, but assumed to be there. And then they photographed the Milky Way from the Hubble and found, Larry told me, not a comforting wall of red stars at all, but large dark holes, through which they could glimpse other galaxies.

Ashes to ashes. Dust to dust.

The man from the funeral home ushered my mother out of the car. Dark matter. That part of the universe we can't see. Something that holds us together, taken on faith.

They all said the ancient prayer of obedience: *Our Father, . . .*

Larry and I, eyes open, listened while Mom and Adele mumbled furiously.

. . . and forgive us . . .

·°☙°·

The scientists are listening, Larry told me. Carl Sagan and a bunch of others. Radio satellites are pointed toward the stars, searching constantly for other life forms.

Except, now, Carl Sagan is dead.

Occasionally, a seemingly meaningful pattern of radio waves bounces back to them from out of the darkness, but, for the most part, the universe is silent.

"At Grandpa's funeral they had real ropes," my mother said. "Remember that, Karla, how they lowered him down?"

Who will listen to the stars now that Carl Sagan is dead?

"I don't like this motor thing," she said. "It's so impersonal."

The coffin descended.

"You know what it reminds me of?" she said in a stage whisper. "One of those grease racks they have at service stations."

Everyone was looking at her.

"What?" she said.

The minister took her hand and led her to the grave. She looked frightened, as though she thought they might throw her in. "They do that in other countries," she told me once. "India, I think, is where they do that."

He placed a lump of earth in her right hand. She looked at me, uncertain; she looked at Larry.

She was *stricken*—that was the word. She hadn't understood this thing before, and now she did. The minister whispered something in her ear, and she nodded. Tears were streaming down her face. She tossed the dirt lightly on top of the casket.

Larry pretended to be amused. Although he had lost the most, he refused to grieve. He kicked a clod of earth toward me, soccer-style, but I ignored him; I knew I had to choose.

So, I moved forward and tossed my little handful just like Mom.

Then Adele did the same. Then aunts and uncles and cousins and neighbors and friends. Guys from the union, Pop's old boss. The honey oak began to disappear.

Mom wailed dramatically. Adele joined in. They clutched at each other, they patted, they stroked. Larry called my name like a question: "Karla?"

Women surrounded my mother and sister, gathered them in. "Karla?" They gathered me in. An arm reached out and scooped me inside the circle.

The game had been called on account of darkness, but Larry couldn't let go. Night came on. Like playing tennis alone. Larry's eyes were wide open, dry—they always had been—and though I reached out to him, by then, he had drifted too far away.

Three Weeks in Italy and France

"It's absolutely the show of the season." The woman who spoke was holding a vodka gimlet. "Here's to Vermeer."

She lifted her glass. The vodka rocked and splashed over the rim. "Now look what I've done," she said, brushing her skirt.

Twenty-one Vermeers at the National Gallery. Rose simply had to see them. "They say Vermeer is sheer poetry."

"Well," Sunny said. "I'm game."

"We could all drive down," someone said. "Get up a caravan."

"No, the train."

"Sloshed in the bar car."

"We could get compartments. Do they still have compartments?"

"Somebody phone."

It was one of those gentle summer evenings. Pale sunlight retreated across the deck, leaving the circle of guests lounging half in shadow. Rose heard the sound of a power mower cutting through the dusk.

"So, Rose," Sunny said, "what are you working on?"

In fact, Rose was working on the garden. The gladiolas had just begun to bloom, a series of scarlet gashes along the fence. She wanted to make them even more startling by ripping out the ivory impatiens that grew at their feet and substituting some hotter color—purple, yellow—she wanted the shock of color she remembered from France.

"I'm afraid I'm not painting now."

"What?"

Rose smiled self-consciously, shrugged her shoulders.

"Oh, but you must, dear." Sunny's thin auburn eyebrows crashed together in dismay. "You have to paint. Everyone, doesn't she?"

The telephone rang inside the house.

"Joe's got it," Rose said.

She heard her husband pick up the receiver.

"Yes? Yes."

The rise and fall of his voice, staccato answers. Whatever it was, Joe would handle it. And, if it was important, he would stop tossing the salad or pouring the wine or whatever it was he was doing in there and walk out through the heavy glass sliding doors to the deck and tell her.

"Rose?"

It was Joe at the door, holding the phone out to her, his hand over the mouthpiece. "It's for you."

She excused herself and went inside.

"She's dead," he whispered. "Marnie."

Rose said nothing.

"Did you hear what I said?"

She took the receiver. "Yes?" It was Marnie's mother in Iowa. "Mrs. Flynn?" Standing with her back to the party, Rose listened.

". . . didn't know who to call, and it was so sudden. I mean . . . It was and it wasn't."

Marnie. Whenever Rose spoke of her, Joe would frown and repeat her name as though he'd never heard of her before.

"Mary Maureen Flynn, the girl I went to Europe with. Back in art school. My best friend?"

"Oh, Marnie," he'd say. "Marnie. Of course."

"I'm so sorry." Rose spoke softly into the phone, saying the obvious thing, but the truth was, she didn't know what she felt. It wasn't as if they'd stayed in touch over the past twenty years. It was hard to say now whether they still were "close."

"What was it?" Rose said.

"What?"

"The cause of death."

"Oh, that." There was a pause. "Cancer," Marnie's mother said. "Breast cancer, at first." Another pause. "That is, she had cancer. I thought you knew."

"No."

"She had it for years, in and out of the hospital. She lost one breast . . . when was it? 1992, I think. I remember because she had just turned forty. And, they thought they got it all, but . . ."

Marnie. Marnie in black and white: the black turtleneck, the leotards; Marnie driving that little white Fiat through Paris—a demon, Rose had called her, but with love. Marnie painting, how her hair flowed perfectly over her shoulders, like dark water, how her sapphire eyes narrowed in concentration.

"I believe . . ." The woman broke off.

"What?"

"I think she was just completely exhausted. The cancer. And all the rest."

There was laughter out on the deck. Someone was telling a story.

"Art is such a difficult career."

Rose said nothing.

"It breaks you," Mrs. Flynn said. "It can."

"Yes."

"Well, as I said, I didn't know who to call, so I'm just going through her book."

There was a long pause.

"The funeral is Monday," Mrs. Flynn said finally. "It's not even a funeral really, just a service. At the graveside. It's what Maureen wanted."

"Mrs. Flynn . . ."

"We don't expect you to come, of course. All that distance—not that you wouldn't be welcome."

Rose felt her eyes fill with tears.

"Are you still there? Hello?"

"Thank you," Rose said. "Thank you for calling."

"Certainly."

"I can't say right now . . ."

"No, of course not."

"But probably not," Rose said. "Don't count on me."

"No."

"I'll let you know," Rose said. "Thank you again."

She replaced the receiver.

Joe took her in his arms. "How you doing?"

"Don't say anything."

Laughter floated in from the deck. She looked back over her shoulder.

"They'll be all right," Joe said. "Forget about them."

"She had cancer," Rose said. "Had it for years, her mother said. Marnie. I never knew."

❧

Those mornings in Paris, chilly and gray. Rose never forgot them. A trace of rain in the air, the cobblestone pavements almost silver in the light. Rose drank expresso. Marnie had her tea. The waiters in tight black pants, crisp white aprons, gossiped in the open doorways; old men in black berets read the morning papers at zinc-topped tables. The shops began to open. The sound of iron gratings rising rang along the streets.

Two delivery men wrestled a side of beef from a gutted Citroen, their dingy white coats wet with sweat and blood. The dogs were out, keen and hungry. The smell of the first cigarette of the morning still hung in the air.

"God, do you ever want to be anywhere else?"

Marnie sat with her back to the door, her elbows on the table, reading a map. She looked up and smiled.

At the pension, they'd met a frazzled German woman who told them there was sun clear down to North Africa. "Verrückt," she said. Italy was restless and unpredictable. "Hot!" She threw her pudgy hands in the air and rolled her eyes.

❧

Joe straightened the collar of Rose's blouse, smoothed her hair. "And that was your first trip to Europe."

Rose nodded.

"How did you manage it?"

Her eyes darted up at him. "I manage things."

"I didn't . . ."

"Actually, Marnie did everything. Booked the plane, rented the car. She spoke French—thought she did anyway. And a little Italian." Rose dried her eyes. "She had a book. God, we were so earnest, so young."

"I wish I could have known you then."

"Why?"

He looked away. "I don't know." He let her go. "I don't know what I mean."

Rose walked to the kitchen window and looked out over the lawn. Guests chatted on the deck or strolled through the dusk to the rock garden. Some sat at the edge of the pool, dangling their legs in the turquoise water and sending silvery rings of light wobbling across the surface.

"It was comic, really," Rose said. "Two girls, alone, drinking cheap wine in famous places, ticking off 'sights' on some pretentious mental list of must-sees. She was twenty-two. I was twenty-one. We had three weeks and a road map and about a thousand dollars, I guess, between us."

"And each other."

The lawn was deep, solidly green. The guests in their bright summer clothing seemed like flowers.

"So," Joe said. "What did you see?"

She saw the Impressionists. Cézanne, Pissarro, Monet. Everyone sees the Impressionists. Everyone loves them. Certain, focused, effortless artists, blessed by light and color. They didn't seem to need anyone, anything else, except the light and the paint itself and time.

Rose took a knife from the drawer and began to slice bread. *You're pressing too hard,* she told herself, and there were tears again.

"Hey," Joe said. "Talk to me."

They drove south in gentle sunlight. In Burgonne, they had a wonderful meal in a town they called Intredit because of a funny sign they saw there. "I remember clean white linen," she said, "and thick steaming soup, potage, and real bread, not like this."

Joe took the knife from her hands.

And in every village, somewhere near the center of town, there was a bronze statue enclosed in an iron fence and the simple inscription, *Mort pour France.*

"It was beautiful," Rose said. "We thought. To die for something."

The farther south they drove, the crazier life became. The gentleness disappeared; the smiles faded. People no longer responded to their questions. It was hot, mad, as the German woman had said.

There were too many people in Cannes, too many in Nice. The traffic was crazy. Drivers blew their horns and fought for position, fought for a parking space. Order broke down in a mad scramble for space.

"At least there's the water," Marnie had said.

She peeled off her T-shirt. Her body was hard, angular; she was thin, and her skin was smooth and the color of honey. She wore a plain black swimsuit. The straps were halter style and showed off her perfect square shoulders. Rose was pale by comparison.

"This is it, Rosie. The Riviera."

They found a spot, back from the water, and spread their towels. "Tits and ass," Marnie said. Everywhere it was women. Old women, yellow-toothed, with blood-red polish splashed on their stubby fingernails; young women, slim and haughty, strolling the beach with that arrogant, distant look they had learned from some popular fashion magazine.

"You can't be too thin or too rich," Rose said.

Marnie poured amber suntan oil into her hands and rubbed it over her shoulders.

The gray-green hills behind them were hung with villas, each one pure white, each one capped with an orange terra-cotta roof. Below, elaborate high-rise hotels rimmed the beach and hid the view of the water from the poor, who lived on the flat, scruffy stretches of sand across the road.

"Wouldn't you love to be rich?"

Marnie scowled and said nothing.

"I don't think I could stand not being rich."

Near the Italian border the Mediterranean turned a bright cerulean blue. The coastline grew rocky and colors went hard; the heat intensified. The camping site they were assigned their first night in Italy was

off a dusty gravel road and barely cleared of brush. Stubble pierced the
floor of the tent and let the dampness in. Insects swarmed incessantly.
The washrooms were crowded and dirty and miles away from their
tent, and for this they paid twice what they had in France.

A field of bright-colored nylon tents—orange, blue, army green—
and children everywhere. And, in the tiny tents, bouncing and swaying, more children were being conceived by thin men and frowzy,
sun-bleached women. The women's bath was a horror: sharp-eyed
women waiting for their chance at a dirty, cold-water basin, elbowing
in, a lack of awareness of the others the best technique.

"Look," Marnie whispered. "Aren't they great? I wonder if anyone
would pose for me."

Women stripped to the waist or completely naked, their breasts
swaying, heavy and slug white against their suntanned bellies.

"The French women were slim and straight. Even those who were
thick with work were still proud," Rose said. "But those Italian wom-
en . . ."

Joe smiled.

"They had this 'breeder's walk.'" Rose waddled across the kitchen
to demonstrate.

"Womb-centered," Rose said. Like the Italian Madonnas: the same
heavy lap, the useless arms.

They washed their breasts and arms, their armpits, their crotch in
mindless mechanical motions, then, slipped their feet into canvas
shoes—run over, caved in at the heel—and slapped out through the
pools of dirty water.

"Honestly, Rose," Marnie had said. "You make everything into a
moral argument. It's only the body, the human body. You're just not
used to it."

Rose flared. "What's that supposed to mean?"

"I've camped before. That's all I'm saying."

Rose sighed. "Our whole day is: 'What are we going to eat, where
are we going to stay?' And the mind is so . . . dragged down."

"Oh, screw the mind."

Rose remembered the balconies of Paris, the open doors where, be-

hind the intricate wrought iron railings, the floating sheer white curtains, gentle light suggested a higher, more intellectual life. She loved
to look up at those windows at twilight and imagine quiet couples, be-
spectacled and dressed in fine dark woolens, talking, really talking to
one another.

The mind needs clean sheets and hot water. "The soul costs more
than a motor car," Rose told Marnie. "George Bernard Shaw said
that."

Some sort of spirited discussion had erupted on the deck. Rose
could hear Sunny's voice raised about the others.

"I think we'd better get back outside," Rose said.

"They're all right. The barmen are out there."

"We're the host and hostess."

"Tell me about it, Italy," he said.

"Why do you want to know?"

He leaned against the counter and smiled at her. "I'm learning
something."

They went on to Florence, where the art seemed predetermined
and documentary. A patron's face always seemed to intrude in the lower right-hand corner of every fresco. "Art on the backs of the people,"
Marnie had said. Turkish slaves cut the stone for the Medici chapel.

"There was a static quality about the work in Florence. It came
from all that wealth. I mean, even in the best things, you could always
sense, somewhere in the background, the thick fingers of the mer-
chants, counting."

"Don't knock wealth," Joe said.

She stopped. "I don't. I don't knock it. It changes things, that's all."

"Oh, I don't know," he said. "If I lost everything tomorrow, it
wouldn't change who I am."

"Don't be silly. Of course it would."

"I'd still be happy," he said. "I'd still have you."

Rose glanced away.

"Marnie hated it, too," she said, "but the thing is, I was completely sucked in. A fever took hold of me to buy things, to own. I don't think you know what that is because you've always had money."

"I know," he said.

"No, you don't." She arranged the bread in a large sweetgrass basket. "It's painful. It hurts."

Like on the Riviera, Rose thought. Your guts twist, and a raw, bitter taste comes into your mouth because you know that a lifetime of doing . . . whatever it is you do wouldn't buy you a single day in one of those clean white villas—or the arrogance to enjoy it.

She set the basket on a tray. "You don't belong—that's what it is. You can never have the really fine things. Always pecking around for crumbs, looking for the cheaper shops, the markdowns."

The shopkeepers looked up expectantly when Rose and Marnie walked in, Pavlovian at the sound of the bell. But it was only two college students, poor American girls, who would finger the merchandise and never buy. "Their faces fell," Rose said. "We saw it. They knew who belonged."

He reached out and tried to touch her, but she wouldn't allow that. "What is it really?" he said.

Rose remembered the martyrs, in the churches along the side walls, tucked in their small niches, the martyrs—shot through with arrows, burned or beheaded, abused in a thousand delicious ways—the people loved the martyrs. And the queen of the martyrs was the Madonna, the done to, the uncomprehending.

Women are nothing in Italy, and they are everything. It frightened her. A country steeped in flesh, absorbed in the body—tortured in the middle ages, swarming, and rubbery in the Renaissance. Spirituality comes through the senses, only. There is no route—except perhaps wealth and the power it buys—that can put the body aside, and woman is the route; hence the cult of the Madonna, the sensual path to the father. Truckers on the auto route have lighted Madonnas in the cabs of their trucks. There are roadside shrines to her everywhere.

The best art money could buy. Costly and finely crafted, astonishing in some ways, but lacking intelligence. Mindless ornamentation in floors and walls and tables; endless flowing draperies, sculpted around inconsequential portraits.

"We were sick of it, and I kept nagging for us to go on to Venice. Then on the last day we saw the *David*."

"Wow."

"Marnie wanted to see it, insisted we see it. She was so eager, for everything. Anyway, there was this corridor of unfinished work, slaves, just emerging from blocks of stone—twisted postures, the way they were struggling . . ."

"This is Michelangelo, right?"

"We turned a corner . . ." She looked up. "I mean, I had seen pictures of it, in school. We'd studied it. But this . . ."

Joe smiled.

"I mean, . . ."

"I read somewhere . . ."

"And I was so glad," Rose said. Tears stood in her eyes. "I was so happy. Completely. Isn't that silly?"

❧

The pilot of the vaporetto from the Fusina campground over to Venice was good-looking and friendly and let the kids on board steer the boat in open water. Rose saw him watching Marnie, and not just from the corner of his eye. Watching, wide-eyed and hungry, the way that animals watch.

"Want to drive?" the boatman said. He pointed at Marnie. "You."

Marnie smiled. Rose knew that smile. "I'm not a child."

"Most definitely."

Marnie stood at the wheel and he stood behind her, his arms over her arms, his face next to hers. The water, severed, threw a veil of spray on either side, and the bow of the boat reared and plunged. Rose held on.

For over three years she had been a spectator in Marnie's romances, a conspirator in some seductions, a go-between. When things fell apart, as they usually did, Rose consoled her. Rose was the source of wisdom. "He wasn't good enough for you," she would say. "You can do better." Usually, it was true.

The boatman put his hands over Marnie's hands.

"You camp? Fusina?"

Rose watched as Marnie smiled and nodded.

"In a little blue tent?" he teased.

Rose watched Marnie tilt her head, letting her hair swing loose, looking up at him with her practiced smile.

"You come early," the boatman said. "Is good. The piazza is *senza popolo*. You see?"

Venice rose from the water, seeming to float, its lacy architecture a delicate salmon pink in the early light. Fragile, ancient. It seemed to glow.

He cut the engine and spun the wheel in a hard right turn, and the boat reversed and slid neatly up to the dock, rolling gently in its own wake. He helped the women passengers—some of them—Marnie, but not Rose.

"Well," Marnie said. The women stood awkwardly on the pier. "Thanks."

He said nothing, let them walk away. Let them take a few steps— Marnie, Rose guessed, knew exactly what he was doing. And then, at the last minute, he called to them: "Hey, you two. American girls."

They turned.

"Your name."

"Don't tell him."

"Marnie," she called back. "I'm Marnie. Mary Maureen. And this is Rose."

He smiled. He had straight white teeth and a heavy mustache. He wore the striped T-shirt that tourists expected, a sort of flat sailor's hat. He pointed to his chest with his thumb. "Carlo."

Marnie put her hand to her ear, shook her head, teasing.

"Carlo. Carlo."

He stood up in the rocking boat and spread his legs for balance. He leaned forward, smiling back, and cupped his hands to his mouth: "I am Carloooo."

❧

The piazza was almost empty. The waiters in the cafes along the arcades were just setting out the tables and chairs. Pigeons strutted on the steps of the basilica. A wonderful stillness hung in the air. The stones beneath their feet seemed almost alive.

"Let's just walk," Marnie said. "Let's not do the tours."

They left the square and got lost immediately.

"Of course, we didn't realize it at first."

The twistings and turnings of the narrow streets led them further and further away from the tourist center around the square, deeper into the dark heart of the city.

"Where are we?" Rose said.

"Don't worry."

Marnie had a camera, a small instamatic, and snapped pictures methodically.

"Don't you love it, Rose? God, there's like . . . intrigue everywhere. Lord Byron lived here, he lived in a palace or something. And the Brownings."

"And Cole Porter," Rose said.

Marnie frowned.

Rose felt it, too, of course, the tragic sense of decay and loss, the romance. It was impossible not to. "But I blocked it," she told Joe. "I wouldn't let myself be sucked in at first. Because it was just exactly what was to be expected, and it was so Marnie. I tried to be wise."

Joe smiled. "A wise twenty-one-year-old?"

"To have given in to it would have meant I was her, *trying* to be her, at least, and I couldn't do that, and yet, I could see it, of course."

They wandered into a little shop that sold cheap glass beads and papier-mâché masks.

"Look," Marnie said. She held a pearly white half-mask to her face.

"*Volto*," the shopkeeper said.

The nose was beaklike, the eye slits tilted upward, oriental. It gave her face an amused, haughty expression.

"She was mocking me. Even then."

Marnie bought the mask and wore it. People turned to stare. She was wearing a white dress of thin Indian gauze that floated around her ankles. Her hair was loosely bound with a white ribbon.

"A man offered to buy her a glass of wine. Another to take her picture." She jumped up on the ledge of a fountain and danced. "She was beautiful."

And then the sun began to go down, and it was cold in the narrow streets, and they were lost and getting hungry.

"Let's sit down for a while."

They sat outside a cafe. Marnie counted her money.

"Don't do that."

"Why?"

"Someone will rob us."

"Rose. For twenty dollars?"

"Your friend is right."

It was a male voice, familiar. They turned, and it was Carlo, smoking a cigarette at the next table.

"For ten dollars," he said. "For five, for one. For a single lira they rob you."

"Who?"

"Everyone," he said. "All." He swept his hand in a brief arc to include and dismiss the whole world at once.

"What are you doing here?"

He shrugged. He gave his coffee cup a gentle quarter turn.

"Did you follow us here?"

Only Marnie would ask that, would be sure enough of herself to ask.

"You are lost?"

"Sort of."

"Sort of, sort of. What is 'sort of?'"

"Yes, we're lost," Rose said. "Can you tell us how to get back to San Marco?"

He smiled. "Lost." He studied his cigarette. He ran his eyes along the tops of the buildings, seeming disinterested.

"Well, can you?"

"Of course, of course." He stood up, dropped his cigarette, and ground it into the pavement. He dropped a few lire beside the coffee cup on his table and a few more beside the coffee cups on theirs.

"Come," he said. "Come, come. I show you."

"And she invited him back to your camp," Joe said.

"How did you know that?"

"I know a good story when I hear one."

"I think we should get back outside," Rose said.

"In a minute."

That was the beginning. Marnie and Carlo, walking arm-in-arm, slightly ahead, turning, when they thought of her, to ask, laughing, "Rose, are you okay?" Laughing when they said it, between themselves, laughing, as though she, Rose, were their child.

"And they would explain everything to me," Rose said. "What was on the menu and what the street signs said, what everything meant, like little tour guides, and Marnie didn't know any more than I did, and Carlo . . ."

Then at night, Rose in the Fiat, reading by flashlight, while silhouettes of the two of them, Marnie and Carlo, squirmed on the roof of the blue tent, the muffled sounds, laughter, and Rose getting more and more tired and unhappy sitting in the car.

"And then, the way he would come out, come out of the tent, and smile and say something pointless and transparent, as though they hadn't been . . . as though they had just been drinking wine and talking, just been looking at picture postcards . . . I don't know."

"You were jealous."

"I guess."

"I can understand that," Joe said.

Marnie was the pretty one. They had agreed on that. And Rose was the intellectual, "cerebral," Marnie called it.

"It made things easier, I suppose," Rose said.

Still, it walled her in. There were limits, under this system, to what she could openly feel and what she could do. She was not expected to respond to the romance of Venice. That was Marnie's department.

"I don't understand," Joe said.

"Men compete." Rose wrapped a kitchen towel around a sweating bottle of chilled white wine. "Women compartmentalize. One is the 'career woman'; one is the 'stay-at-home'; one is 'practical,' and one is 'flighty.' There's no competition that way, no hard feelings."

"So you were the intellectual."

"I was the rational one."

"Practical."

"Yes, I guess so."

"And that meant . . . what?"

"I wore jeans instead of dresses. I read Henry James. I preferred Bach to Mahler, that sort of thing. I just fell into it, because . . . I don't know why."

The constant smiles and innuendoes, the secret communications, the way she changed, Marnie, the way she lorded it over Rose, pushing her deeper and deeper into that schoolmarm identity.

"And I was pretty, too," Rose said. "I don't mean beautiful," she said quickly. "But . . ." She poured herself a little wine. "We never know, when we're young, how beautiful we really are."

And, she could never just walk away, leave them, smiling and whispering, leave with no subtle message intended, and wander the city alone because, after all, she and Marnie, they were best friends.

"Carlo's not serious," Rose told Marnie. "He's laughing behind your back."

"I don't think you're in any position to judge."

And he was an ignorant man, not worth her attention. Cruising the Grand Canal, he dozed, he smoked, he never looked at the city at all. And there were fabulous doorways, frescoes; there were palaces, for God's sake.

"Who lives there now?" they asked him. Carlo shrugged. "Are these homes? Offices?" The windows of the buildings were blank, like empty eyes. "Who lives there? Are these buildings occupied?" He shook his head. The question meant nothing to him.

At the Basilica di San Marco, Carlo insisted they pay three hundred lire apiece to see the Pala d'Oro, a gem-encrusted altarpiece hidden behind the main altar. "*Troppo d'oro*," he kept saying, all of gold.

"It's garish," Marnie said. "A clutter of loot from the crusades."

"*Troppo d'oro*. A masterpiece."

Carlo suggested they buy a booklet on the Pala at the gift shop. "For study," he said. "To remember."

"No," Marnie said.

They had their first fight then, on the steps of the church.

"It's just . . . money," Marnie said. "Just what money can buy."

"Of course," he said. "Beautiful."

"No," Marnie said. "Corrupt, like Florence."

She overstated, of course. She always did. She had no idea then what money could buy. Still, Rose understood what was at stake for her. Some higher dream, art, a dream of beauty. They didn't quarrel, Rose and Marnie, ever, about ends; only their means were different. Marnie was young. The Pala d'Oro was, to her, exactly the sort of thing a tourist would buy.

Carlo was puzzled. "But you are," he said.

❀

Sunny leaned in through the open patio doors. "What's going on in here, you two?"

"We're coming," Joe said.

"Something came up."

"Well, we're all starving out here." She smiled to indicate she was teasing. "It's nothing serious, I hope."

"No, no. We just started talking."

"And forgot all about your guests."

"Never."

Rose took Sunny's hand in her own and squeezed it.

"What were you talking about? The Vermeers?"

They walked out through the sliding glass doors. "Italy."

❀

Venice sold gilded plastic gondolas, glass, gaudy beads, silver, and guidebooks; postcards, and cold, raw coconut for one hundred lire a slice. It sold leather and silk and seafood; it sold itself.

"Do you know what I remember about Venice," Sunny told Rose. "The light. That quality of light. I always thought Canaletto was sentimental. And then I actually went to Venice and saw it. Well, the man was absolutely accurate."

"I remember how, in the Piazza San Marco, old men would shake a handful of corn in a tin can to attract the pigeons," someone said. "The tourists loved it."

"The whole place is covered in pigeon shit."

"I had my picture taken there," Rose said.

"You and everyone else in the world."

"With . . . a friend of mine."

Just as the shutter opened, something startled the birds. They lifted up in a swirl of blue-gray wings and with the heartbreaking sound of wings, which is like time rushing away, like no other sound that Rose had ever heard. Marnie laughed, and the camera caught her, gazing up, her arms outstretched, and the sleeves of her thin white gauze dress floating, a look of absolute, perfect joy on her face.

"There's such a piercing simplicity in the really old things," Sunny said. "Like the Zeno doors. Did you see those?"

"Yes."

"A lack of self-consciousness, a purity of purpose and vision."

"Get you," someone said. And Sunny laughed.

"Society is a solvent," she said. "It erodes and dilutes the artistic purpose."

"And where did that wisdom come from?"

"So is love."

⚜

Across the piazza, past the sea of bright umbrella tables, flocks of American tourists followed the uplifted cane of an officious tour guide. Hawkers assaulted the tourists on either side, flipping the pages of souvenir books as they passed, waving maps, "Signore, Signora, look, look please, very cheap."

"Coffee costs two thousand lire here," Marnie said.

"I don't care."

Rose sat down at a cafe table.

"Two thousand, Rose."

"Marnie, I'm tired."

They sat at a table outside the Florian. It was dusk. Rose thought about Paris, how cool it was, how calm and intelligent.

"Do you know what I think," Rose said. "Form is the mind's peace. I just made that up."

"Wonderful." Marnie was sulking.

"Skill holds the mind, thought and design and form. Not *'troppo d'oro.'* Not tricks."

The bells of San Marco began to toll, deep-toned and absolute. In the twilight they seemed profound and as though they were speaking to Rose alone, positioning her at the center of her life, exposing her for what she was, small and pretentious and greedy in the face of such beauty, not beautiful herself, inconsequential.

"Carlo says, . . ."

"Oh, please, please. Enough about Carlo, okay?"

"What's the matter with you?"

"Carlo this and Carlo that. I'm just sick of hearing about him, that's all."

Rose was tired of the twisted streets, the pushing, the babble of languages. Tired of the constant struggle just to be cool and quiet, the expense of time and money and strength. She was tired of the oldness of things, the broken feeling, even the beauty, all passion, the useless hotheaded slogans scrawled in red on the villa fences.

"I want to go back to France."

Marnie looked up. "Are you crazy?"

"I'm tired of all this."

"Well, I'm not."

Rose looked at Marnie. She had that sinewy kind of beauty, tough; and, no, she would never be tired, never be scared or uncertain. Marnie would never lose her way, and Rose knew then that she loved that strength in her and that she depended upon it.

"I love you," she said,

The blue eyes flashed up at her. "Sisters."

"Now and forever."

"Until we're old, wise women with nothing left but our paintings and scandalous memories."

She was so beautiful.

"Yes."

The light was dying. The square had gone cold. An old woman and her son were packing up their souvenir stand for the night. First, the woman put away the pennants and maps, the books and the postcards in battered cardboard boxes. Then she began to wrap the cart in a heavy green tarpaulin.

"Souvenirs," Rose said. "All this . . ." She looked around her. "You buy a picture of it, a dozen pictures. You think you have it then, forever. You don't."

The old woman secured a rope and went around and around the cart, lashing down the canvas while her son—who was in his thirties, balding—looked on helplessly.

"Oh, Rose. You're so dramatic."

The old woman pulled the rope tight and knotted it. She brushed her hands on her skirt and turned and walked away. The son picked up the worn wooden handle of the cart and began to drag it after her.

"Carlo's just another souvenir."

The woman and her son passed slowly down he length of the piazza, passed beneath an archway and entered the shadows of one of the narrow side streets.

༺✿༻

Rose sat on the patio, listening, her hands curled loosely in her lap and half-hidden under the folds of her skirt. Habit. Her hands were usually battered and paint-stained. She welcomed winter, in a way, because she could hide her hands then in sleek leather gloves.

"Well, it's decided," Sunny said. "We're all going down to see the Vermeers."

"Wonderful."

"You know the piece I read in the paper said he left—what was it, Dick? Thirty-five paintings or so. Dick, was it thirty-five?"

Her husband shrugged.

"Well, anyway, whatever. The point is he left so little. So few paintings."

She paused and looked around her. "I mean, isn't that . . . sad. Or something?"

"He died penniless," someone said. "That's the astonishing part."

"Well, that won't happen to you."

You squeeze a life dry, Rose was thinking, for your work. You throw your health and your love life, and your friends, into that work, gladly. Nothing else matters. And, in the end, you get thirty-five or so miraculous paintings. And, the astonishing thing, the really astonishing thing, is that it's worth it.

"I was at the gallery the other day," Sunny said, "and you know we have the Charles Manning show now, and, I mean, he's just such a craftsman. And I'm walking through and I hear this absolutely midwestern voice."

But what if the work isn't good?

"It was some tourist," Sunny said, "and, I swear, this is a quote. He says to his wife or his girlfriend or whoever she was, 'You know, Babe, this guy's stuff don't look like it would be all that hard to do.' "

Sunny roared. "Not all that hard to do," she said. "Charles Manning."

The guests smiled, laughed. Joe laughed along with them. "Manning," they said. They shook their heads. "Charles Manning."

⁂

"Do you know who is the great Venetian," Carlo asked Marnie, "long ago?"

They were crossing the piazza. The sun was low and sinking into the dark blue water.

"Casanova," he said.

He leaned over Marnie, whispered in her ear, "Casanova. You know? The great lover."

"The great libertine."

"Of course. Venetian." Carlo smiled, softened his voice. "Like me."

His boat was docked at the foot of the Grand Canal. No tourists waited.

"We have all for ourselves."

He started the engine and maneuvered the boat out into open water. A perfect quarter moon was rising, bright silver against the darkening sky.

"I've never seen a sky like this," Marnie said. "It's almost violet."

Carlo put his arm around her and pulled a bottle of something from his pocket. Out on the water it was dark, cold. Rose huddled in the back of the boat and braced herself against the wind.

Carlo drank from the bottle; then Marnie, then Carlo. They passed it back and forth. Once they offered the bottle to Rose, but she shook her head, refusing. By the time they got to Fusina, Marnie was sick.

"What was that stuff?"

Carlo smiled. "Only wine."

"It was so sweet." Marnie said. "God. I feel awful."

"Go lay down," Rose said when they got to the campsite.

Marnie looked at Carlo.

"Just for a minute," Rose said. "God, you can do without him for just one minute."

"Go," Carlo said. He was building a fire. "Rest." He smiled at her. "I wait for you."

⁂

"Well, they're not painting like Vermeer anymore." Sunny had been an art dealer for over twenty years. "Except for Rose," she said. "Rose is my first, best 'find.'"

Rose shook her head. "I'm afraid I've let you down. Lately."

"You're in a slump. That's all. You're taking time out to recharge your batteries. Everyone does it."

"I haven't painted a decent canvas for months," Rose said. "It's over. My promise. I should ask for my pictures back. You should make me take them."

The guests grew quiet.

"I don't think it's all that bad," Joe said.

He wasn't even looking at her. He said it automatically. It was a reflex that came out of years of support. Long-suffering Joe. Rose suddenly hated his blind faith in her.

"How would you know?"

"Excuse me?"

"What do you know about painting? What do you know about me, for that matter? What did you ever really know about me?"

"What do I know? What do I know? Nothing," Joe said.

"You . . ."

"I'm just the guy who pays the bills."

Profound silence fell over them all.

"We all love you, Joe," Sunny said finally. "We don't tell you that often enough, and that's our fault."

"Oh, stop it." Joe stood up. "I know what you all think of me."

"I'm sorry," Rose said.

"No, you're not."

Joe looked around the circle. "You're all just so damned . . . sure of yourselves, aren't you? So polished. I mean, you know everything, don't you? Everything."

No one spoke.

Tears stood in his eyes. "And the funny thing is, I really admire you. All." He turned and walked quickly into the house.

❦

"You are also a student," Carlo said. "Like Mary Maureen." Clearly, he didn't care what she was.

"Yes," Rose said. "We're classmates. At Iowa."

"Iowa."

"Where the tall corn grows."

He smiled politely. He didn't know what she was talking about.

All around them campers were talking, laughing, cooking late-night suppers and drinking wine. They had nothing to say to each other, Carlo and Rose.

"You're cold?" he said.

"No."

"You are. I see the geese marks . . ."

"Goose bumps."

He shrugged. He slipped off his coat and offered it to her.

"No. Thank you."

"You don't like me," he said.

"I don't know you."

"You think I am . . . the Casanova."

"I think you think you are the Casanova."

A flicker of recognition passed over his face.

"I am a simple man." He pulled his lower lip down in an exaggerated scowl, shook his head. "I am no one."

Rose said nothing.

"The tourists come and they see me . . ."

"I think you make too much of yourself."

He looked up, surprised.

"Not everyone is looking at you," Rose said. "Not everyone thinks you're romantic. Only the very young."

"Like Mary Maureen."

"She's easily taken in."

"And you are not."

"No."

"I love her," Carlo said.

Rose laughed out loud.

"Do you know what love is?" he said.

Sunny put her hand on Rose's shoulder. "Go after him" she said.

"No."

"Don't worry about us."

Everyone could hear Joe, up in the master bedroom, not crying exactly—some muffled sound. The light from the bedroom filtered down to the deck.

"Go up to him," Sunny said. "We're all right here."

Carlo offered Rose a drink from the bottle. It was a dare, and she understood it as such.

"Do you?" he said again. "Do you know love?"

"I think I do. I will."

"When it comes."

"Yes."

Carlo spat into the fire. "For ever and ever?" he said. He was laughing at her. "No," he said. He took a drink. "Love for a moment, a night.

What you feel, now. Is no forever."

Rose said nothing. She stared into the yellow heart of the campfire, past the leaping flames to the core of it.

"What *do* you feel? Miss Rose," he said. "Now?"

She felt lost. She felt small and plain and provincial. Not alive the way Marnie was alive, not open to life, not pretty and all that that implied. A hopeless outsider, walled in and cold to everything.

"Now, Rose," he said softly. "Now."

He took her in his arms. His flesh was incredibly warm. He was solid and smooth and graceful. He kissed her lightly.

"You have nothing to say?"

He swept her up in his arms, carried her to the car. In the back seat of the car—it was cramped; it was cold; it didn't matter. He was inside her before she knew what was happening, swept along. His kisses were hot on her neck, on her breasts. He didn't undress her. Not completely. She was "disheveled," as in some charming, innocent nineteenth-century genre painting, her clothing pushed aside, with art, in such a way that she felt natural, sexual, for the first time in her life.

❦

Rose opened the door quietly. Joe was lying face down on the bed. She sat down beside him and stroked his back.

"What is it?" she said.

His answer was muffled.

"I can't hear you."

He turned to face her. "It's you. It's always been you. You're everything to me, and I'm nothing to you."

"That isn't true."

"I'm . . . You have this other life. Sunny and your work and . . . You don't even love me."

Rose said nothing.

"Do you?"

She couldn't respond.

"You see?"

He stood up abruptly, walked into the bathroom, and splashed cold water on his face. "I always knew it," he said, his back to her. "I thought, I hoped, I guess, it might change, but I always knew, I always knew it wouldn't."

"Why are you doing this?"

He turned to face her. "Why am I?"

"Yes."

"Did you love her?"

"What?"

"You heard me."

"Who?"

"Oh, Christ, Rose. Marnie. Did you?"

"I don't know what you're talking about," she said.

❦

They fell asleep in the car. Marnie discovered them the following morning. They were tangled together in sleep, covered, only partially, by Carlo's jacket. The sunlight pierced the windows of the Fiat, and they looked up into her blue eyes, staring in through the glass.

"Is nothing," Carlo said, climbing out. "Is nothing, Mary Maureen."

"I guess not." Marnie turned her back on him. "I was silly, wasn't I? Thinking it was."

He put his hand on her arm. "Mary Maureen."

She started to cry. Surprising. It was usually the men who cried. Marnie wasn't used to being the person who got hurt.

"So?" Carlo leaned forward, teasing, trying to search her eyes.

She stood alone in the sunlight, crying silently, her mouth straight, tight, her eyes wide open.

Carlo shrugged, shook his head. He ran his hands over his tight belly. "Hungry," he said.

Marnie turned to stare at him.

"What? What you look?"

"I don't believe you," she said.

Rose struggled out of the car.

"And you," Marnie said. "You, Rose."

Carlo squatted beside the campstove. "Coffee," he said. "Makes the day to begin."

Rose tried to put her arms around Marnie, but Marnie shook her off, and they stood, the two of them, side by side, looking down at Carlo, squatting on the grass.

Carlo looked up. He squinted into the sunlight for a moment, then went back to the coffee. "You American girls," he said and laughed.

❧

"You think that's all there is to it," Rose said. "I-love-you, I-don't-love-him, her. That settles everything, doesn't it?"

She stood up and paced the length of the bedroom. "It's not about love, not all about love. That's such a simple word for what it really all is. Love."

They heard a car horn in the drive.

"I'm simple, I guess," Joe said. "I'm not 'the intellectual one.' I love you, and that's it. It's simple for me."

The horn again. "Who *is* that?" Rose said.

She went to the balcony. Sunny was standing beside her car; the motor was running. The door was open and light spilled out from the plush interior.

"Rose?"

Rose stepped out on the balcony.

"We're going," Sunny said.

"Oh, Sunny, I'm so sorry."

"It's nothing."

"Let me come down."

"No, no, don't bother. We're on our way."

Rose was silhouetted against the light. Sheer, white curtains drifted in and out of the room. She put her hands on the railing and leaned over, looking down. Her hair tented her pale, angular face. In the reflected light from the pool, she was beautiful.

"You look like a picture," Sunny said. "Something I've seen, not recently. I can't remember what it is."

"Woman Wrecking Party with Domestic Quarrel."

Sunny laughed. "I'll call you."

Rose nodded.

"Night, night."

❧

Up in the mountains the air seemed cooler, cold. Marnie was driving. The road was narrow, like a tunnel, and it went steadily up out of Italy. They traveled into cold air and gentle light, ice-blue lakes and green, secluded pastures nestled in the shelter of pearl-gray rock. They drove without speaking, crossed at Susa and were back in France again. They camped at Lanselbourg, under the mountains, and Rose had delicate mountain trout with butter and lemon, alone, at a nearby cafe. The tablecloth was so white that the light reflected from it burned her eyes. Tears came. The wine glass in her hand was squeaky clean.

❧

The charcoal in the barbecue had turned an ashy white. The power mower had stopped. The dinner guests, still hungry, had struggled out of their lawn chairs and departed.

Joe came up behind her. They stood without touching.

"I am sorry," she said. "Again."

"I know." He took her hand and kissed it, kissed her cheek. "Okay?"

She nodded.

"So then what happened?"

"Nothing, really. Everything."

On the flight back, Marnie was distant, pretending to read, pretending to sleep.

"It just happened," Rose said.

"Don't say anything."

"I didn't mean . . . It didn't mean anything."

"Oh, Rose," Marnie said. "Of course it did."

Marnie turned off the overhead light, and in the darkness, Rose began to cry.

"Don't leave me," Rose said. "Be my friend."

"I am your friend."

"Whatever I do."

"Rose, . . ."

"Stay faithful."

"Yes."

The plane was dark. Everyone else was asleep.

"It doesn't make any difference, does it?"

"No, little Rosie," Marnie said. "Nothing ever really makes any difference."

⁕

A single light gleamed on the patio where the barmen were packing up. White shirts, black trousers. Young men from the college where Rose taught.

"She sent me some slides," Rose said. "A few years back."

"Slides of what?"

"Her work. She was working in pastels then. Tricky business."

"Why did she send them to you?"

Rose shrugged. "I don't know. I think she wanted . . . I don't know."

Whatever I do.

The letter was written on fragile ivory paper, folded in thirds: ". . . really appreciate any help you can give me . . ."

Yes.

"Were they any good?"

⁕

Two weeks after they returned from Europe Rose met Joe at a wine-and-cheese party. He was just finishing up an MBA. Joe was solidly built, Rose's own height, dark, but with clear amber eyes. He didn't talk much, and that was all right. Joe knew exactly where he was going.

Suddenly Rose was busy all the time. They still met, of course, now and then, Marnie and Rose; they had lockers side by side in the dingy basement of the art building. They would chat distractedly for a while, about their lives, about art.

But always, at some point, Rose would begin to fidget and glance away. "Gotta run, kid," she would say. "I'll call you. Really."

She never did.

Graduation. Rose and Joe posing for pictures on the steps of the auditorium. Marnie in a pale blue dress, her dark hair pulled severely

back from her face. She had a fellowship somewhere—where was it?
California? Oregon? Still the starving artist. Rose had Joe.

"You know the rest," Rose said.

"Only a part."

The false smiles, the final, sure excluding of one another.

"Then what?"

Rose finished her wine. "I don't know."

Maybe she had gone on the way she was, naive and unselfcon-
sciously talented, wearing her theatrical clothing and painting only for
herself. Maybe she got married. Maybe she did. Maybe she had children, lots of children, as Rose never did, slim, elegant, beautiful dark-
haired children, and kept them safe in a big white house by the sea.
Maybe she was wonderfully happy, Marnie.

"We sort of lost touch."

That day she had smiled down on Rose—she on the top step, still
the pretty one, Rose and Joe at the bottom, looking up. "Rose," she
said. "Rose, we finally made it."

❧

Rose watched Sunny and Dick's silver Lincoln glide up the lane. It
seemed to float. It took the gate and swung left, slipping away through
the trees.

"So. Were they any good?"

"What?"

"Come on," Joe said. "The slides."

"They were wonderful."

Rose looked up. The sky had gone from tangerine to peach, from
peach to a subtle blue-mauve, impossible to match. A slender moon
was rising. The shadows of night birds swung across the corner of her
vision.

"Sun's gone," Joe said. "It's almost dark."

Rose slipped her arm though his and felt again how solid he was.
She leaned her head on his shoulder and closed her eyes. "I didn't realize it had gotten so late."

Part Two

Me and Ray and Bud

The squirrel stuck its head out through a hole high up in the tree. I didn't think of it as anything but a target. Then it came clear out and hung upside down with its legs spread and its tail twitching, watching us.

I snuggled my cheek against the stock of the .22 and tried to keep both eyes open.

"Lean into it," Bud said. He was standing so close behind me that I could feel the sour warmth of his breath on my neck. I was seventeen and Bud was two years older.

"Squeeze," Ray said. "Don't jerk it."

I took a breath and held it and squeezed the trigger the way Bud showed me, shooting tin cans off a sandbar down on the Raccoon River. It gave easily. I hardly felt the kick, but over the sights I saw the squirrel open up, and a thin jet of blood spattered the tree.

"Hot damn, she hit it," Bud said. "Jesus, what a shot."

"That's my baby sister," Ray said. "Deadeye."

The squirrel didn't drop, but hung on, swaying, for a minute, and before Bud could get his gun up to shoot it again, it jumped back into the hole.

"Shit," Ray said. "Why didn't you shoot?"

"Why didn't you?" Bud said.

I put the safety on the way Ray had showed me. "What happened?"

"You missed." Bud spit on the ground. "You only got a piece of it."

"It'll hole up now," Ray said. "Probably a female. Probably got a nest in there."

"Will she die?"

"You hope."

Bud walked away, disgusted, and sat down under a tree, his legs crossed Indian style and his rifle across his knees.

"We'll have to wait it out," Ray said.

"You said I got her."

Bud lit a cigarette. "Well, you didn't get her good enough."

My brother and I sat down under a cottonwood tree and waited. It was cold, and Bud was pissed off having to wait.

"Ray?"

Bud scowled. He put his hand over his mouth and pointed at me.

"Just be quiet," Ray whispered.

A wire fence ran behind the tree with a fallow corn field beyond it; dark furrows cut through the snow and wandered away toward an empty horizon. I'd just gotten my period the day before, and my guts felt heavy; my legs ached.

"I'm sorry," I said.

The blood on the tree began to turn dark.

"Ray?" I said. "I'm really sorry."

"Hey, shut up," Bud said.

The squirrel began to bark in high, wavering shrieks that ricocheted through the woods, and we all stood up silently and willed her to come out. And then she did come out, suddenly, squealing and wild with pain, and Bud and Ray and I all raised our guns and shot at the same time.

The squirrel fell into a pile of leaves and snow at the base of the tree.

"Finally," Bud said. He walked over and picked up the squirrel by the tail. "Not much left of her." The elegant nails on the forepaws were bloody and broken; the soft, white belly torn away, as though she'd dug herself open, looking for the pain.

"Hey, Baby Sister's ready for pheasants," Bud said. "No shit. Hell, man, she's ready for deer."

Ray didn't answer.

"Oh, yes, indeedy." Bud winked at me. He had on the same kind of canvas jacket my father used to wear hunting, the edge of the pockets dark with old blood, the same kind of orange cap pulled low over his eyes. "Mag, we'll make a gunner out of you yet."

Bud took out a hunting knife and dipped the point in the blood. "And now for the ceremony."

"Come on," Ray said.

"She's got to be baptized."

Bud held the knife in front of my face. "I'm supposed to draw a cross with blood on your forehead and say, 'Today, you are a man,' or some shit like that." He looked me up and down. "But, obviously, you're not."

"Cut it out," Ray said.

"Who's gonna make me?"

Ray hesitated.

"Oh, Christ." Bud flipped the knife and it stuck in the ground between his feet. "This ain't shit," he said. "This is fuckin' cowboys and Indians, man."

"You wanted to go hunting."

Bud went silent.

"What?" Ray said. "What now?"

"Bobbie Saunders went," Bud said. "Did you hear that? Huh? Two weeks ago. And Richie. And Harvey Giles. 'Member old Fatso Harvey? Jesus, Ray."

Ray said nothing.

"Even old Crazy Nordell, and he's—what, a whole year younger than me and you."

"So?"

"So, Vietnam, man," Bud whispered.

Ray shook his head.

"Vi-et-nam, Vi-et-nam." Bud began to chant softly. "That's where it's at, man. Vietnam."

He lifted his gun and sighted along the horizon, sweeping the barrel in a swift half circle. "Pow, pow." He fired off cartoon rounds.

"My old man says war is like . . . like somethin' happenin' every single God-damned minute."

"I don't know."

"Pussy."

"Okay, fine."

"Chicken shit, commie." Ray said nothing. Bud lowered his rifle. "God damn, Ray. We're gonna miss it."

They stared at each other. Bud was taller, heavier, more at home in the woods. The gun was part of him, the whole thing was.

"You want to just keep on sitting around, waiting to get called?"

"I don't know," Ray said.

Bud squatted down and picked up the dead squirrel. "We got to eat this thing."

"Not me," I said.

"That's part of it. Your first kill."

Bud used his knife to slit the skin along the belly and down the legs and cut neat circles around each foot so that with one hard pull the skin slipped away from the squirrel's flesh, leaving little socks of reddish fur on the paws.

"I'm not eating that."

"You got to." Bud pulled the guts out and dropped them on the ground. "That's why you killed it in the first place."

"Just leave it," Ray said. "Or bury it or something. Nobody's eating that thing. Jesus."

Bud tossed the squirrel into the air, and it spun in a lazy loop and dropped at our feet. "Have it your way."

He pulled the clip from his rifle and reloaded it, snapped it back in. Then he drew a bead on the squirrel and started blasting. Ray and I jumped back, and Bud slammed five or six rounds into the carcass, making it jump and splattering bits of flesh.

"The incredible dancing squirrel," he said. "Neat."

The wind stirred the dead leaves. A thin covering of gray-blue snow drifted across our boots. The squirrel was like the pulp of some exotic fruit, laid open, the heart and lungs and liver a glistening dark ruby red.

Ray turned away and picked up his gun and walked back up the narrow path to the road.

"Pussy," Bud called after him.

Ray didn't answer.

"Chicken shit."

Ray walked over a little rise and disappeared in sections: first his feet in heavy hunting boots, his legs to the knees, his thighs and beltline, shoulders, head—like lifting the silver-gray film of a Magic Slate. I glanced at Bud, and when I looked back, Ray was gone.

"Hey, Maggie," Bud said. "I know this place? Really cool. Out by the quarry. Jillions of rabbits, man, I ain't shittin' you."

"I don't think so."

He grabbed me by the wrists, tight.

"Bud, don't."

"Don't, don't."

"I just want to go home," I said.

"Are you gonna give me trouble?"

He pulled my arms up over my head and kissed me.

Little Brothers

A heavy summer rain had washed the afternoon. Neon reflected jagged pools of color on the sidewalk, and streaks of lime and vermilion flashed on the windshields of passing cars. Chris and I had taken a seat by the window to watch for Ray.

It was 1975 or '76. Chris was working at Carsons then—one of those flawless beauties behind the Estee Lauder counter—and my brother was looking for work, or so he said. I visited them in Chicago for a week, and every morning Ray made an elaborate show of checking the want ads. He'd snap the *Tribune* open, one eye on Chris and me, and spread it out on the kitchen table to read, then shower and shave and leave early for interviews he probably didn't have. "An academy award performance," Chris called it.

"Good evening, ladies. Will you ladies be dining with us tonight?" The waiter had two red paper menus tucked smartly under his arm.

"We're waiting for someone," Chris said.

We ordered beer and sank back into the booth, neither one of us wanting to talk right away. The bar was cool and quiet, tucked in under the Lake Street El tracks. Every few minutes we'd feel the pulse of it, trains passing over our heads, and Chris would put her pale, slender hands flat on the table to feel the tremor, then look up at me and smile.

"So, where's the interview this time?"

She sat back abruptly and reached for a cigarette. "Some metal-stamping plant out in Franklin Park, wherever that is."

"He *is* picking us up."

"Sure. I guess."

The waiter brought the beer, dripping in heavy frosted mugs.

"Sure you won't be eating?"

We shook our heads. I started to rummage for cash.

"That's okay," he said. "I'll run a tab."

He wore denims and a pale cotton shirt, frayed and faded but freshly washed, smelling of starch and the iron.

"I see you," Chris said.

"What?"

"Checking him out."

"Pure research," I said.

She sipped her beer, using both hands to lift the mug. "You got troubles?"

"Yes. No. I don't know."

"None of my business, of course."

I drank and said nothing.

"So, what'd you do all day?"

"Same as always," I said. "The Art Institute, the Palmer House, and Wimpy's."

Wimpy's World Famous—it's gone now. The place was crazy, packed to the ceiling, but the waitress, an easygoing, caramel-colored lady with sassy freckles, refused to be rushed. She leaned across the counter as though she had all the time in the world and looked in my eyes. "What you want, Baby?" she asked me.

"I miss you guys," Chris said. "I wish you could move here, you and Bill."

"I'd like that," I said.

"Maybe if the amnesty goes through. You guys could stay with us until you found jobs. It'd be like the old days."

The dynamic duo, that was always her name for the two of us. In grade school, high school, we were inseparable. And then, when I started dating Bill, we became the fantastic foursome: Bill and me, Chris and my brother.

"Might straighten Ray out, too," she said. "Being around Bill."

"I don't know." I circled my finger in the sweaty ring from the beer mug.

"Don't you miss the states?" she said.

"Sure."

Beyond the cartoon street, beyond the yellow haze that hovered

over Chicago, I could almost feel the land stretching out and running
in easy ripples toward the horizon. The sun was setting; windrow pines
faded against the fences, and, along the farm roads, the people were
lighting lights. Men washed up for supper—I could hear the slap of
water in the basin—and mothers called their children home. The
screen door slammed. The yard lights came on, outlining ghostly gray
pickups and chicken sheds, spreading circles of light that linked to the
next one and the next one down the road—a chain across the darkness under Orion. Yellow squares of light appeared at the windows, silhouettes in the doorway. An old black and white shepherd barked,
noncommittally, at shadows, at the stars. Satisfied, he circled twice on
the front porch and settled his heavy head on his paws for sleep.

Chris glanced at her watch.

"What's with Ray?"

"Oh, he's always late," she said. "He'll show up."

"No, I mean, what's with him, what's the story? He seems so different."

"I don't know. I don't think he's really looking for work for one
thing. Why should he? After all, I've got a job."

"What does he say?"

"Oh, that maybe he wants to move to California," she said. "Or
Texas. Or Idaho. Some place where there aren't any people."

"No people in California?"

She shrugged. "It's different every day."

A silence always settled over things when we talked about Ray. She
loved him, I think. He certainly loved her. It's too dramatic to say that
the war came between them.

"Ray was always so . . . I don't know," she said. She lit another cigarette and offered me one.

"I quit. Remember? Two years ago."

She gave me a mock salute.

"He wakes up in the middle of the night," she said. "Not exactly
screaming, but, you know, like he's dreaming and stuff." She stubbed
out her cigarette. "And then he can't get back to sleep again, and neither can I."

She signaled for two more beers, even though the first two were barely half gone.

"You know what I used to like about him best?" she said. "The way he smokes. He smokes a cigarette just like Humphrey Bogart. Instead of holding it at the tips of his fingers like I do, he tucks it in close to the palm of his fist. Like this." She took a fresh cigarette from the pack and demonstrated.

"Hardly a career."

Cars glided past outside the window, none of them Ray's.

"You think it's just the war?" I said.

"I don't know. Bud wrote me once that the Vietnam War was 'the most meaningful thing' he'd ever done," she said. "Of course, it killed him."

I didn't say anything. I didn't say it killed Ray, too.

Buddy enlisted, he and my brother, both deluded by their fathers' dreams. Ray vacillated for months, but Bud kept saying, "God damn, Ray, we're gonna miss it," till Ray gave in or gave up or whatever it was, and the two of them hitchhiked to California and joined the Marines.

Bill and I left for Canada at about the same time. Married at nineteen. My mother and father refused to see us off.

"I just can't go," Bill told my father. "I can't explain it to you. I just can't go."

My father shrugged. "Love it or leave it," he said.

At the bus station we sat on cardboard boxes packed with our clothing and books—we didn't own a suitcase then—and Bill's father and mother stood over us, reasoning, as they called it, until the bus was ready to pull out.

"What if your notice comes?" Bill's father said.

"Ignore it."

"We can't just throw it away."

"Mark it 'return to sender' then. It won't be addressed to you."

"Just like that?"

"Yeah, I guess so."

They shook hands. Bill's mother refused to kiss him good-bye. We got on the bus—the station was still down on Fifth Avenue then—and left the country.

Bill said practically nothing for the first hour or two, pretending to sleep till we got to Iowa City. A dozen college kids got off the bus there, most of them eighteen, nineteen years old, like us. One boy in particular caught our attention. He seemed lost and kept squinting up at the street signs.

"Deferred," Bill said. "Probably just as well."

The bus was almost empty when we pulled out for Chicago, past the limestone Capitol building, lit to a ghostly white by a dozen flood-lights; a cluttered bookstore; a row of cheerful, crowded, amber-lit bars. The residential section of town dissolved in a scatter of houses; the lights fell away, and we rode on into the darkness, the tires hum-ming steadily on the pavement. A full moon was rising over the fields. Bill leaned over and kissed the bridge of my nose. "Well, kiddo," he said, "we're on our way."

"Maybe we shouldn't worry about him so much," Chris said. "Ray, I mean. Either he'll find his way out of this or he won't."

Ray served his tour and came home. He married Chris and they moved to Chicago where, Chris thought, they could make a better start. Their daughter, Beth, was born—a surprise—and Chris quietly promised her everything.

Bill and I moved into a house on Major Street just west of the uni-versity in a section of Toronto called the Annex. We shared it with some other Americans—a Jewish philosophy major from Rochester and a quiet, dark-eyed girl from Buffalo.

Bud Leech did a second tour.

I heard from him now and then: *Fire fight, beaucoup gooks,* that sort of thing. He loved the jargon and wrote me, I sometimes imagined, just to be able to put the words on paper.

Bill and I enrolled at the U. of T. and lost ourselves in the library stacks: reading Robert Graves and Thomas Hardy for seminars—Faulkner, James, Thomas Wolfe for ourselves—translating *Beowulf* from the Old English, line by murky line. There were a lot of Americans then. It seemed okay for a while.

"I don't know," Chris said. "Ray's changed. We all have. Maybe now things are just beginning to surface."

"Meaning?"

"Things are different now." She made a sudden wave of her hand, dismissing the whole question. "I haven't made love in a public place for days and days," she said. "I hardly ever dance on the table anymore."

"Slowing down?"

"Just the opposite,"

A good, three-piece string band was playing the bar, and a girl with long, dark hair, dressed in second-hand clothes—an *interesting* girl, we used to call that type—was walking among the tables, passing the hat. It was old Joan Baez stuff, vintage Dylan. They knew their audience. Bill and I tried to stay contemporary—Rod Stewart, Willie Nelson, whoever—but mostly we still played the same old songs. I knew what Chris was talking about. I, too, was ready to move on.

"Excuse me, Ladies." The waiter appeared suddenly, his shadow falling heavily over the table. "There's a party of gentlemen at another table who would like to buy you some wine."

I felt myself straighten a little.

"A party of very young gentlemen."

We followed his eyes and saw three boys, all about eighteen, sitting at a table near the door. They had scrubbed, eager faces and very short hair.

"You're kidding."

He shook his head and smiled, half sympathetic.

"Not exactly what I had in mind," I said.

The man in the museum that afternoon had been forty or so, a little paunchy. Probably some corporate type, playing hooky. Lonely women visit museums—I'm sure that's what he thought. He trailed me up the marble stairs and through the impressionists, into the room with the great Cézanne, the Van Gogh *Room at Arles, The Old Guitarist.* We stopped in front of the big Seurat for a showdown.

"*Dimanche,*" he said. He stood just behind me and whispered in my ear. "What does a beautiful woman do, I wonder. During those long, hot afternoons?"

"Tell them that's very nice of them," I told the waiter. "But we were just about to leave."

Chris sighed dramatically. "Maggie, you have no sense of adventure."

The waiter went away, and we watched him talking to the boys, their faces tilted up to him in the light.

"Can you believe it?" Chris said. "They can't be more than nineteen."

It *was* sort of funny, at first. They were eighteen, maybe nineteen. I was twenty-eight. Ten years. It seemed like more somehow.

Chris ran a comb through her hair. "Brace yourself," she said. "I think Ronnie Howard is headed our way."

The boy who approached our table was well-fed, almost chubby, with reddish hair and honest, soft blue eyes. He was wearing some sort of loose chino pants stuffed into the tops of stiff, elaborate cowboy boots that made his feet splay out at the ankles and appear to be headed in opposite directions. His fingernails were bitten to the quick.

"Excuse me, ladies," he said. He spoke loudly. "I don't want you ladies to get the wrong idea, but me and my friends were just wondering if you ladies would like to join us for a drink." He pointed toward the other table.

"Oh, listen, thanks, really . . ."

"I just want you ladies to know," he said, his voice taking on a deep seriousness, "that me and my friends don't have any intentions."

I looked at Chris.

"We're just here on leave." He brightened up, losing some of the murky southern accent that, obviously, he had put on with the boots. "From the army? We're stationed at Fort Hood," he said. "That's in Texas."

I looked at Chris, who for no good reason had begun to paw aimlessly through her handbag.

"Would you like a cigarette?" He produced the most unrumpled, clean-edged pack of Marlboros I had ever seen.

"Help yourself."

She took one and he lit it with a flashy, chrome-plated lighter.

"I have two packs," he said.

I looked at Chris. She was weakening.

"We don't get to see many smart city girls down in Texas," the boy said.

There was a long pause.

"I have an eight-year-old daughter," Chris said.

"That's okay."

"And a husband," she said. "Sort of." She laughed.

"We don't have any intentions," the boy said. "Honest."

❧

There were three of them: Dwayne, Kevin, and Greg. One was dark, one was thin, and one was talkative. They ordered what looked like a milk bottle full of what looked like apple juice.

"We're only having one," Chris said. "I'm waiting for my husband."

"Sure," Greg said. "That's okay."

"This is a nice place," Kevin said. "Do you come here often?" He pronounced the "t."

"Not really," Chris said. "I'm just showing my friend around. She's down visiting me from Canada."

"Canada?" one of them said. "I was in Canada once. They talk French there."

"Not all of them. Just in Quebec."

"Ever been to Red Lake?"

I shook my head.

"It's in Ontario. I think. Maybe Manitoba. Me and my dad used to go fishing there. It's a great place to fish, but the gas is expensive, wow."

"Dollar forty a gallon," Kevin said.

"It's not a real gallon," the other one said. "It's a bigger gallon."

The conversation foundered.

"I don't know what they call it."

I stared at the maze of stitching on Greg's boots, an arabesque of red and white thread from which now an eagle's wing, now a star struggled to emerge, faltered and fell back into the web.

He leaned toward me. "Were you originally born in Canada?"

I stared at him for a long time, at the milky blue eyes like the gentle eyes of animals, the hair so short it seemed no more than a faint red stain on the fragile skull, and for no good reason—I still don't understand it—I lied.

"No," I said. "I was born in Ohio."

"Where at in Ohio?"

"Canton," I said. "I went to school at Kent State."

"Is that anywhere near Akron?" Greg punched Kevin. "Remember that time in Akron?" He turned his empty eyes to me. "We went to Akron one time? Right after graduation. Kevin's grandma lives there."

Kevin looked up. "It's about half an hour, he said.

"The way you drive."

The name had meant nothing to him. We were simply going through the old American ritual of finding out who lives where, who knows what towns, connecting the dots on the map. Springfield, Cheyenne, San Francisco. Kent, Chicago, Saigon. They were just places to him, made for him. Nothing had ever happened in any one of them, and nothing would until he got there. Looking at his sweet, comic Norman Rockwell face, I wanted to reach over and slap the silly kid happiness out of him. I remembered Ray and Bud, shipping out for San Diego, high on some sappy top forty song about "California girls," dreaming of motorcycles.

"So, how do you like the army?" I asked Kevin.

"It's okay. I'm in diesel school."

I tried to assume some appropriate expression.

"A lot of people put it down, you know?" He smiled. "But, I think, hell, it's a good deal. I didn't want to go to college."

"Look at me," Greg said. "When I get out, I'll be a qualified diesel mechanic."

"There's always a demand for them."

"Right. And what do you think they make?"

I shook my head.

"Well, what do you think? Guess."

"Ten dollars an hour?"

"Thirteen." He smiled broadly. "That's what they make in Texas anyways."

They had each ordered big, bloody hamburgers with onions and relish—neither Chris nor I had felt like eating—and devoured them in half-a-dozen bites. The plates lay like casualties on the table, stained with ketchup and sesame seeds.

"So, what do you say, Dwayne?" I asked the quiet one.

Tipped back in his chair, his eyes half closed, he reminded me a little bit of my brother: the same defensive thoughtfulness, the eyes.

"I don't know," he said. "The army's okay. But, it's just killing time, you know? You ain't gettin' no better and you ain't gettin' no worse."

Photographs: A young man, Vietnamese, braced against the bullet, his eyes squeezed shut and his mouth twisted. A soldier has a gun to his head; he has just pulled the trigger. The young man's brains are a delicate mist just beginning to spray to the right of the frame.

A little girl, naked, her sex open and vulnerable, running, the first in a pack of terrified children, running down a road with her flesh on fire.

The wine was almost gone, and I was signaling Chris with my eyes to drink.

"Doesn't look like your hubby's gonna show," Greg said. "Hey, are you two beautiful girls really married?"

"Sometimes I wonder," Chris said.

"Let's have another." Greg put his hand on my arm. His fingers were soft and damp, like a little boy's hand.

"Not for us."

"Aw, Ladies, . . ."

"We really can't." I was suddenly angry. I pushed my chair back, stood up and grabbed my bag. "I have to go home early in the morning."

⁂

The subway station was dim and smoky; it was old. An old black man was hosing down the platform. In the car, the lights were needle bright, reflecting my face in the flat black windows as we wailed through the empty stations.

When they brought Bud Leech's body home, it was Christmas. The snow glistened that year like a Hallmark card, and Mom had a wreath on the door. I came home on the Greyhound bus, and when Dad met me at the depot, there were tears in his eyes. "Cold enough for you?" he said.

Going back to Toronto, I sat next to a boy in uniform. The driver, in cowboy boots, his belly hanging over a brass belt buckle, mothered him all the way to Kalamazoo.

Where you stationed, soldier?

I leaned my head against the rattling window and listened to them talk.

Necessary Fictions

Prologue

I dream sometimes of a soft, feminine face, half formed and floating in a thin, uncertain light, and I know that it is Donna and that she is all the dreams that never came true. So frequently does she visit me that Bill can detect my sister in my eyes on those mornings when she seems to hover close. In the convenient way that dreams collapse meaning and condense it into easy, acceptable answers, Donna surfaces occasionally as a touchstone, an unspoken parable of our lives. I would miss her if she were gone, although her ghostly presence doesn't really explain anything.

Donna had my father's sandy hair, my mother's pale skin and steady eyes. Even as a newborn her gaze was so knowing that my parents used to amuse themselves by imagining her thoughts.

"She's thinking about life," my father would say. "She's thinking, 'What's it all about?'"

"She's thinking about lunch," my mother would say.

"And, you know, I bet she knows something, too."

"The wisdom of the ages?" my mother would say.

"Something like that."

Trailing clouds of glory, new-minted and unbelievabley perfect down to the tiny half moons of her fingernails, Donna was rightfully cherished. It seemed impossible that she could die.

She leads me up the stairs of the house on Delaware, empty now, and down the hall to my room, still so naively feminine, just as my father designed it. The pink rose wallpaper, the little vanity table my father made. I lean my cheek against the cool, white enamel of the window frame and remember.

Outside, my brother and Bud Leech are practicing hook shots on the asphalt driveway, using Bud's basketball, the regulation hoop still only imagined above the garage door, not due to appear in our lives until Christmas. It is late afternoon. My mother is at the dining room table downstairs, hunched over the Singer and growing round with Donna, still a promise; and my father, with Duke at his feet, has set up his battered sawhorses out on the drive. Building, dreaming, he is completely himself, lost in the intermittent whine of the power saw.

It is summer, hot and hazy. Grandma is still alive. The sun is just settling in the limbs of the horse chestnut tree, which is still thick with leaves, which has not yet burned. Everything is back in place and waiting, and when the shadows strike the dining room wall at a certain angle, my mother will put her sewing machine away and set the table and call us all in for supper.

I

My brother is an alcoholic. That is the most recent explanation. For almost a year now the talk about Ray has been centered on "dependency" and "addiction." What we have is a medical situation.

"Diseased," Ray says sometimes. He points to his head and smiles.

This is the latest story he tells about himself, and it dovetails so neatly with the facts of his life—the war, the divorce from Chris, the endless succession of temporary, dead-end jobs—that it's become almost impossible to refute.

"Well I, for one, don't believe it," my mother said when Bill and I tried to explained it to her. "He's trying to gain our sympathy for some reason."

"I wonder why."

"I am *not* responsible," she said. "I refuse to take any share of the blame."

"No one's blaming you."

"And what is this *helplessness?* Why is he *helpless?*"

"It's just a way of talking about it," Bill said. My husband is quasi-medical; he keeps up on these things.

"Of course, he may really be . . . troubled," my mother said. "That would be understandable, I suppose."

My father had died eight months before. He died on the gentlest Sunday morning I had ever seen, in April when the grass was still a tender uncertain green and the daffodils were just beginning to show. He died in his car, a one-car accident. Opinions varied as to exactly what happened.

"Ray was all right until your father's . . ."

"Accident?"

"He just can't accept it," she said.

After Dad died, my mother talked for a while about getting a job, volunteering, joining a club. As it turned out though, she did none of those things. Instead, she simply lived on, like one of those mysterious air plants that seem to need no water, no light. And then her sister, Estelle, moved to Florida.

"It's called a condo," Mother said. "I always think of that other word."

"What word?"

"You know," she said, whispering.

Mother had decided to sell the house. "It's really the only sensible thing to do," Estelle informed her over the phone. "It's just too much for you now, Ruthie," she said. "All alone."

"Well, . . ."

"And so expensive. I don't know how you've managed."

"Plus the worry," Mother said, "that's the worst of it."

"Well then," Estelle said, "the time has simply come."

My father was a carpenter. He stayed on top of the maintenance and did everything himself—painting, plumbing, even roofing the house one summer, he and Ray. But, after he died, the paint began to peel. The ash gray shingles he nailed down weathered and curled. The plumbing groaned and complained until the bathroom tap ran only a trickle of cold rusty water. My mother would phone in a panic, but nobody knew a good plumber, and the man she finally got—out of the yellow pages—charged her a hundred and seventy-two dollars just to fix the faucet.

"And it still doesn't work right," she said.

Seams opened up; a network of hairline cracks began to fan out across the dining room ceiling.

"Get Ray to look at it," I'd tell her. "He's the carpenter."

"Ray?"

"Your son. Raymond Gerhardt Junior. Remember him?"

"I wasn't sure to whom you were referring."

Something always needed to be tightened or tacked back in place. Mother worried constantly—about the wiring, about the furnace.

"Don't look at me," Bill said.

So, as my mother says, "the decision was made." Estelle found a condo in Clearwater, near where she and her husband, Floyd, were living, and Mother took it sight unseen. The same day she got Estelle's call, she telephoned Iowa Realty, the firm that had sold my parents their house back in 1958.

"Of course, you know the neighborhood's changed," they told her.

"Oh, yes," she said, "yes." But she didn't know.

They told her that, at the right price, the house should move quickly.

"Fine," she said, "fine. That's . . . wonderful."

In the meantime, Mother was staying with us, sleeping on a rollaway in the small second bedroom of our apartment, the room my husband likes to call "the study." Estelle and Floyd were supervising the other end of the move in Florida and had already directed the unloading of the Mayflower van at my mother's new home.

"Just leave everything packed," my mother told them. "I'll handle everything when I get down there."

Estelle and Floyd knew that Mother, despite her bravado, could not "handle" things of that magnitude, and there were good-natured quarrels over the phone in which Mother claimed that they are doing way too much for her, and they replied, always, "Well, what are families for?"

The furniture from the house on Delaware was much too large for the condo, Estelle told Mother. The sofa crowded the patio door, and the cherrywood hutch that held her china and crystal blocked the hallway and towered over the little Formica kitchen table they bought for her at a yard sale.

"Well, I just can't get rid of everything overnight," my mother said. There was an edge to her voice.

I have the matching cherrywood dining room table and the six Queen Anne chairs that were grandmother Carlson's. It was obvious even to my mother that they would not fit in her tiny Clearwater kitchenette, and, besides, it had always been my responsibility to fill those heirloom chairs with two or three healthy, normal children, something Bill and I neglected to do.

❦

"Kaymus?" my mother said.

"*Mais, non, Madame.* Ca Moo. Make like a cow. Ca." Bill held up his index finger. "Moo."

"Ca moo." My mother laughed. "What's it about?"

She was standing in front of the book shelves in the dining room. "All these books," she said, to no one in particular. "Have you really read all these books?"

Bill, in fact, has read all the books, and I have read many. Instead of children, Bill and I have books, films, records, prints. And we have Barbara Stanwyck, Bill's cat, the most recent in a long succession of feline starlets with the orange tiger-stripe markings Bill admires: Rita Hayworth, Lucille Ball.

"Books," my mother said. "They certainly collect the dust, don't they?"

In Canada, Bill and I read through the long northern winters: American history, American lit. Everything from Hawthorne to Joseph Heller. We read our way through the end of the war, through two assassinations, through Watergate.

"*The Myth of . . .* I can't pronounce this word." My mother held the book with both hands, clearly intrigued by the wispy little stick man on the cover, pushing a cartoon rock up a steep incline. "What's it about?"

"Dinner's ready."

"Is it a novel?"

"No."

"What is it then?"

"It's hard to explain." Bill glanced away. "It's a dated argument, really, in some ways . . ."

"It's about suicide being the ultimate question," I said finally. "It's my book."

"Oh," she said. There was a long pause.

"Is life worth living? If not, why not. That sort of thing."

"I can't believe you'd waste your time on something like that, Maggie," she said. "I mean, unless you're contemplating suicide."

Opinions varied as to exactly what happened. The car was a 1989 Bonneville, a bronze four-door, traveling, the older policeman estimated, at eighty-five miles an hour. My father was not wearing a seatbelt. My father always wore a seatbelt. When the car hit the bridge abutment, it flipped and lifted over the guardrail.

"Let's all just sit down and eat," Bill said.

"And how is the question answered?" My mother was standing her ground.

"I can't remember," I said. "It's been a long time since I read that book."

My mother flipped the pages. "I like my questions answered," she said.

Bill took the book from her hand. "It's time for dinner."

We seated ourselves at the dining room table.

"Anyone want coffee? Mom?"

She lifted her hand, palm out, stopping imaginary traffic. "Not for me, Dear. I'd be up all night."

We huddled at one end of the oversized table, shuffling bread and salad and pasta between us.

"Why do you read those books?" my mother said. "I mean, I can see liking a good story."

We raised our voices as we spoke, as though that would help clarify matters between us.

"I don't know," I said. "It's just an old paperback."

She waited for an answer.

"Tell her," Bill said.

"What?" My mother stiffened.

"I don't think I should," I said.

"What?" Alarm was growing in her voice.

"Well, see, Mom, God is dead," I said. "And the system is breaking down."

"The infrastructure is crumbling," Bill said darkly. "It always does."

"Traditional family values . . . kaputt," I said. I shook my head in dismay.

"And we just want to know what to do about it."

My mother never knows quite how to read us in this mood. She stabbed at her salad.

"I want to see Ray," she said.

Ray was just out of jail, driving while intoxicated. It wasn't his first offense. He had a court date early in January.

"I said, I want to see my son. I know he probably doesn't want to see me."

"He never said that."

"Not in so many words." She pushed her plate away. "He blames me, I suppose. Well, we did the best we could."

"Nobody blames you. He was angry," I said. "We all say things we don't mean when we're angry."

"And that makes it all right, I suppose," she said.

She rose from the table dramatically. "I'm not hungry, Margaret," she said.

❧

Bill was stretched out on the bed, watching *Invasion of the Body Snatchers*, the old one with Kevin McCarthy, on the black-and-white in the bedroom when I came in.

"Well, I got the dishes washed. Mom's gone to bed."

Bill said nothing.

"The sound of dishes clattering in the sink didn't disturb you, I hope."

He scowled.

The pods were running amok in Santa Mira, and Kevin McCarthy was out on the freeway, frantically pounding on the windshields of passing cars.

"Think they'll stop them this time?"

"There were two endings to this," Bill said. "One where they believe the guy's story and call out the army and one where they don't."

You fools, Kevin McCarthy said, *You're in danger. Can't you see?*

"Which one is this?"

They're after you, . . . They're after all of us. You're next!

"Well, there's just one movie," Bill said, "but the thing is, they forced a happy ending on Siegel. The director. His original ending's ambiguous."

I slipped out of my jeans and sweater, pulled on my old chenille bathrobe, and settled in beside him.

"Do you ever feel like that?" I said.

"What? Like a pod?"

"Sort of hollow."

"Sometimes," he said.

"Mom says . . ."

"We've been over this. Let her think whatever she wants to think."

"'I want my questions answered,'" I said. "Like hell she does."

"It's possible you're wrong, you know."

"I don't think so."

"What do you want, Maggie?"

"I want the truth."

"Want your ledger to balance?"

"Yeah, I do."

Silence. Close-up of Kevin McCarthy.

"Is that so bad?"

Bill put his index finger to his lips, pointed at the set. "Just watch."

Only by chance was the hero's incredible pod story believed. In fact, they were about to cart him off to the loony bin when an accident on the highway dumped a truckload of pods on the pavement.

Where was the truck coming from? someone asked.

Santa Mira.

Now the man in the white coat was on the phone, calling the state patrol, the FBI. Kevin McCarthy sank against the door frame. The screen went black.

"Another cataclysmic disaster averted," Bill said. He switched off the set. "Thank God they stopped them in time."

At two o'clock in the morning the phone rang.

"Hi, Merry Christmas, I have cancer."

"What? Wait. Let me get a light."

It was Chris. She was crying, clearly drunk. "Oh, Mag," she said. "What the hell's the point?"

"How bad is it?

"Bad as it gets."

Bill struggled awake. "Who is it?"

"Nobody," I said. "Go back to sleep."

"Oh, sure."

"It's Chris. She's got some trouble." I switched on the light. "Chris?" A muffled laughter seeped through the telephone line.

"Going, going, gone. Those perky boobs. The near north side is devastated. Men are jumping out of hotel windows."

"Let me talk to her," Bill said. He reached for the phone.

"Leave us alone, for once. This is none of your business."

Stanwyck flattened her ears and hightailed it off the bed.

"Okay, okay," he said. "Jesus, Mag." He got up and put on his robe and slippers. "I'll make some coffee."

"Actually, they're only taking one," Chris said. "They say I'm lucky. Hasn't spread yet. Isn't that a laugh?"

The crying had stopped. "Are you alone?" I said.

Silence.

"I'll come in. I'll get some time off work. When are they planning . . ."

"Maggie? Don't tell Ray."

"Of course, you defend him," my mother said. "Both of you." It was the next morning. When Bill and I got up and stumbled out to the kitchen for coffee, my mother was already dressed to go out and resumed the conversation of the night before as though no time had elapsed.

"We don't defend him," Bill said. "We just don't blame him. Ray has a disease. He isn't any happier about it than you are."

"And he's *helpless* against alcohol," she said. She tossed her head abruptly, dismissing the thought.

We carried our coffee into the dining room and sat down at the table, Bill at one end with the newspaper in his lap, me midway down its length, across from Mom.

"And I don't want to hear any war stories," my mother said. "My goodness, when we were young, your Dad and I, the whole world was at war."

She stirred her coffee with quick, angry swirls of her spoon. "Have you met this woman? This what's her name?"

"Courtney."

"Courtney." She handled the name of Ray's new girlfriend the same way she might have handled a squashed cockroach in a Kleenex.

"That's what she calls herself. I think her real name is Sharon or Cheryl or something."

"Why do they all have such funny names these days?" my mother said. "Sounds more like a destination to me."

"It's a fad. Supposed to sound classy, I guess. Whitney, Tiffany."

"Chutney," Bill said. "Piccalilli."

"She's much too young for him," Mother said. "A cocktail waitress? She has a child, I understand."

"Yes."

My mother has a way of settling her shoulders, as if she were shrugging off some unpleasant garment.

"It's not against the law to have a child," I said.

"Well, one would think it is around you two."

"Okay." Bill slapped down the paper. "I'm going to go shave." He walked out of the room, leaving my mother and me staring across the table at one another.

☙

Ray and Courtney lived in a house trailer—mobile home, my mother corrected me. As we approached, a wiry mongrel sitting near the stoop snarled and feinted an attack, then retreated behind the fragile latticework that concealed the tenuous footings of the trailer.

"Hi," Courtney said. "Hi, you guys." She held the storm door open, balancing a grimy toddler on her hip. "Ray's still sleeping. Come on in."

My mother took the middle of a worn plaid sofa that spanned the end of the narrow living room, and I perched on a kitchen chair. The kitchen area was distinguished from the living room only by the presence of linoleum on the floor instead of green shag carpeting. A tiny, useless sink hung on the wall.

"You guys want some coffee?" Courtney said.

"We want to see Raymond," my mother said.

I smiled at Courtney; I smiled at the baby, but Mother held firm.

"Ray," Courtney yelled down the hall.

The trailer was tossed and dark, like the cave of animals. Dirty dishes were scattered over the kitchen counter; toys littered the floor. I saw my mother wince as Courtney put the child down on the carpet, which was stained and fuzzy with lint.

"This is a cute place," I said.

"It's kind of messy now," Courtney said. "We're fixing it up."

We stared at each other. "Ray!" she yelled, her eyes still fastened on me.

Just as she started to yell again, my brother appeared, barefoot and shirtless, at the end of the hall. His hair was wild from sleep, and he had a dark growth of beard.

"Hey," he said. "Mom."

He was obviously hung over. He poured himself a cup of coffee and sank down on a chair beside me at the kitchen table.

"You're not working today?" my mother said.

"That's right, Mom," he said. "I'm not working today." He let his lack of an explanation hang in the air.

"I thought you'd be working," my mother said.

"Why did you come over then if you thought I'd be working?"

"Well, I didn't come for a fight," my mother said.

Courtney scooped her child up and melted into the far end of the trailer.

Ray sipped his coffee. "Well, good," he said. "Good."

My mother wanted Ray to take the house. She thought it would steady him. And she was reluctant to see it go. Bill and I "refused" to own a house—my mother's word—a form of blasphemy she could not understand. My mother thinks that, because we went to college, we can afford anything we want.

"How's Little Sister?" Ray said. He smiled at me. "Come over to help scold me?"

"No."

"How's old Bill?"

"He's okay."

"Old Pecos Bill," Ray said, putting on his cowboy accent.

Courtney returned with a tray of coffee cups and some Oreos on a plastic plate. Mother ignored her.

"How's Aunt Estelle?" Ray asked my mother, pouring on the good-old-boy accent.

"She's very well."

"How's old Uncle Floyd?"

My mother straightened her spine. "I don't find this one bit funny," she said. Tears were starting in her eyes.

Ray looked down, gave his coffee cup a quarter turn. "I don't either," he said.

My mother stood and walked out the door so fast that no one had time to stop her. I heard the car door slam and knew she was sitting stiffly on the passenger side, waiting for me and crying silently.

"You could talk to her," I said. "You could try."

Ray looked away from me, and when he spoke again his country-boy accent was gone. "How's Christine?" he said. "Still hear from Chris?"

II

My mother slipped her key in the lock and the door gave easily, as though the house still knew us.

"I could never leave a dirty house," she said. "I always thought that was such a trashy thing for people to do."

With everything gone, the house had a hungry quality. The living room carpet was crisscrossed with darker traffic patterns, senseless now that the furniture was gone, and in the kitchen each vanished cup and drinking glass had left a ghostly print of itself on the shelves. My mother intended to scrub those rings away and line the shelves with fresh, bright paper.

"I'll start in the kitchen," she said. "Maggie, why don't you start upstairs."

Clearing out the house had been a continuous battle, with Mom at first wanting to hang onto everything, then wanting to see it all go, then wanting it back.

"You can't take everything," I told her.

We fought over every lamp and end table, had stormy, drawn-out discussions over ashtrays and Tupperware. Once she started to cry. "You want me to explain everything," she said, "how every little piece fits in."

"You're right," I said. "Pack it."

"No, *you're* right. I can't take everything."

As it turned out, she took way too much. I could imagine her condo down in Florida, bulging with overstuffed chairs and elaborate bric-a-brac, forlorn and out of place in the streamlined efficiency of her new home.

We had frequent spats, followed on both sides by hours of childish sulking.

"You can't understand what it's like," she said once. "You and Bill. We raised a *family* in this house."

In my parents' room four indentations in the carpet marked where the bed had stood, a few stray hangers remembered their clothes. Their lives were still there, just beyond perception. The room recalled the routine of forty years, the way people grow into each other and into a place. Even the knots in the drapery cords, the checked paint on the windowsill had meaning.

"You know, I can't remember your father's face," my mother said. This was only a month or two after he died. "It scares me. It's as though he never existed."

"Sure you can," I told her. But the fact was that my father's face was slipping from my mind, too, and yet he seemed close, a presence. I

sensed him in the quiet of a shadow, in the heavy, humid air of a summer night. A wayward breeze could make me believe that he was passing my door, and I saw him a dozen times in the streets, haunting the
bodies of stocky, faded redheads who looked a little bit like him or had
his way of completing some small gesture. He was everywhere and
nowhere. I rifled my memory for a good story, something to hold him
in place.

"And I'm so angry with him," my mother said.

After my father retired, he began to have stomach pains, shortness
of breath. He woke up often during the night, worried about money,
my mother said. He'd dream that fire was breaking out inside the walls
of the house, that the roof was leaking. She would wake at three or
four in the morning, and the kitchen light would be on, filtering up
the stairs to their bedroom door.

"Of course, I never went down," she said. "I wanted to."

That was when the night driving began. My father would take the
car out and drive alone for hours along the interstate. Once he drove
all the way to Omaha and might have just kept going if the car hadn't
blown a fuel pump as he headed on west for Lincoln.

"Did you ever go with him?" I said.

"He never asked me."

And then he died. A one-car accident. Opinions varied as to exactly what happened. The car was going eighty-five miles an hour. When
it struck the bridge, it flipped and lifted over the guardrail. My father
wasn't wearing a seatbelt. My father always wore a seatbelt. "I'm sure
there's a perfectly logical explanation," my mother said.

The car landed upside down in a shallow riverbed, not deep
enough to allow it to sink. Of course, it filled with water, fairly quickly, but still . . .

The younger policeman noticed that there were no skid marks on
the pavement, that the car apparently hadn't swerved; but my mother
prefers to remember what the older policeman said: that my father
probably fell asleep at the wheel, that the car had just drifted toward
the bridge.

"That makes sense," my mother said. "Doesn't it?"

It was five o'clock in the morning. The sun was just coming up over Leech's garage; the lilacs were bathed in a misty light, and there was dew on the grass.

ಿ಼ೢೢೖ

I wandered downstairs. Ray was caulking the Formica countertop in my mother's kitchen, running a thin bead of polymer along the joint where water from the sink was seeping down into the wall. Suddenly he stopped and raised his head; he put down his caulking gun and opened the back door.

A helicopter skimmed the horizon, a giant dragonfly. "Ever time I hear one of them things, I say to myself, 'This time I ain't lookin' up.'"

He closed the door and smiled. "And I always look."

"Life Flight," I said. "From Methodist."

"Not old Bill's hospital."

"Nope."

"Vets had enough chopper rides," he said.

Bill is an orderly at Vet's hospital. "The Shit Can Man," he calls himself. Mother can't understand it. "A person with his education," she says, "choosing, *choosing*, Maggie, to throw his life away."

Ray sat down heavily on the kitchen floor and leaned back against the cupboard doors. "Good old Pecos Bill."

Beside him was an apple box that my mother had packed with photographs and papers and smaller boxes filled, no doubt, with still more photographs, more papers. The box had a large smiling Jonathan apple printed on the side above which she had printed in black Magic Marker: "Important Papers."

Ray rummaged through the box and pulled out a black leather jewelry case. "Hey, I wondered where this thing was at." Ray won a Bronze Star in Vietnam. Again, accounts varied.

"You know, Mom's still talking about the accident," I said.

"Maggie, don't you know about sleepin' dogs?"

He took the medal out of the box and dangled it in the light.

"I was the only guy in my squad who wasn't wounded," Ray said. "Only one, ever tell you that?"

I sat down beside him. The linoleum was a gray swirl of stylized marble, faded and worn thin over the years. I traced the pattern with my finger. I remembered the day Dad put it down.

"Ever tell you how I got this?" he said.

"Many times. And no two times the same."

He hunched down, squinted, extended his right hand as if to say, "Picture this."

"Mom's ready to leave."

"There I was, wounded in every orifice and hopelessly outnumbered."

"Ray."

"Surrounded by gooks and dinks and chinks and Charlies, hordes of 'em, Maggie, the yellow peril, ready to gut me. Oh, it was fearsome."

"Ray . . ."

He rolled his eyes toward me. "This is a goodun."

"Better than 'The Phantom of Danang'?"

"Oh, lots better'n that."

A silence filled the kitchen. He was waiting. "You gotta help me out," he said.

I was tired of playing the wide-eyed listener: *Gee, Ray, golly, what'd you do?*

"You need to tell the real story," I said.

He shrugged.

"Give you a handle on it," I said. "Try."

He leaned back against the cupboards and closed his eyes, thinking, then popped them open again. "I should wear this," he said.

"Why?"

"*The Scarlet Letter.* Ain't that a book?"

"That's a book."

He took the medal out of the box and pinned it on his plaid flannel shirt. "Pin this puppy right over my god-damned heart."

"What's the point?"

"Help me out here."

Together we got the medal positioned over his left shirt pocket.

"Point? I don't know. Only thing I ever did, I guess."

"I wouldn't say that."

He looked at me.

"There's Beth."

"Oh, yeah."

Beautiful Beth, my brother's only child. I pictured her chubby baby face in my mind, pale and bright-eyed like Chris. Then later images, a string of them: Beth as the homecoming queen, in the high school band. Junior Achievement, Computer Club. Beth, unlike her mother and me, seemed to know from the very first what she wanted. College scholarships, business major. Fresh out of school, she got a job as a customer-service rep for a bank in Chicago. She wore navy blue suits and bought herself diamond earrings and heavy gold chains. She had her hair precision cut and invested her money. Her mother and I were frankly amazed. So sure of herself.

"She's a pistol," Ray said. "She gets that from me."

Now she planned to marry, a boy with the same annoying confidence, the same irrational expectation of wealth. They were looking at houses in River Forest—"for investment," Beth said. She would have children, she said, of course. She would have everything.

"She votes Republican," Bill said once, "and believes everything they tell her."

"Looky here," Ray said. He held a picture: baby Beth in the arms of a beautiful girl. Christine Leech Gerhardt Davis. Ray's ex-wife.

He rubbed his thumb over the surface of the photo.

"I should of never let *her* go," he said.

"Oh, did you *let* her?"

"Not exactly."

He turned the picture end for end; Chris and Bethie slowly revolved in his hands. "Lotta water under the bridge," he said.

III

There used to be a small, dignified piano store called Hunsicker's four blocks from our house on Delaware. Pianos arrived there once or twice a month, packed in wooden crates the size of double beds and three- or four-feet deep. These crates were perfect for forts and Kool-

Aid stands—for building of any kind—and they were highly prized by the neighborhood boys.

My brother, Ray, and his friend, Bud Leech, would begin to haunt the store in early May, hanging around the back doors, part of a group of scruffy, restless ten- to twelve-year-olds, waiting for a piano to be delivered. Ray was the tallest among them, a lanky boy with straight brown hair and, by default, the leader because he was the oldest and the best builder among them.

You had to be there right at the moment when old Mr. Hunsicker and his only son, Leo, carried a crate through the double doors in the back and on out to the alley. Then you had to ask, politely but with a touch of indifference, to take possession of the crate, and you had to call Mr. Hunsicker "sir."

Mr. Hunsicker had no interest in the affairs of the neighborhood boys, and as long as he was addressed politely, he gave his permission to haul the crates away. But Leo, a flabby, overgrown boy himself, liked to play games.

"This crate?" he'd say, eyeing each boy in turn. "This crate here?"

You had to humor Leo.

"What you want it for?" he'd say.

The bravest boy—and this, whatever Bud said, was always my brother—would explain that they were planning to build a tree house.

"What you want a tree house for?" Leo would say. "Are you a monkey?" Leo stood watching them, rolling his tongue in his mouth and making gentle sucking noises. "Are you a chimpanzee?"

The trick was to stay silent and motionless. Sooner or later old Mr. Hunsicker would come boiling out the back door, looking for Leo.

"Boys, we're busy here," he'd say. "Take the damned thing and go home."

Girls were never invited to go on piano-crate expeditions. This was serious business, requiring at least four boys—six worked better—and two or three coaster wagons. Girls did not have the muscle or the brain power to haul piano crates, and it was only when there were absolutely no more boys available that my brother would allow me to tag along.

First, the wagons had to be positioned, one facing home, the other behind it, but pointed in the opposite direction. Then the wheels had to be stopped with good-sized rocks to keep the wagons from rolling out from under the box when the weight came down. This done, a boy would lift each corner and, like pall bearers, carry the box to a position of precise balance over the wagons and lower it carefully. It helped to have an extra boy to supervise, someone to run around the box, checking its position as it came down on the wagons.

Then one boy lifted the handle of the front wagon and another took the back. One would pull, one push his wagon in perfect synchronization, while the other boys steadied the box from the sides.

Curbs, of course, were a problem. Any bump might disturb the delicate balance and send the crate sliding off the wagons. No boy was strong enough to stop a box from falling once it began to shift, and at least one boy every summer had his bare toes crushed beneath a falling crate.

Though the crates were large and cumbersome, they were oddly fragile. Made of an amazingly thin and flexible two-layer plywood, they protected the piano, I suppose, more from dust and scratches than from major damage. The plywood was attached to pine one-by-twos that formed the supports of the box, but these, too, were flimsy, and the whole thing was a little like the eggshells we prepared at Easter time: incredibly tough when the egg was intact, fragile once the egg was blown from the shell.

My brother and Bud were the best at conning Leo out of the crates and best, too, at the complicated logistics of transporting the boxes home. Sometimes partners in securing these prizes and sometimes rivals, Ray and Bud were able on one occasion during the summer of 1958 to secure two crates at the same time and balance them one on top of the other on four wagons. This was difficult and required an army of boys, but the construction it made possible—a fabulous double-decker tree house wedged in the swaying branches of the neighborhood's oldest and most stately horse chestnut tree—was, undeniably, magnificent.

Ray and Bud were never able to cooperate for long, however, and once the excitement of securing the crates had passed, fights broke out over who was to be the boss. Wiry and good-looking, with a monkey's cleverness, Bud was the leader of a rag-tag group of four or five boys who had nothing much in common except their limitless energy and an uncritical eagerness to accomplish whatever building project they dreamed up for themselves. Mother referred to them as "that gang of boys" and worried constantly that Bud might lead her own son astray. There were, she said, "concerns" in regard to Bud Leech.

Bud's mother had died some years before, a fact that advertised itself in the Leech's dirty windows and cluttered, overgrown yard; and Bud's sister, Christine, had been enlisted to take her place. Sometimes she accepted this role, and sometimes she rebelled, flatly refusing to cook and clean, spending her time instead painting her fingernails and setting her hair in big pink rollers. By the age of eleven, she had discovered my brother.

Bud's father was an over-the-road trucker. He was gone most of the time, and when he did come home, drunk and belligerent, there would almost always be a fight, a sort of free-for-all among the three of them, which would end only when Christine stormed out the front door, wearing that awful brown hand-me-down coat she wore back then and carrying a battered dark blue train case. Chin up, refusing to cry, she would march across their scruffy lawn, squeeze through the hedge, climb our porch steps, and spend the night with me.

Balanced between Bud and Ray was Crazy Nordell, who lived in the house just west of us. Intelligent, but a "weirdo," Joe Nordell was a dreamer who spent his time inventing strange gadgets and writing exotic South Sea adventure novels. He buried things and drew complicated maps to show their location, scorching the edges of the paper to simulate aging parchment. He trapped fat, gray pigeons in an elaborate wire cage he built, intending to train them to carry messages across the country in a special little leather pouch he'd stitched together. (This enterprise, he said, would make the federal postal system obsolete.) He drew strange tattoos on his arms with a straight pin and doused them with blue Scripto ink until the color seeped into the wounds and stayed there. Ray and Bud built their clubhouse in the horse chestnut tree that marked the property line between Nordell's lot and ours because it was the only tree in the neighborhood big enough and with a suitable configuration of branches, but Joe Nordell was not invited to help.

Sometimes Mrs. Nordell would send Joe out to the tree house construction site with a pitcher of red Kool-Aid. She hoped, I suppose, that this transparent bribe would insinuate Joe into Ray and Bud's boyhood activities and wean him from his eccentric loneliness. But Ray and Bud hauled the Kool-Aid up on a makeshift dumb waiter and sent the glasses down again to Joe without even a thank you.

That was the summer my mother was pregnant with Donna, her third and, as it turned out, her last child. To prepare for the new arrival, my father took on a lot of overtime work for Cappelli. He even hired a helper, Mickey Tanner. Swinging his toolbox, Dad would depart every morning in a swirl of activity, leaving us, my mother and I especially, to spin ever more slowly in the eddy of his absence. Ray would leave for the tree house shortly thereafter, and with both of them gone, a stillness would settle in.

My mother had wanted to be an English teacher before the war came along. Instead, she took a job at the Chamberlain-Mylor plant where the other girls taught her to roll her hair in a wide crown above her forehead and coaxed her into going with them down to Babe's on Saturday nights to dance with the soldiers from Fort Des Moines. That's where she met my father; that's were she told him, gliding across the hardwood dance floor, that she would wait for him.

The only remaining trace of my mother's ambition was her tendency to speak too formally and her habit of reciting poetry from a worn green volume called *The Family Book of Best Loved Poems*.

"How do you like to go up in a swing, up in the air so blue?" she would recite to me.

And I would answer: "Oh, I do think it the pleasantest thing ever a child can do!"

"And the poet?"

"Robert Louis Stevenson."

She had a beautiful throaty voice and a natural ear for rhythms:

There are hermit souls that live withdrawn
  In the peace of their self-content
There are souls, like stars, that dwell apart,
  In a fellowless firmament;
There are pioneer souls that blaze their paths
  Where highways never ran;
But let me live by the side of the road
And be a friend to man.

"And the poet is?"

"Robert Browning."

"Wrong."

"Ella Wheeler Wilcox."

"Wrong, wrong." She gave me the name like a piece of candy: "Sam Walter Foss."

We seldom had actual conversations. Talk happened when there were men in the house, when my father came home, bringing his stories back from the bigger world, improbable, thrilling everyday adventures, wrapped in the buzzing rhythms of his voice. Without him, there was a loneliness to our lives, and though, through the day my mother and I kept busy—washing, ironing, peeling potatoes for supper—all the while we were waiting for the sound of his car in the drive, his shadow leading him back to the house at sundown. He walked in the door and started our lives again, like flipping a switch.

Coming on slowly with a long, teasing spring, summer exploded in color that year about the middle of May. Lilacs bloomed early, and the lawns ran wild with dandelions, and almost before we could get the porch screens up, it was already June. Racing toward summer, kids roller-skated down broken, sun-dappled sidewalks and marked the succession of firsts that shaped the season: the first trip to the Frost Top for ice-cold root beer in heavy, glass mugs, the first barefoot walk over a lawn sprinkled with heady lavender clover, the first fumbling game of worky-up that brought in the long, dust-grimy stretch of real baseball.

By mid-June, the grass was a startling green and, screened through a veil of humidity, the landscape shimmered. When real summer came on—July and August—the lawns bleached to a pale butter yellow and acquired a ghostly fragility, like the delicate ash of burned paper.

This was before houses had air conditioning, when housewives shuttered their windows against the heat and put their children down for their naps in twilight bedrooms where the blinds were drawn and an oscillating fan lapped waves of tepid air over the sheets. The women did their cooking early in the morning while the kitchen was still cool, making deviled eggs and potato salad for cold-plate suppers. Once or twice a week they made hamburger steaks with grilled onions, corn on the cob, and ripe tomatoes for supper; they made skillet meals like Spanish rice or mixed a can of tuna with egg and cracker crumbs and fried it a crisp light brown in margarine. The women drank iced tea and listened to their stories on the radio and ironed clothes in the basement where it was twenty degrees cooler. Young wives dragged a blanket out to the back yard around noon to lie out in the sun in bathing suits. They put a little peroxide on their hair with an old toothbrush and read *Life* and *Photoplay* while their hair bleached platinum in streaks and their arms and legs, wet with baby oil, tanned to the color of honey.

I spent my afternoons that summer upstairs in my grandmother Gerhardt's room, where, despite the western sun, there was always a faint breeze floating between the corner windows. The pine tree was still in place then at the corner of our lot and provided a view of sorts, and Grandma had an abundance of peppermint candy and magazines. We would sit, reading sometimes, or sifting through my grandmother's photographs. Often we simply watched a thin, pale triangle of slanting sunlight ease across the bright oriental carpet.

None of the men in our neighborhood was lucky enough to work in one of the air-conditioned office buildings downtown except John Nordell, Joe's father, who was an accountant for Bankers Life. Most, like my father, worked outside, shirtless or wearing only a white cotton T-shirt with a pack of Luckies rolled in the left sleeve. In summer each man carried an extra steel thermos of water or iced tea along with the usual thermos of black coffee, and his wife folded a tablespoon of salt into a square of waxed paper and tucked it into his lunchbox. The men burned to a deep mahogany tan or, in the case of my father, an angry red. His pale eyes grew intense and raw, set in his reddish summer coloring, and lost the sad tranquillity they seemed to have in winter.

Ray and Bud Leech secured the two piano crates in late May, when the weather had just turned warm. My mother was against their building the tree house and issued her usual vague hit-and-run warnings; but Ray ignored her, and Dad backed him up.

"He's a carpenter, Ruthie," Dad said. "Chip off the old block."

To make matters worse, the boys stripped off their shirts and worked bare-chested and went without their shoes for most of the day, something my mother considered uncivilized. Their hair, buzz-cut like my father's, bleached blond, and their arms turned dark, speckled with mosquito bites.

They lived like savages, their minds deep in construction. Bud no doubt imagined a lofty fortress, a vantage point from which he could spy on the mailman and the meter reader, something to give him the edge, finally, over his enemies. But Ray had his eye on Christine Leech as he built, and I believe he imagined a home in the tree for the two of them.

"It's a miracle to me," my mother said one evening over supper, "that you boys have not been killed—Maggie, pass the green beans— monkeying with that thing.

"And I am equally puzzled," she said to my father, "that you don't put your foot down, Ray."

"Aw, Ruthie, I don't think . . ."

"No, you certainly do not." She rose abruptly and cleared the table, whisking the plate from under my father's fork.

My mother's defense in all unpleasant matters was a chilly, sulking anger, which had to be coaxed out of her, kindled like a weak spark until it burst into flame. She expected to be pursued in arguments and would drop a hint of annoyance like a handkerchief. When—and this was usual—my father didn't stoop to pick it up, she would cold-shoulder us all for days, radiating fury through a calculated silence.

The funny part was that, despite her fuming, Mother was terribly proud of Ray's construction. She didn't tell him, of course, but I overheard her bragging to her sister, Estelle, on the phone. "Stell, you wouldn't believe it," she said. "The boy is simply a born architect."

IV

It was a dry summer, 1958, full of long, hot afternoons when the air grew sullen and motionless and the sky always seemed to be just on the verge of rain. That spring a forest fire had taken hold in the Black Hills, threatening Keystone and Hill City, where our family vacationed the year before; a series of small mysterious fires broke out in the apartment buildings my father and Mickey Tanner were working on for Cappelli. A grass fire got out of hand near Mitchellville, shrouding the highway in smoke and causing a chain-reaction traffic accident that claimed two lives. The whole world seemed dry and brittle and ready at any moment to burst into flame.

In the heat a faintly unpleasant odor had begun to be noticed. There was no doubt it was coming from Grandmother's room.

"What in the world is that smell?" my father thundered.

"Shhh."

"What is it?" he whispered.

Mother shook her head.

It was no secret that Grandmother hoarded things: newspaper clippings and photographs, remnants of fabric, magazines, buttons and zippers torn from old clothing to use again, greeting cards, tinfoil, steel pennies and pencils and safety pins. After what had happened—she was widowed the year before when my father's father died of pneumonia, and her oldest son, Earl, my father's rival, sold the farm quickly, not exactly with her consent—it was natural that she clung to whatever was left. Still, the clutter of her bedroom always gave my mother a turn. There was too much dark old-timey furniture, and it was piled with too much clothing, too many blankets and quilts. There were too many pictures on the walls. Stacks of magazines—too many—nestled in the corners; boxes of books and papers were hidden under the bed.

"It's unbelievable," my mother said.

Mother occasionally attempted to dislodge Grandmother Gerhardt and clean the room thoroughly, but Grandma would not budge.

"Open a window then, Mother Gerhardt, please."

I was the only one who knew about the food. In fact, I was responsible for some of it, bringing Grandma crackers and oranges and tea bags from the kitchen. She never ate any of this, as far as I know, just stored it in a box on the closet shelf. When one box was full, she would start another.

The resulting odor was not unpleasant to me. It had, some days, a wicked fruity smell, like wild honey, and seemed appropriate in the swelter of spring. I liked the smell, but I was alone in that judgment, and when it got unbearable, Mother and Dad confronted Grandma directly, knocking ceremoniously on her bedroom door one evening and demanding to search the room.

"Tomorrow," Grandma said. "Tomorrow, Ray."

When my father pushed his way in and saw the full extent of Grandma's clutter, he hit the roof.

"Jesus," Dad said. "Will you look at this?"

He turned on the glaring overhead light, something Grandma never did, and began pulling open drawers and pawing through the mess on top of the bureau, Grandma protesting, grabbing his arms, and he shaking her off.

One item that especially offended him was Grandma's soap collection. Whenever my mother discarded a sliver of bath soap, judging it too slender for further use, Grandmother retrieved it and saved it with dozens of others in a Folger's coffee can.

"You can melt those down," she told my father. "And use them up. They're still perfectly good." My father dumped the can in the wastepaper basket.

He pulled up the spread and peered under the bed. "Unbelievable. Why do you do this?"

He opened the closet door and a small avalanche of clothing tumbled out at his feet.

"I never dreamed it had gotten this bad," my mother said.

Dad pulled a box off the closet shelf and opened it, and the fumes from Grandma's hoard flooded the room.

Mother was peering over his shoulder and jumped back from the stench. "Oh, Ray," she said. "My Lord."

A shriveled orange and a stack of crackers green with mold were the only recognizable contents of the box.

"Well, it's just a mess," my grandmother said. "I know it is."

"Living like a bunch of god-damned Okies."

Grandmother reached for the box, but Dad had already dropped it in the trash.

"Ruth, for God's sake, get rid of this stuff."

Grandma was evicted the next day and quartered on the upstairs sleeping porch while Mother tried to scour down her room. The house filled with the pine scent of cleanser. Mother eventually burned Grandma's curtains when three washings in Oxydol failed to restore them, and she would have dragged the oriental rug out to the alley for the ragpicker if Grandma had not protested.

Grandma fought, too, to save the magazines. There was a long, convoluted discussion about them that afternoon as Grandma paced the hallway watching my mother clean.

"We will refer the matter to Raymond," my mother said finally. Referring debates to my father was always Mother's last resort. "You can tell him what you think should be done, and I will tell him what I think should be done."

When my father got home, my mother did refer the matter to him, telling it, to give her credit, fairly, but not failing to mention either her own efforts to keep our family on some semblance of a normal footing.

"I'll straighten it out," my father said.

"It isn't that I haven't made concessions."

"I'll straighten it out."

Mother and I followed my father upstairs. It was just about suppertime. Grandma was on the sleeping porch, sitting in the plain, mission oak rocker. Her head was tipped back at a slight angle and her eyes were open as though she were trying to remember something, something probably not all that important.

"Oh, Ray," my mother said. She put her hand to her mouth.

Sunlight was flowing in. Grandma's hair was down, and against the bare white walls of the porch she looked fragile and alone in her death and, curiously, as though she were fading, her clothes bleaching to white and even her skin growing pale and translucent. Outside my brother was shying grounders against the garage door. The impact of the ball striking solidly, followed by its return to the leather glove sounded hollow in the silence, a mockery of a heartbeat.

V

Only certain people were allowed up in the tree house. Some had an obvious right to be there; others bribed their way in. I was not a member of either camp, but, of course, Chris was.

"You know, Maggie," my mother told me, "the girl who gets all the attention isn't necessarily the lucky one."

Christine was permitted to paint her fingernails; Christine got the lead in the Easter pageant.

"Well, boo hoo hoo," my mother said. "I don't know what you think I can do about it."

She dismissed me with Emily Dickinson:

I'm Nobody! Who are you?
Are you—Nobody—Too?
Then there's a pair of us?
Don't tell!

And Christine was admitted to the tree house. She got her first kiss there, from Ray, she told me once, looking out over the roof of Nordell's garage.

I never saw the view from that lofty perspective, however, and, instead, had to imagine it. From that height I saw my world as an orderly pattern of tight gray roofs beneath the dapple of twirling horse chestnut leaves. I imagined how Mrs. Nordell would look from my bird's-eye view, and it seemed I could almost peer down into the loose French twist she wore as though it were a marbled sea shell, brown and yellow-gray. Her heavy shoulders, slumped in permanent resignation, her arms, covered with a plain, long-sleeved blouse, would contrast sharply with my mother's willful, military posture, my mother's arms, bare and solidly muscled. I imagined that the sidewalk would unfold below me like a board game and that, suspended between the earth and the sky, I would be too high to hear my father's relentless power saw or my mother and Ray bickering over the dozens of trivial points they chose to contest with one another.

In my mental tree house, I was myself, gloriously, alone. A usurper in the castle the boys had made, I watched how the sunlight tumbled through the windows, printing butter-colored squares on the white pine floor, and knew it was working in its brightness to weather the tree house brown as the tree itself. The smell of sunlight on wood is a little like citrus, a dry, peppery smell that is sharp in my mind. Like wild honey, it was as real in my imagination as the breeze through the rough-cut lookout windows, the sway of the horse chestnut tree.

I brought up my books and crayons and settled in, listening to a gentle wind twist the fragile plywood and chanting lines from "Evangeline" the way I had heard my mother do as she worked alone in the kitchen:

> *This is the forest primeval. The murmuring*
> *pines and the hemlocks,*
> *Bearded with moss, and in garments green,*
> *indistinct in the twilight,*
> *Stand like Druids of eld, with voices sad*
> *and prophetic,*
> *Stand like harpers hoar, with beards that rest*
> *on their bosoms.*
> *Loud from its rocky caverns, the deep-voiced*
> *neighboring ocean*
> *Speaks, and in accents disconsolate*
> *answers the wail of the forest.*

I came by my love of poetry through my mother, who recited to me with such sweet rhythms in her voice that I acquired, even before I knew what the words meant, an absolute faith in the kind of reconciliation with life that linguistic form could make possible. My mother was a poet. I imagine that, with training, she could have been quite good. Strangely, however, as the years went on, she suppressed her

artistic side, even seemed to mistrust it, and let her love of books be si-
phoned off in the reading of magazines. She had three or four sub-
scriptions: *Women's Home Companion, Better Homes and Gardens.*

Only occasionally would I find her scribbling verse on an old envelope, humming a meter softly to herself or weaving it in the air with
a yellow pencil. Only occasionally would she browse through her
book of familiar poems and chant them under her breath, her eyes
closed, her thick brown hair swinging to the meter.

Free verse of the type I wrote later in college was unthinkable to
my mother, or would have been had she known about it. Order was
the mark of achievement, and expression must find its place in traditional order. Once I showed her a copy of "The Wasteland." She was
genuinely horrified and countered with Robert Frost.

"It's pure gobbledegook," she said. "It doesn't mean anything at all."

Ours was a disciplined home. Romance was kept in check, and anything unfamiliar was "handled" immediately. Following advice from
the women's magazines, my mother attempted to approximate for herself the orderly life she sensed existed somewhere, in less chaotic, bet-
ter-run households. If my father's standard was newness, my mother's
was normalcy, the efficient rightness of family life that she read about
every month in *Woman's Day.* "Let's all just sit down and eat like normal human beings," she would say when turmoil swirled around the
dinner table; and when Ray and I would act up, she would plead with
us to "just act normal for a change."

In the glossy folds of the magazines, housewives in high heels and
stockings served solid, normal meals of thrifty casseroles to handsome
men in white dress shirts like the ones that Mr. Nordell wore. Normal
children, a girl and a boy—the girl was always younger—beamed up
at this normal housewife, respectfully offering to help her set the table.
They lived in normal houses where interesting picture books always
lay open at an inviting forty-five degree angle on the polished coffee
tables. Fresh-cut flowers, flanked by silver candlesticks, graced the dining room tables in normal homes. Fathers who looked a little like John
Nordell sat in tasteful wing-back chairs and read to scrubbed, chubby,
bright-eyed children while mothers looked on, smiling, from the
kitchen.

This was the life she wanted, but my father was not Nordell. Under the circumstances, Mother's battle to make our home match the ideals of the women's magazines was decidedly uphill and made her seem a little severe at times, set her mouth in a tight, determined grimace of resolve that only dissipated when she was baking or sewing or otherwise engaged in achieving the normal. Her one consolation was that, atypical as our family was, her children, thank goodness, were not as bad as that crazy Joe Nordell.

Joe was a constant irritation to Mother, and she criticized his mother at every opportunity

"That woman is completely ineffectual," my mother would say. (Mother's lost ambition to be a teacher caused her to look upon every utterance she made before us children as an opportunity to build our vocabulary.) "She does not restrain him in the least."

What alarmed Mother most were Joe Nordell's constant "experiments"—the mechanical manned-flight venture, for example, in which Nordell strapped a large pair of canvas-and-coat-hanger wings to his back and jumped off the garage roof. Mother censured him and his ineffectual mother, but she was fascinated by Crazy Nordell, too.

"Who does he remind you of?" my father would tease. Of course, he meant himself, Mother's bad-boy choice of a husband, the man her own father, John J. Carlson, would barely agree to share a meal with. Mother's father had been a retail clothier, very polished and normal in every way, and he had looked upon Dad as "unsuitable."

"Well, he ought to know," my father said. "He is a tailor."

"Merchant," my mother said.

Mother was strong-willed. She married Dad, a carpenter, against her family's wishes. She was only nineteen. It was, perhaps, the audacity of her decision that made her rigid in pursuit of a normal life. Having cut herself off from her old family, she had a need to prove that her new one was sound, as cheerful and clean and content as magazine families, thanks to her efforts.

Mother sensed from *Ladies Home Journal* that civilization rested upon her shoulders. Men made the world, and women maintained it. The house, the children, cleanliness and health, sex appeal and security were all left to Mother; and when anything went wrong, she had failed in her role. She was to blame, and of the making of occasions for guilt there was no end. If she were not vigilant, her family might suffer from headaches, split ends, bad breath, tooth decay, diarrhea. Their diet might be lacking in one of the essential nutrients. (Over half the children in American don't get enough vitamin C.) The home itself needed constant monitoring for germs in the toilet bowl, mildew and static cling, ho-hum meals, fingerprints, and dinner plates in which one could not see one's own reflection. Anything that could go wrong would go wrong.

Children were almost totally the product of their mothers' care and wisdom. Ironically, however, too much maternal concern could make children overly dependent on their mothers, a particularly disastrous possibility for boys. Girls raised themselves, easing into their mothers' patterns and becoming, in effect, almost their sisters. No special care need be taken of girls, but, with boys, mothers were required to achieve a difficult balance in which, on the one hand, the boys were encouraged to seek adventure while, on the other, their natural savagery was discreetly curbed. This was called nurturing their development, and this was the fine line that, according to Mother, Mrs. Nordell had failed to walk with Joe.

Mother blamed Mrs. Nordell for Joe's erratic behavior, railing at her secretly through his bottle-rocket stage, when no roof was safe from the flaming debris that Nordell launched from his upstairs window, and tracing it back to earlier afternoons when Joe spent hour after hour pounding caps with a tack hammer on the sidewalk in front of his house. It was then, my mother said, that Mrs. Nordell should have "nipped this thing in the bud."

This thing was fire. Almost every endeavor that attracted Joe Nordell had fire or explosives connected with it, and by the time he was eleven, that summer of 1958, he had accumulated a number of burn scars, including a fiery brand just above his right eyebrow where a cherry bomb fragment had caught him two years before.

Fireworks were illegal in Iowa, but somehow Joe always managed to get them. It was one of Joe's Roman candles, in fact, that had sent the ragpicker's horse careening down the alley the previous summer.

"Someone might have been badly injured," my mother said. "That boy's parents simply must take a firmer hand."

To be fair, Mr. Nordell did try to impress upon Joe the gravity of this episode by confining him to his bedroom for a week, but this was hardly a punishment for Joe. We would see him up in his window, reading, tinkering with some gadget. Joe was constantly sending away for things: crystal radios and magic tricks and, once, a live chameleon, a wonder of nature direct from the Amazon, which was dead on arrival, curled in a knot like a fiddlehead fern and smelling like Roquefort cheese.

In 1958 Joe ordered a Super Sleuth detective kit from the back of a *Classics Illustrated* comic book. It included a large magnifying glass, a paper deerstalker hat, a badge, a book, and a periscope. The information Joe would gain by using this "scientific investigative equipment" was guaranteed to amuse and amaze his friends; but, of course, Joe had no friends, just an intermittent alliance with Benny Wolf, the only son of the only Jewish family on the block.

Joe spied on everyone; he was, he said, writing an exposé. Women working diligently in their kitchens would suddenly be aware of a cardboard periscope poised at their windowsills; they would find their mail rifled, the ragged red petunias by their back doors trampled where Joe had hidden in order to observe them. The other women on the block criticized Joe himself, but Mother knew that children are never to blame. They merely reflect their upbringing, the sole responsibility of their mothers.

"Joseph has an inquiring mind," my mother said, "and the boy's mother should nurture his development."

VI

The day after my grandmother's funeral my father built a bonfire in the backyard and carried out the clutter of her room, marching relentlessly back and forth with my mother right beside him, protesting, his mouth set in a tight, grim smile.

"Don't you think we should look this over?" she said. "Just to see what's here."

"I know what's here."

When the stack of debris on the grass had reached almost the height of my head, he sat me down on a cardboard box in front of the fire and handed me a broom handle. It was my job, he said, to feed the fire, tossing on more papers as the first ones were consumed.

"One at a time," he told me. "Don't pile them on or they'll never burn. And if it starts to die down, give it a poke. Like this." He jabbed at the burning papers to illustrate, and they flared up, angry.

I started with the clippings, which burned quickly, seeming almost to dissolve in midair; then I burned the other papers, not bothering much to examine them. I burned the magazines and the scraps of cloth, and when there was nothing left but the photographs, I sailed them, one by one, into the fire, the way I'd seen my brother sail a deck of cards into an upturned hat.

They were mostly of men, men in groups, men posed severely in tight, black suits, seated, with comic bowlers balanced on their knees, or standing, both feet rigidly aligned. When there were women in the pictures, they stood demurely at the back of the photograph, fading away in white dresses, their eyes wide, like curious animals. All except one woman, Ellen, who stared out boldly. There were several portraits of her, and in each one she looked directly into the camera, defying it to capture and define her.

My grandmother was one of two sisters, not the pretty one. She was the hard worker, who packed the picnic lunch that Ellen took when she went, with first one boy and then another, to hear Sousa at the band shell in the square. Or she went to see the fireworks; it was the Fourth of July. They lit up the night. Oh, they took your breath away, they were so lovely. My grandmother, Esther, heard secondhand how sweet the cider was at the sociable, how silver and serene the moonlight was when the gentlemen escorted Ellen home. As though beauty and brains could not be contained in one woman, our family split these traits between the sisters, crowning Ellen with femininity, heaping duty on Esther.

Ellen was fair; Esther was darker, "cursed" she said with the reddish coloring that my father and I both inherited from her. Ellen was fragile. In the spring of 1908 she contracted scarlet fever.

"No one would help us nurse her," my grandmother said. "Every-one was afraid that we were contagious. When Ellie died, the under-taker refused to bury her, and Papa took her out to the meadow beyond the barn in the wagon and buried her himself on a little hill."

It was a wet spring, and constant rain had turned the fields to mud. Halfway up the hillside the horses faltered, one fell. The wheels of the wagon were sunk so deep in the mud that they wouldn't turn.

"There was no one to help," my grandmother told me. "My father and my mother carried her on."

Grandmother survived, a survivor. Her eyes did not challenge the camera in the one formal portrait I found of her and rescued from my father's homemade hell. Instead there was an inwardness, an almost belligerent rootedness in the physical fact of her being. Her eyes were flat, her mouth uninviting; a reluctance to join in the narcissism of portrait photography was evident in her posture, and there was a cer-tain impatience in the turn of her head.

"A stubborn woman," my mother said, pausing to peer at Esther over my shoulder. "Just like your Grandmother Carlson."

The afternoon lengthened into evening, and the sky turned peach and robin's-egg blue and then a neon orange behind the black branch-es of trees. The fire sank down slowly into a smoldering glow.

"Is that everything then?" my father said, giving the ashes a final stir with the toe of his shoe.

Out of all of Grandma's treasures, her scraps of cloth, her photo-graphs and yellowed clippings, I had saved only a lacy Christmas card from 1917 that showed two horses—a black and an ivory white one—pulling an old-fashioned sleigh; a small American flag; a purple cam-paign button; two photos, one of Ellen and one of Esther, and another I found later in the ashes, passed over, apparently, by the flames: a girl who, I realize now, may not even be Grandma, perched bareback on a plow horse in a feed lot somewhere, maybe near Albion.

"Well then," my father said, "that's that."

VII

It was late at night. My brother and I were sleeping on army cots on the screened-in front porch to catch what little breeze there was, and my mother and father were talking earnestly in low voices at the dining room table. I drifted in and out of dreams, aware at one point that my mother had come out to check on us and then aware suddenly of light.

It was not an ordinary light, nothing I'd seen before, but a glow like morning, only more intense and jumping crazily on the sky-blue enamel ceiling of the porch.

I knew what it was.

"Oh, my Lord," I heard my mother say. And then she was calling, "Raymond, Ray." My father was still at the table.

He came out on the porch with a bottle of beer in his hand. "What is it?" he said. "Ruth?"

My mother turned and ran back through the house. She threw the back door open, and light flooded in. "Oh, my Lord," she said.

The light was fire. Fire was climbing the horse chestnut tree between our yard and Nordell's. It whipped through the branches and played in and out of the windows of the tree house. Ray and I reached the back porch just in time to see a blazing limb disengage from the tree, drop and crash on the concrete of the alley.

"Call the fire department," my father said. My mother seemed frozen. "I'll do it," he said.

John Nordell came out of the house next door wearing a white dress shirt with the sleeves rolled up and carrying a newspaper folded under one arm. "Where's Joe," he said. "Where's Joe?" His wife came out and began to call, "Joseph, Joseph."

Mr. Nordell started to run for the tree with Mrs. Nordell hanging on his arm, and just then we heard a siren and a window opened upstairs at the Nordell house.

"Cripes," someone said from above. It was Crazy Nordell. He was leaning out the window watching the tree burn, the fire high and wavering like a torch.

John Nordell turned and yelled something up to Joe.

Mrs. Nordell said, "John, don't lose your temper."

Joe came out wearing baggy camp shorts with several pockets and a football helmet with a flashlight attached to the top with electrical tape. It was a sort of homemade miner's hat Joe had designed and constructed for himself in order to leave both hands free for catching night crawlers.

Mr. Nordell spoke to his son briefly, but before Joe could answer, his father grabbed him by the shoulders with both hands and began to shake him. Joe was a skinny blond kid, almost an albino, with thick, steel-framed glasses, and he rippled under his father's hands like a scatter rug being shaken free of dust.

"I knew it," my mother said.

We advanced across our backyard tentatively: Dad and Ray first, then me, then Mother, a little behind us. All of the neighbors were there: Bensons, Nordells, Leeches. We could see clearly inside the blazing piano boxes, and although the tree house was empty, mothers counted their children over and over and held them under crossed arms tight against their skirts.

Ray started forward, and Dad restrained him. "Just stay put," Dad said. "There's nothing you can do."

Firemen arrived and bossed us all back behind an imaginary line. They hooked up a hose and a floodlight and arced a golden curtain of water over the burning tree. The fire by this time had settled into a steady blaze, marked intermittently by the fall of flaming fragments or the sudden crack of burning wood that sent an exultation of sparks shooting upward. There was a terrible beauty in it; and, wrapped in my mother's arms, I thought—arrogantly, I suppose—that possibly I was the only one there who could see it.

I was wrong. Joe Nordell kept edging close to the fire. Each time he got within twenty or thirty feet, a fireman or Mr. Nordell or Mrs. Nordell would grab him by the arm and pull him back. Joe's glasses caught the reflection of flames; fire leaped and twisted in his eyes. Clearly, to me, he wanted to know the fire.

A heap of charred, glowing debris had accumulated at the base of the tree, and thin, isolated flames licked in and out of the crevices. The planks were blistered a silvery black, edged in white, lacelike; the wood had swollen and split into raised squares, and, in between, glowed tracings of orange and vermilion. Joe, unguarded for an instant, walked straight toward the tree, stopped and lifted his hand, and reached deliberately into the fire.

Mrs. Nordell screamed, and both my father and Mr. Nordell ran forward.

"Oh, my God."

They pulled him back. His hand was red and the fingertips of his index and middle fingers—Joe was left-handed—had started to blister badly. Thanks to the quick reactions of the men, Joe had not managed to actually grasp the wood, but the audacity of what he'd done shocked us, even the grown-ups, and I remember the whole crowd of neighbors began to swirl. A buzzing went up, voices, amazed and terrified.

"He's in shock," someone said.

Joe was unperturbed. Never said a word, just stood there, smiling. Crazy Nordell.

Joe's father carried him to the car—Joe's mother trailing, hysterical—and the car took off like gangbusters, careening down Delaware. The nearest hospital was Broadlawns off Hickman Road, and they must have taken him there. It was two o'clock in the morning before we heard Mr. Nordell's Chrysler pull into the drive.

My father got my weeping mother back inside the house and poured a shot of bourbon down her, which, despite the fact that she seldom drank, had no effect. "Oh, my God," she kept saying. "Oh, my God." She grabbed first my hands and then Ray's, kissing our palms, pressing them to her belly.

No one suggested that sparks from my father's bonfire might have ignited debris at the base of the tree. Firemen hosed down the nearby garages and the mulberry bushes that lined the alley to keep the fire from spreading. People drifted away, and the force of the fire died down. Finally, around midnight, the platform of the tree house fell in a flaming square of light and crashed in our yard.

VIII

"This will be like a picnic," my mother said. We had thrown an old bedspread down on the living room carpet and were waiting for Ray and Bill to come back with sandwiches from McDonald's.

"I just wish . . ."

"What?"

"I don't know. Christmas is almost here."

"You'll be in Florida by Christmas," I told her, "Decorating a palm tree."

"I know, I know. I was just thinking," she said.

Ray's Monte Carlo roared up outside, and Bill and Ray tramped through the front door, ignoring the neat path of newspapers Mother had put down.

"I just vacuumed there," she told them, scolding, "and I *don't* want to have to vacuum again. So, please, boys, *stay on the papers.*"

We arranged ourselves in a circle, and Bill distributed the food. "Le Mac Grand, Madame." He handed me a sandwich. "Le shake au choco-lat."

Ray cradled a six-pack of Miller Draft.

"Aren't you eating?"

"Not hungry," he said.

There was an awkward silence. Mother started to speak, then stopped. Her voice died away in the room.

"Fast food still seems like a treat to me," I said. "Like when Dad used to take us all to the Frost Top."

"Huh," Ray said. "Where you been? Kids grow up on that shit nowadays." He kicked the empty bag and toppled it. "That's all old Courtney ever feeds her kid."

We all fell silent.

"You're always remembering shit," he said. "Why you always re-membering shit?"

Mother shot me a look.

We ate in silence, none of us looking up.

"The big thing when I was a kid was Porky's hot dogs," Bill said fi-nally. His voice seemed a little strained. "They cost about a quarter, I think. They were fabulous."

"You can't buy a good hot dog today," Mom said. "They're all saw-dust and pig squeals."

"Do you remember"—I glanced at Ray—"that summer Dad poured the patio? And built that brick barbecue? We could have cooked a whole side of beef on that thing."

"Everything had to be the biggest and the best or your father was-n't happy." My mother rubbed her forehead, sweeping the palm of her hand down her left temple. "I'm going to have to see about new glass-es," she said.

"We cooked everything on it for weeks," I said, "until the new wore off."

"I remember that so well," my mother said. "And other things are so . . . vague."

"It's been forty years," Ray said.

"You know, when Mickey Tanner's wife started that fire, and that little girl died, your father took that very hard," she said. Bill and I glanced up at her, surprised.

"I thought it was wiring," Bill said.

"What?"

"Wiring, defective wiring started the fire," Bill said.

"Oh, no," she said. "Why do you say that, Bill? You weren't even in the picture then."

"Well, I've heard the story," Bill said.

"That's what I thought, too," I said. Ray said nothing.

"Oh, no," my mother said. "No, it was her, I can't remember her name. Mickey Tanner's wife started the fire. She was cooking, I sup-pose."

She stopped and seemed to be thinking. "Yes, that's what the paper said." Ray nods. "And something caught fire. Maybe a dish towel." She stopped again. "It could have been a dish towel."

"Rashoman," I said.

"What?"

"Nothing. Go on."

My mother seemed confused. "Well, just that," she said. "This was our home."

She hugged her sweater around her. It was an old white cardigan with an open work pattern that showed the faded print of her blouse underneath. "I hate to see it go, kids, I'll be honest." She scanned the room, and her eyes filled with tears. "I wish I could afford to just give it to you," she said. "But I can't, and that's a fact." She looked at Ray.

"I just don't want it, Mom," he said. "What the hell would I do with it?"

"And then there's the maintenance," she said. "Your father was so conscientious, and he could *do* anything. He never hired a single thing done—brick work, roofing."

Ray was silent.

"The place is so run down now."

Ray drained his beer.

"That faucet," she said. "I think all he did was put a washer in it."

"Who are you talking about?"

"Or was it a trap? I can't remember. Of course, if you were living here . . ."

"I'm no plumber," Ray said.

"No," she said. "No, I supposed not." She picked at her sandwich. "I thought that you and Courtney . . ." She seemed back on course now.

"Uh, uh," Ray said. "No."

"Now that she's expecting," Mother said.

Courtney's condition was an open secret, but Ray was surprised that Mother mentioned it, so openly, so matter of fact.

"She *is* expecting," Mother said.

"Oh, she's expecting all right."

"Ray, can't you . . ."

"Just stay out of it," Bill told me.

"She's expecting more than she's gonna get."

"You know, you are nothing but a common drunk," my mother said suddenly. We all fell silent.

"You do it to thwart me," she said. "You always have."

Ray looked away.

"I did the best I could, I know you don't believe that, but you never . . . loved me," she said. "I don't know why."

"Mom, . . ."

"And I can't count on you two," she said, meaning Bill and me.

"We just can't afford it, Mom," I said.

"Maybe you two and Raymond together."

"Oh, no. Bad idea." Ray popped another beer.

"First of all, as you say, there's the maintenance," Bill said. "A big place like this, the age it is . . ."

My mother put her sandwich down on its paper, started to rewrap it and stopped. "I'm very well aware . . ."

"Besides, it's *your* house," I said. "*Your* way of living."

This surprised her, surprised us both.

"Maybe if Christine and Beth were here," she said.

Ray bristled at this.

"Bethie and her new husband could live in the house."

"Beth lives in Chicago," Ray said. "She grew up there, remember?"

"I know, I know. I'm only saying, the place needs a family."

"Well, I'd like that, too," he said. "Don't you think I'd like that, too? Go back twenty years—hell, go back to high school. Why not?" He crossed his arms, sulking.

"I hear Christine's divorced that Randy Davis," Mother said.

Ray said nothing.

"I'm trying to help you."

"Let's just drop it."

My mother seemed suddenly angry. She tried to stand up and fell back, sprawling. One leg kicked out, and a soft drink cup went over, spilling Coke on the carpet. "Maggie, Maggie," she said, but it was Ray who caught her.

"*Why* didn't you love me?" she said.

Bill was on his feet and running, churning up the newspaper path as he went. He knew at once what was happening. The phone was disconnected. He had to run to Nordell's house next door.

"I'll get an ambulance."

The door flew open, hitting the wall, splashing a slant of sunlight across the carpet.

IX

"Typically, we see a fairly rapid development of a neurological deficit," the doctor said, "which then evolves at its own pace, depending."

"Depending on what?"

"I've ordered a series of X-rays," he said, "which will give us a picture of any infarction, and then we can go from there." He began to back out of the room like a fading image. Infarction, infarction.

"An infarction is necrosis of the localized tissue," he said, continuing to melt into the hallway. "I'm afraid there's just not much more I can tell you at this point."

And he was gone.

Necrosis, necrosis, death. Necromancy, necrology, a list of the dead.

"She's not going to die," Bill said.

"How do you know?"

"Because. She would have died already. In the ambulance, at home."

Ray sat on a green, vinyl sofa in the waiting room, his hands limp between his knees. His head drooped as though he were at prayer.

"This is all your fault," I said.

"There's no point in blaming anyone." Bill took my hand. "Let's just sit down."

"Why can't they just tell us? Why all this 'necro' jargon?"

"They *are* telling us," he said. "You just don't speak their language."

"Oh, sure, defend him."

"Who?"

"What the hell do you know about it?" I said.

"Sit." He sat himself and patted the sofa cushion beside him. "Please."

I sat, at the far end.

"A stroke is most often a blocked blood vessel," he said, "usually from a blood clot, although it can be a burst vessel, too. Infarction just means that when the blood flow is interrupted, some cells die. Not the patient," he said. "The patient doesn't die."

"The damage is like a bruise," he went on. "It's an injury, what a physician would call an insult, but the word doesn't mean anything by itself."

"So?" Ray said.

"So we just have to wait."

I stood and paced to the window and back.

"Look, imagine the circulatory system is a road map," Bill said, "and the blood vessels are highways. Now imagine one road is closed.

Okay? Traffic is diverted." He fumbled; his figure of speech broke down.

"So what?" I said. "What the hell are you saying?"

He tried out a number of metaphors—mechanical, bloodless explanations.

"The brain is living tissue," I told him. "Raw meat." Emotions are physical; they have mass, weight, extension. Sorrow is like a toxin that runs through the blood, builds until it becomes so potent the vessels cannot contain it. Bill doesn't know this sorrow, rage. The powerlessness, the waiting; and somebody else is always in control. Betrayal. It's physical, like an explosion. And bitterness is like memory, like a bruise.

⁖

The doctor ushered us into a darkened room where the walls were lined with X-rays, my mother's brain repeated endlessly, like a pattern of wallpaper. The arteries, injected with some sort of chalky fluid, showed white against a cloudy gray, gray matter, which was the brain.

"As we suspected," he said, "there's an aneurysm." He pointed to a white spot about the size of a dime that appeared in each picture, seen from several angles, but the same menacing star shape in each, the eye of the storm.

"Which," he said, "is simply a weak spot in an artery wall. Under pressure from the pulsing of the blood—and, over time—it stretches, grows thin. Then, one day, it balloons, and . . ." He tossed his hands up gracefully, a silent explosion.

"So, she might have had this condition for some time," Bill said.

"Oh, undoubtedly."

The pictures wavered against the light behind them, advancing and receding. The white arteries confounded themselves into a spidery pattern, a nest of confusion. I could not remember what it was I wanted to ask him, and Bill said, "What's the next step?"

The doctor was thin, polished, tall, gray at the temples. He used a pen to doodle imaginary lines over one of my mother's many white-lined brains.

"What we propose is to lay back a section of the skull, here." He pointed. "Like a little trap door." He smiled. "It sounds worse than it is."

"And?"

"And remove any blood clots and repair the artery."

I stared at him.

"We would clamp it," he went on. "I can show you what we would use."

"How bad is it?"

"There isn't a lot of time," he said.

I said nothing.

"We just can't know what we're up against until we go in," he said.

"Well, what do you think you're up against?" Ray said. He was slouched against the wall, his face shadowed, so that all that showed in the thin light from the X-rays were his arms locked tight against his chest.

"Undoubtedly," the doctor said, "there's been some memory loss, some loss of motor functions on the right side. Hemiplegia or hemiparesis, we can't be sure. There may be speech difficulties. It's impossible to say."

She might have had this condition for some time.

It's impossible to say.

This condition, this condition. We just can't know.

It's impossible to know, impossible to say.

We just can't say.

"So, do we have to sign anything?" I said.

"The nurse has the form."

"Which says she could die," Ray said, "and if she does, it ain't your fault."

The doctor gave Ray his best professional smile. "Something like that," he said.

≈≈≈

My mother's skull was opened with a series of burr holes, which Hayes—that was the doctor's name—then connected using a Gigli saw. There was massive bleeding. It was necessary to cut through the temporal lobe to reach the aneurysm.

The operation took five hours, during which Ray and Bill and I sat in the waiting room drinking coffee while a parade of pretend problems and Tide commercials passed before us on TV.

"Funny," Bill said. "It's a hospital soap. In a hospital. It's like the Quaker Oats box that has a picture on it of a man holding a box of Quaker Oats, that has a picture on it of a man holding a box of Quaker Oats. Et cetera."

I kept thinking of Bill's father, who died of a stroke in 1971, and how his mother wrote him tersely, *We will understand if you don't come home*. And how Bill's father for years before that kept calling and writing and coming up to Toronto, trying to lure us home, how he would say, *I can fix it. Bill? Just come home.*

It was almost six o'clock when Hayes came in. "We found pretty much what we expected to find," he said.

X

I called Estelle in Florida.

"I'm not surprised," she said. "Ruthie takes on way too much. She always has."

"And she's such a worrier," I said.

"Well, she's had some reason."

Estelle had never approved of our family. She found my father's energy "disruptive," his rage for building a kind of escape from what she called "adult responsibilities." They used to have terrible fights about politics. "Your father is a racist," she told me flatly one time.

"How's Ray handling this?"

"Well, you know Ray."

"Maggie, I want you to tell me exactly what happened."

"What do you mean?"

"Well, I should tell you that I have my suspicions."

"What?"

"Well, he was bad before."

"Bad?"

"The drinking," she said. "But since your father's . . ."

"Accident?"

"Were she and Ray fighting?"

I hesitated.

"Were they?"

"Not exactly."

"Because she has talked to me, you know. You must have guessed that. And at some length."

"About Ray?"

"She has been terribly worried about him, Maggie, and hurt, and I don't blame her. And then, well, you know. She's been nursing this business about your father."

"What business?"

"I think you know."

My father didn't drown. The water was incidental. The trauma of the crash killed him; that's what the autopsy showed. If he'd been wearing his seatbelt, . . .

He wouldn't have lived in either case, Bill told me.

He wanted to crash against it. Whatever *it* was. He wanted the impact. He couldn't have not imagined how it would be.

"You know, Floyd was his executor," Estelle said.

"Yes."

"Did you know that?"

"Yes."

"You *did* know that."

"What are you getting at?"

"He'd paid everything off," she said. "Sears, Amoco, everything. He had all the receipts. Stapled together. Everything in order. What does that tell you?"

In the nursing home where I worked there was a woman named Mrs. Steele, whose husband, Leonard, committed suicide by running a length of tubing from the exhaust pipe of his car to the driver's-side window. He started with a full tank of gas and the car ran for hours, three or four hours. Mrs. Steele was away. She was shopping, I guess. When she found her husband he seemed to be asleep behind the wheel, his head resting on his chest, his eyes closed. On the seat beside him were some papers: mortgage, insurance, that kind of thing. The radio was playing.

"Why are you telling me this, now?" I said.

"I'm only stating the facts."

"Stell, I know," I said. "I've always known."

She was silent.

"So, your little bombshell is a dud."

There was a long pause.

"Aunt Estelle?"

"In the old days," she said, "they wouldn't have even buried him with Christians."

XI

From the time Ray was a baby until the spring of 1958, my father must have bought and sold half a dozen "handyman specials" like the one we owned at 1629 Delaware, crumbling, pre-war houses with empty windows and overgrown yards, which Dad would buy below market value, remodel, and sell at a profit. And, for every house he bought, he prowled through a dozen others, looking not just for a bargain, but for a promising structure, a form that could be made to contain the many romantic notions he had then about the perfect American family.

Every Sunday morning he would scour the real estate section of the *Des Moines Register and Tribune*, his cigarette forgotten in the ashtray, his coffee going cold. He'd circle the promising ads with a red china marker, and we would spend the rest of the day driving down unfamiliar streets and wandering through open houses where the scent of another family's life still haunted the empty rooms. The sense of promise we felt as my father paced the rooms was almost unbearable. Sometimes I would notice a cigarette burn on the kitchen countertop or a speck of dried shaving cream in the bathroom sink and imagine my father, content at last, smoking a Lucky in that kitchen while the coffee brewed, shaving in a cloud of steam in that bathroom.

One house, I remember, had a den with wall-to-wall bookshelves.

"Those would have to come out," my father said. No one needed that much room for books.

The unspoken assumption was that, eventually, we would find the perfect house, the house with possibilities so endless and intriguing that they would content my father for a lifetime, but each house disappointed him. Each was not quite right. Or maybe it is more accurate to say that his vision of the American home was so vast and complicated that no one house could content him.

My father's dream was to live in a perfect house, a house where every closet had a light, where every bathroom tile was stuck down tight, where paint never blistered and linoleum never curled. He wanted every window caulked and every door to shut with a snap, and more than that, he wanted built-in storage space and picture windows and poured-concrete patios. He wanted to live in a house that was finished, isolated, self-contained, safe, a place where a man could rest and raise his family; but, of course, he never did. Our house was always emerging from one of my father's dreams. My brother and I would go to sleep to the roar of a circular saw and wake to steady hammering, never surprised to find a new half-bath where a closet had been or a door opening suddenly through what once had been a solid wall. My mother called it the "someday house," our home that was always becoming, never quite was.

While the remodeling was under way, we would live in whatever house it was, camping out in the gutted rooms among power tools and scrap lumber. My mother made do, cooking one whole week, I remember, over a Coleman stove and keeping the milk and butter cold in an ice chest while my father did some rewiring. Estelle, a no-nonsense licensed practical nurse who had lived for several years in a trim brick bungalow west of us, described our houses as "war zones" and refused to visit us except in summer, when we could sit outside in lawn chairs, away from the clutter.

When a house was finished and still adazzle with fresh paint and brand new linoleum, my father would sell it and buy another that needed just as much work. To convince my mother to move, my father would pick the current house apart. The kitchen was too small, he would tell her; we needed a laundry room. If our house then was a two-story, the ideal house was a ranch. If we happened to be living in a ranch house at the moment, then a two-story really would be better.

The profit from all this effort was never much, and never the real reason behind my father's relentless remodeling. Fixing up houses for resale was simply one way for a working man to build up a little nest egg, my father said. Of course, it was more, a kind of faith. The future was my father's real home, and he saw it, as a child might envision Oz, shining in the distance, almost attainable—certainly attainable—with just a little belief and a little more effort. He raced ahead, his dream for his family's home like a distant music, something perfect that only he could hear. The dream was real; it was American. All we had to do was lend ourselves to it.

With every sale, there was always a small celebration. My father would put on a clean white shirt and hustle us all out into the car for a ritual drive downtown. We'd park on Walnut in front of the imposing granite facade of Home Federal Savings and Loan and storm through the brass-bound doors like millionaires. There beneath the massive chandeliers my father, with great solemnity, would tuck exactly half of the profit away, proof against that rainy day that he knew would eventually come.

I can barely remember the first house, a one-bedroom bungalow with French doors off the living room and a huge screened-in back porch that was half the size of the house. We lived there for almost a year when I was five, long enough for my father to frame in the porch, converting the bungalow into a more desirable two-bedroom. He sold that house, two weeks before Christmas, I'm told, and bought another on contract, moving us piecemeal through a gentle snowfall.

This episode was far from Dickensian. In fact, my father recalled it as a pleasant winter adventure and liked to tell how he and Floyd Lindquist, Estelle's husband, stacked the smaller cardboard cartons on Ray's Flexible Flyer and pulled them up the walk from the van to the house, pelting each other with snowballs while they worked. My brother remembers that, later, Estelle fixed chicken and home-made egg noodles and apple crisp for dessert and that, after the move, we sat in her tidy kitchen, exhausted, elated, eating from her gold-rimmed Haviland china.

My mother has a dramatic flair, however, and used the story in quite a different way. She told of "trudging, homeless, through the snow" or "dragging the children through the snow," of how we had to take refuge at her sister's. She told this version, with more or less pathos, whenever she wanted to curb my father's appetite for real estate.

Our new house was a stucco two-story, still smallish but large enough for me to have a room of my own. My father completely re-modeled the kitchen of that house, added a half bath downstairs, and painted inside and out before he sold it.

The next house, on Thirty-fifth Street, needed a lot of work, but it was large enough for my father to make a small apartment upstairs. We lived downstairs and were the landlords to a succession of drifting young men and uncertain women until my mother put her foot down and my father sold the house, the only income property he ever owned, to a developer who—my father liked to point this out to my mother—eventually got rich with a string of similar make-shift apartment buildings north of the loop.

In the years right after the war, houses sprang up overnight, twenty at a time, whole streets at once, and young families moved into them as fast as they were built. Without history or any connection to place, these projects were named, often, for the developer's wife or daughter: Delores Circle, Linda Lee Lane. Or they bore some mimicked generic label that promised the buyer upward mobility: Oakwood Knolls, Briarcliff Estates. The names suggested a woodsy New England landscape, but, of course, there wasn't a tree or a shrub in sight.

Adapting to this building boom, my father learned rough carpentry, and, in his forties, liked to drive through the west-side developments and point out to Ray the houses that he had built. For a while, just before Donna was born, he had a crew of ten or twelve men working under him, a makeshift collection of college boys and re-trained veterans, working shirtless high in the rafters like sailors working the webbed riggings of sails. Like Dad, Ray loved any kind of construction, and the best treat for him was the rare, bright Saturday morning when Dad would take us with him out to the job. On the treeless mud lots west of town, where a line of raw wooden skeletons broke the horizon, any kind of future seemed possible.

My father was a carpet layer by trade, but he started out as a floor sander in the days when houses still had hardwood floors. Later, when he came home from the war and America was crazy for nylon and plastic and synthetics of all kinds, he learned to set plastic tile and to install the hard, gleaming pink Formica and the bright chrome trim that was everywhere in the fifties. He did a lot of what he called "commercial work"—hasty, makeshift refurbishments of restaurants and motels and cheap apartment houses for people who seemed suddenly to be always on the move. But he saved his craftsmanship for his own home.

In my favorite photograph, my father has a thick, sandy-colored mustache, an affectation he sported briefly just after the war and eventually shaved off when my mother complained that he looked like a desperado. His hands are jammed self-consciously in his pockets; an Adams hat tips forward on his head. Staring out from the shadow of his hat brim, his eyes have a hurt, half-frightened, half-curious look. But there is also something about the hat and the way he wears it that expresses authority.

When my parents went out—just the two of them—my father had a way of setting his pearl gray hat on his head. The New Yorker, I think the model was called. He would pull the brim low, slanted over one eye, a gesture that shielded his face and gave him an air of mystery. Then, cupping his hands, he would shape a wedge of hat and air, running his palms forward along the edge of the brim in a twisted salute. The brim would curl perfectly, a part of his profile. In the set of my father's hat his whole life seemed balanced, and on the day, years later, when I noticed that he no longer sculpted his hat, that it sat square and lifeless on his head like a flowerpot on a table, I knew that he was irredeemably old.

In the palmy days, my father owned two cars. There was the pale blue Plymouth station wagon, rusted out at the wheel wells, with the outrageous orange flamingo hood ornament—my father's work car. And there was the brand new sea green, impossible three-hole Buick. Riding in the Buick, smelling the clean, plastic efficiency of it, the glue and oil and crisp paint, we were rich and special and isolated from the world of want, as my father intended for us to be. They built cars like tanks in those days, and the joy my father took in owning an automobile like the Buick seemed a total justification of what he called "the American way of life."

My father did some work for a rich Italian developer named Cappelli, who owned a dozen tumbled-down buildings across the river and who was so cheap, my father said, he wouldn't pay a nickel to see Lake Erie burn. The work for Cappelli was mostly remodeling, chopping up old Victorian homes to make cramped, low-rent apartment buildings. The buildings were pretty run down; it wasn't easy to bring them up to code, especially since Cappelli—"that cheap guinea son of a bitch"—used shoddy materials and, when he could get away with it, unskilled nonunion labor.

My father hated this, what we now call "cost cutting" measures. Cheap lumber warped and split; cheap metal and wiring were dangerous. You never knew how they'd hold up. Cappelli and that "bunch of knuckleheads" who worked for him—subcontractors, men Cappelli had hand-picked, sometimes for family reasons—represented compromise to my father, an obvious form of weakness and the worst sin of manhood.

Cappelli paid well, however, and in cash. It was nothing for my father to have three or four twenty-dollar bills in his pocket, a form of braggadocio that worried my mother sick. She, on the other hand, liked to put every cent in the bank and measure it out with a checkbook. In one of the pictures I keep of her in my mind she is washed in the overhead light at the dining room table, a thick green ledger book open before her, a pile of bills on the left hand, a pile of crisp white envelopes on the right.

"Put a stamp on these, Maggie," she'd say, placing a stack of plump, finished envelopes in front of me. I'd lick the stamps and paste them on precisely, impressed with myself for reasons I did not then fully understand. I was part of that elaborate ritual that, somehow, kept the family safe.

Cappelli loomed large in our imaginations, my brother's and mine, and I think that even my mother was a little afraid of him. Cappelli's back Cadillac would sometimes cruise to a stop in front of our house around suppertime, and a dark runner would scramble out of the front seat and sprint up the walk with an envelope in his hand: the week's pay for my father.

Cappelli never came in, never got out of the car, in fact. My brother and I, playing Monopoly on the screened-in front porch, swinging mindlessly to the creaking of the glider, saw his profile, the folds of fat neck flesh beneath the heavy homburg, the glowing tip of a big cigar; but Cappelli was no more to us than a menacing silhouette, a shadow puppet.

"Why doesn't he just mail it to you?" my mother would say. She didn't like the big, black Cadillac idling at the curb. She didn't like opening the screen door to Cappelli's messenger.

"It's cash," my father would tell her. "You don't mail cash."

My father had such energy. It was nothing for him to work eight or ten hours a day, to work Saturdays and Sundays for Cappelli, and then to come home at dusk and work another two or three hours on his own home. Sometimes, late at night, I would wake and open my bedroom door and wander down the hallway to find him—measuring, hammering—the shadow of his head and massive shoulders fanned up on a sheetrock wall behind him by a harsh work light. My mother would be sitting on a nail keg, smoking a cigarette and talking with him, and their voices, like the faint, woodsy smell of her cigarette, would swirl around my head as I settled back into sleep.

My father had a helper named Mickey Tanner who worked with him on the big jobs for Cappelli. Tanner was a laborer who lived in one of Cappelli's flimsy apartment buildings with his wife and daughter over across the river on Montrose Street. A short-coupled Irishman, not very old, not very bright, Tanner had been a lightweight Golden Gloves champion three years running and had taken more than his share of hard punches. His eyes were squinty, and his balance was gone, but he was a good worker. My father trusted him.

Tanner's daughter was what they called then a Mongoloid. I didn't know what the word meant, except that I'd seen Mongolians in my grandmother's *National Geographics*—mysterious slant-eyed people wrapped in animal skins—and had been impressed by their example with the vast diversity of the world beyond Iowa. They lived so strangely and in such a remote place, it seemed impossible that they could share the same planet with me and my ordinary family.

My brother also sometimes helped my father. He was big for his age, and my father let him sweep up on the job and carry material in and out and generally act as a gofer and apprentice. Ray was named after my father—Raymond—an honor I was convinced then that he did not fully appreciate or quite deserve. In fact, however, it was the perfect name for him. Ray looked more like my mother, but he thought just like my dad; and the two of them shared, among many traits, a love of construction work, an intense if sometimes misguided patriotism, a beef-and-potatoes outlook on all matters cultural, and a natural, almost intuitive, understanding of the game of baseball.

In 1956 Mickey Mantle had a fabulous year, and Ray became a diehard Yankees fan. When we moved into the house on Delaware, my father papered Ray's room in a wild, gaudy baseball print that ran—bat, ball, glove; bat, ball, glove—up and down the walls endlessly. Ray loved that paper and used to walk his fingers over the pattern. My mother was less enthusiastic, claiming that he would quickly tire of such a dominant pattern, and I pointed out that the bats and balls and gloves were all nearly the same size, that the bat could never really move the ball, that the ball could never nestle in the glove. Nobody seemed to think that it made much difference.

My room, being a girl's room, was papered with roses, full blown, the color of bubble gum. There were endless bouquets of them climbing the walls, each one alike, each caught in a webbing of lace. My father had nailed a three-foot-long one-by-twelve between two upright orange crates to make a vanity, and my mother had painted the plank white and tacked a pink chintz skirt to it that fell to the floor in pleats and concealed the crates. On a glass vanity tray, my barrettes and brushes and the natural Tangee lipstick I was allowed to wear on special occasions were displayed as ritual objects of womanhood.

Pink did not suit me, however, nor did the perfect stasis of the roses. I was uneasy with the promise of womanhood, the duplicity of artifice, the patient pink servitude that I sensed in my mother, and was drawn instead to the silent, intuitive life of animals. There was a liberation in their isolation and straightforwardness, a simplification of the intrigue and endless apologies of being human and, especially, a girl. To my father's dismay, I cut out pictures of cats and dogs and horses from magazines and tacked them up on the pink rose walls of my room.

Of course, we never owned a horse—though we longed for one. Ray used to moon over every horse he saw. Before Grandfather died, we almost had Dad persuaded to let us stable a pony down on the farm near Albion, an impractical plan that Ray and I nevertheless believed was always just on the verge of realization. Then, of course, the farm was sold.

I never owned a cat either (sneaky animals, Dad said) until I married Bill, but we had several dogs when I was a kid. My father was forever picking up strays and, like a kid himself, telling my mother they "just followed him home." In most cases, she could eventually persuade him to send the dog on to the animal shelter or find it a home with someone else in the neighborhood, but one dog eluded my mother's veto.

Duke was a mixed breed, mostly basset, one of those sad-eyed mongrels you can't turn away. Dad found him rifling garbage cans in the alley one day and took him in, and after that, Duke became my father's constant companion, ambling a pace or two behind him, silent and content simply to be in his master's presence.

Nothing rattled Duke but a ride in the Plymouth, the mere promise of which would send him spinning in ecstatic revolutions and elicit a steady melancholy howl. When Dad felt expansive, he would drive Duke to the Frost Top, where, sitting on the passenger side, Duke made the car hops giggle. Dad would order his dog a small vanilla ice cream cone.

"Ray," my mother would say. "That can't be good for him."

Mother sat in the back seat with Ray and me when we went to the drive-in. She refused to share the front seat with a dog.

"Let him have the window," she would say. "He'll take it anyway."

Duke rode like a monarch, hanging out the window with his nose tipped arrogantly, his eyes closed in bliss, his generous ears sailing in the wind.

Because of my mother's alleged allergies and out of respect for the upholstery, Duke was not often allowed in the house. Instead, my father would wander outside sometimes on summer evenings and sit with his dog on the back porch steps, their broad backs hunched up side by side.

Sometimes Ray would join them, sometimes both of us. My father would pat the worn wooden step beside him, a silent and rare invitation, and we would scramble out the back door to be with him. Together, we would watch the evening deepen and the stars blink on and settle into position, and some sensation, almost like a buzz of electricity, would shoot through me.

"Daddy, . . ."

"Shhh." My father would place his finger to his lips. "Let's just enjoy the quiet," he would say.

XII

My mother in those days was thin and flat-chested with wide hips and sturdy, athletic legs, and she had a classic, subtle coloring: pale, clear skin that tanned to a healthy glow and thick chestnut hair. She adored my father, I know that. Twenty-two when my brother was born, she must have been thirty-four years old that summer of 1958 when she was pregnant with what she hoped would be a little sister for Ray and me.

The anticipated addition to our family convinced my father that our house was much too small, and he spent hours that summer drawing plans at the dining room table. Rather than move again, which my mother resisted, my father decided to build his family's dream home right where he was; and, for better or worse, the house on Delaware became our final home, the last of a series of efforts to get ahead, the place my father chose to make his stand.

The Delaware house was a foursquare, a two-story, functional house with a low-pitched hipped roof and a big unfinished attic with a front dormer that looked out over the street. It was probably built around 1910. Foursquares were a popular style of that period, so popular, in fact, that Sears and Roebuck sold foursquare kits through the mail. Designed in reaction to the excessive ornamentation of the Victorian Queen Anne homes of the rich, the foursquare was a working-man's house, a plain square box, thirty-four by thirty-four feet, which, by adding mail-order millwork or varying the belt or the siding, could be adapted to a number of styles. Nordell's house next door, for example, which had the same basic floor plan as ours, was stucco, with a high-waisted belt and deep eaves to suggest the Prairie School, and Benson's up the street—the same house—was Mission style.

Our house, with its clapboard siding and Tuscan porch columns, was a colonial adaptation called The Lewiston, a pretty good example of the style except that my father had removed the delicate railing, closed in the bottom half of the porch and screened in the top to make a so-larium, an alteration that destroyed the open look of the entryway and gave the house a blunt, reclusive facade.

The house had four bedrooms upstairs with a central hallway and a sleeping porch in back that, like the front porch, ran the width of the house. The two large bedrooms in front, each with double windows, faced the street; these were occupied by my parents on the east and, for a little less than a year, my grandmother on the west. The two smaller bedrooms, mine west, Ray's east, were to the back of the house, with a large bathroom between Ray's room and the porch.

My father's plan was to move Ray out of his room, which would then become a nursery for Donna, as he had decided to call my sister-to-be. Ray would take the sleeping porch, which Dad would insulate, and they would cut a doorway between my parents' room and Ray's old room, so that the nursery would adjoin their bedroom. All of these changes, of course, called for new paint and wallpaper, new curtains, new fixtures, and new area rugs; and while my father drew his plans at the dining room table, my mother sat opposite him, thumbing through the Sears catalog.

The centerpiece of my father's plans was a spacious first-floor family room, which would be added on to the south side of the house, extending out from the kitchen in the back to create an open living and dining area. My mother had seen these rooms in her magazines: large, informal spaces, furnished with second best, where families were stashed away in neat semi-circles, content and quiet in front of TV sets. They spilled their snacks and soft drinks there on practical asphalt tile and left the pristine, carpeted living room always ready for "unexpected guests."

My mother favored the empty modern look of the mid-fifties, limed oak and wrought iron, with lots of flat polished surfaces that displayed one perfect piece of Italian glass. While my father priced lumber and got estimates on the cement work, my mother began to look at living room carpet, something neutral, she thought; she was tired of her hardwood floors.

The family room became a mental repository for my father's elaborate dreams, a place where he stored not only the various architectural features he imagined, but his hopes for his family. He talked of almost nothing else that summer. Of course, it would have a fireplace, he said, and maybe wide steps leading down from the kitchen, creating a sort of split-level effect. A picture window—no, bay windows, my father decided—would be set in the east wall to let in the morning light. My mother could have her African violets there. My father said we would all play Chinese checkers in the family room in the evening and make popcorn in the fireplace. We'd buy a color TV set, he said.

Sometime in early June he brought in a man with a trencher to dig the foundation, and my father and Mickey Tanner cut a dark wound into the flesh of our house with a circular saw, ripping the siding off down to the tar paper in preparation for adding on the new room. For reasons best known to my father, the roof of the new one-story addition would not echo the horizontal lines of the existing roof, but would be gabled and jut out away from the house in back, breaking the symmetry. He and Mickey Tanner, therefore, cut out the shape of a squat cube, topped with a wide-based triangle, a flat, black outline of a house such as a child might draw.

My father's enthusiasm was contagious. Yet, my mother worried. "Ruthie, so help me God," he told her, "it's pay as we go."

They were talking in the kitchen while my mother peeled potatoes at the sink. My father set his beer down on the countertop and raised his right hand as if he were swearing an oath. "No more debt."

My father would never dream of taking money out of savings. Instead, to pay for the family room, he took on a lot more overtime for Cappelli. We hardly saw him that summer, except between five and six o'clock in the evening when he'd dash home for supper between jobs. Even then, we heard more than saw him, splashing water up in the bathroom, rummaging the bureau for a clean T-shirt. He'd slide up to the table just as Mother was turning off the frying pan and draining the potatoes.

"Do you think you could slow down a little?" she'd ask him. "This isn't a restaurant."

Supper was over in five minutes or less. My father would end the meal with a folded slice of bread, which he swirled around his plate in two neat half-circles. Tucking in the last bite as he rose from the table, he would grab his cap and his toolbox, pat my mother awkwardly, and be gone, leaving the house silent and almost quivering in his wake.

On Saturdays and Sundays, he'd be gone before Ray and I ever got out of bed in the morning, and it would be sundown before he came home again. With my father working night and day, weekends lost their meaning. His gray Adams hat went unworn, and my mother stopped cooking her elaborate Sunday dinners. Once, out of spite, my mother packed a defiant picnic lunch and marched Ray and me to a nearby park where we swung back and forth listlessly in the wooden swings like hanged men, our feet scuffing the sandy grooves beneath us while other children yelped with happiness. Mother offered to push us, but she could not push us high enough to run beneath the swings like my father could, and she was terrified when we pumped hard, gaining a fierce momentum until we were flying high, almost horizontal to the ground.

"I don't know what you think you're doing," she said to my father that night. The picnic had not been a success. "Children need a father, you know."

My father kissed my mother—*really* kissed her, something we almost never witnessed—and ruffled my hair and played ten minutes of furious, falsely jovial catch with Ray; but the next weekend he was working again for Cappelli on some low-rent eightplexes across the river.

My father's increased absence that summer nettled my mother, perhaps because of the baby, and sometimes I'd hear them arguing late at night. "Can't you get it through your head," he'd say. "I'm doing this for you."

On rare occasions, he gave in, turned down the chance for overtime, and sat sullen in his big, green armchair, drinking Miller High Life out of the bottle and pretending to read the paper. My father was not above raising his voice in order to get his point across, but it was these moments of punishing silence that I dreaded more. The house itself seemed tense, as though any minute the whole place might explode, windows shattering outward into the yard and drawing with them my mother's white lace curtains and chintz sofa cushions. My father seemed to enjoy the brittle atmosphere. "Isn't this fun?" he'd say.

At other times he would get the Buick out, and we would all go for a ride through the steamy heat. Out in the country the roads were so dusty we had to roll the windows up, and the car would get hot as an oven. "Everyone having fun?" my father would ask.

He didn't mean to be unkind. Something drove him. "Just look at this," he'd say, holding up a chipped coffee cup or a worn bath towel.

My mother called worn things "serviceable," but serviceable wasn't good enough for my father.

"I've seen it, Ruthie," he'd say.

My father was born on the farm down near Albion, a town so poor, he used to joke, that they couldn't afford to hire a village idiot. "So everyone just took turns," my father said.

My grandmother had a chicken business, supplying fryers for the local cafe and the county hospital, and it was my father's job to kill and dress the chickens, sometimes thirty a day, while his brother, Earl, the older son, worked the fields with their dad. Not surprisingly, my father left home at sixteen.

He joined a thrashing crew and drifted with rougher boys and men up through the Dakotas, where the wheat was like a whispering sea and practically endless, "so damn thick," he said, "it was almost like water."

He never went back to the farm until after Ray and I were born, and then our visits to Grandma's were brief and awkward. My father would pace the road in front of the house, kicking at black-eyed Susans, impatient with the drowsy pace of the farm.

I was never sure what happened when Grandfather died—I was only nine. But Earl, I guess, after some kind of wrangle, sold the farm; and Dad got a small cash settlement and my grandmother as a permanent guest in our home. But, I am getting ahead of my story.

My father also fought in World War II. This was something he never talked about, almost never acknowledged. What little Ray and I knew about the war we learned in school or from the spate of heroically framed war movies that came out in the late forties and early fifties. Sitting in the dark at the Saturday matinee, we cheered mindlessly as burning Jap planes fell from the sky, and our guys—the mild-eyed Audie Murphy types from Texas and the curly-haired, wise-cracking boys from Brooklyn—stormed the beaches in a swirl of selfless resolve. We could easily imagine our father in uniform, up there on the screen, more handsome than he really was and bigger than life.

Because of men like our father, Ray explained to me, evil was dead, finished, felled before good intentions and a pure heart like a giant in a fairy tale, and an age of goodness and undreamed-of prosperity was on the way under the watchful eye of a nebulous, good-natured personage my father referred to unfailingly as "Uncle Sam."

Yet, strangely, evil lingered, too, in a chilly, hidden war that filtered through to us like smoke seeping under a closed door or sunlight falling through the cracks of drawn curtains, an un-American evil just beyond sight, something insidious that only grown-ups could see, a demon that manifested itself for my father in wear and dust and broken crockery.

And so the new was god. Material—clean, sunny-smelling lumber and fresh paint; plastic and safety glass; aluminum, which never rusted—was a kind of sanctuary. He was a willful builder, my father, stubbornly hoping that wood and concrete would say what he could not say. When my father's mother died, he said almost nothing. "We'd been expecting it," he told everyone, but, of course, we hadn't.

XIII

Labor Day came and went almost unnoticed that summer. September arrived, and the endless, undifferentiated days of summer became the orderly march of fall and winter, marked by holidays and family occasions: Raymond's birthday, September 25; my parents' anniversary, October 9, when my mother, round as a melon by then, wore her short, chocolate-colored mouton jacket and my father, wearing his pearl gray hat, escorted her to the Buick for dinner downtown. The room addition was well past the planning stage by then, stalled while my father scraped together the cash for lumber and nails.

Halloween and Thanksgiving slipped by, and we were into the swirl of Christmas, shopping and sending cards, wrapping gifts in the traditional red or green tissue my mother favored and hiding them under the bed, behind the furnace in the basement, in the trunk of the car.

My father finished one job for Cappelli and started another. He had long since tacked plastic sheeting over the exposed tar paper; but if bad weather held off, he said, he might still frame in the walls of the family room before the new year. Little Mickey Tanner was still his helper, only now Mickey came to the house every morning and waited, cap in hand, at the kitchen door while my father finished his breakfast. I was never sure why, but my father had stopped driving the Plymouth to the job. Instead, Mickey Tanner drove it, and my father rode on the passenger side. My father had stopped eating his enormous bacon-and-eggs breakfasts, too, and usually just had coffee and, when my mother could bully him into it, toast and juice.

"Mickey, don't you want a cup of coffee?" my mother would ask him.

"Nome," he said. At least, that's what it sounded like he said.

"How's your family, Mickey?"

"Fine."

"How's Peggy?"

Peggy was the Tanner Mongoloid. Peggy was the girl my brother imitated, hunching up his shoulders and twisting his face like Red Skelton.

"She's fine," Mickey Tanner said.

Tanner always stared down at the tops of his shoes and turned his cap around and around in his hand. He wore a giant red and black wool plaid coat, frayed at the cuffs. It smelled like coal dust and rotting vegetables. Peggy was not fine.

"Maggie," my mother would coax me, "say hello to Mr. Tanner."

I always managed to mumble something, imagining Peggy Tanner, her flat, wide-eyed face floating, framed in a window of a decaying Victorian house, a place like the one my father and Mickey Tanner would be working on that morning. Then I would wander down the hallway, littered with sawdust and oddly shaped trimmings of wood, enter my own room and shut the door. Enveloped in the heavy femininity of roses, I felt, I suppose, a little superior. I felt, if not accurately defined by my father's house, at least, well protected. I was in my father's house, safe.

My mother always put up the tree exactly a week before Christmas, and no matter how much we pleaded with her to buy some new bauble every year, she always used the same old ornaments, the ones her mother had left her, and two or three that she and my father had made for their first Christmas together.

When my parents were first married, it was war time. My father was due to be shipped out any day. There was nothing in the stores, my mother said—she told us this story every Christmas—no colored lights or ornaments, nothing pretty. She and my father did have an old string of Christmas tree lights, but they couldn't find bulbs for it anywhere.

"Necessity is the mother of invention," my mother always said at this point in the story, right before she told how my father found some small, clear glass light bulbs—the kind they use in refrigerators. He secured them in a vise in his workshop and painted them red and pink and coral by hand with my mother's nail polish. "They weren't handsome," she said, "but they were all we had." (In 1958, we still had a few of them; they still worked. My mother used them on our tree every year until they burned out one by one.)

My mother strung popcorn that first Christmas, she said, and cut snowflakes from plain white stationery. It was all they had, until the second year when my father was overseas and my mother's mother, Grandma Carlson, gave them ornaments of fragile blown glass, several in a heavy maroon color and one with a swirled indentation on each side, and one, Grandmother Carlson's favorite, on which three ghostly wise men and an elegant camel journeyed endlessly around the sphere's pale blue equator, following a star to worship a child.

XIV

Bill stood at the front window, Stanwyck perched on his shoulder. "Is that Ray's car outside?" We had just put up our tree, without much ceremony, and hung a wreath on our apartment door. Bill peered through the open blinds down into the darkness.

"Where?"

"Parked under the streetlight. It looks like his car."

It was Ray all right. "What's he doing here? It's almost eleven o'clock."

I threw a coat on. "Where are you going?" Bill said.

"I'm just going out to talk to him."

"What for?"

"Because. He must have some kind of problem or he'd come in."

"He's got a problem all right," Bill said. "You're his problem. Why don't you just drop this, whatever you're trying to do. Let people be who they are. Think whatever they want to think."

"Why are you always in charge?"

"What?"

"We're not hurting you."

"Maggie."

"I'm going out and talk to my brother, okay?"

"Fine."

"Is that all right with you?"

"That's fine with me." He held the door open, made a graceful sweeping gesture to usher me out.

I knocked on the windshield, but Ray didn't look up. I could hear country music filtering through the windows. The snow fell in a whisper.

"Ray?"

He pointed to the door handle. I let myself in.

"Hi," I said. "What are you doing out here?"

He didn't answer.

"Aren't you cold?"

He shook his head.

"It's cold out here."

And then I saw the gun, laying on the seat between us, a big, comic, old-time cowboy six-shooter. It looked almost like a toy, but I knew it wasn't.

"Maggie, did you ever know our father was a wonderful driver?"

"What?"

"How long do you think he drove a car?"

"I don't know."

"And he never had a single wreck," Ray said. "Drivin'—what?—almost fifty years?"

"Something like that."

Silence.

"So, are you trying to tell me something?"

"Nope." He looked away. "Just weird, that's all."

He fiddled with the radio.

"Probably all my fault," he said.

"How do you figure that?

"I was supposed to hold everything together."

A man walked by with a dog, an Airedale that ranged in wide half-circles, sniffing the ground, while the man, stiff-legged and hunched against the cold, slogged along behind him. Their breath was expelled in short, round puffs that hung in the air.

"What's with the gun?" I said.

"I'm keeping it for a guy."

"What guy?"

"Just a guy I know."

"Is that the truth?"

He shrugged.

Floyd Lindquist kept a gun in his glove compartment; so did a couple of guys Bill worked with at Vets. One in every three people carried guns, the newspapers said.

"I see you still got your star."

He lifted it away from his shirt and studied the inscription. "Ever tell you how I got this?

"Yes and no."

"How I walked on water, saved my buddy's life . . ."

"What's the real story?"

Ray laughed softly. "You're always wantin' the real story," he said.

He lit a cigarette. "You know what they say about Vietnam?" He rolled down the window and dropped the match outside. "Vietnam," he said. "If you weren't there, shut the fuck up."

He took a long drag, exhaled. A cloud of smoke rolled against the windshield and curled back. The radio whined through three or four country songs, and Ray hummed along softly. People went bad and missed their babies, got to drinking on a Saturday night. They couldn't stop loving the people they used to love.

"I still love that woman," Ray said.

"Chris."

"Only one I ever loved."

I would not mention Courtney. Courtney was none of my business. In fact, I was concentrating hard on not mentioning Courtney when Ray said, "Old Courtney's got troubles."

I said nothing.

"You know?"

"If you mean about the baby, everyone knows. Even Mom knew about it, I don't know how."

"She always knows everything," he said. "Got that ESVP or something."

"So, what's she going to do?"

"Courtney?"

"Who are we talking about?"

"I'm damned near fifty-three years old," he said. "Ain't that a hell of a thing?"

"It's not pretty for any of us," I said.

"She don't know what that is."

"How old is she?"

"I don't even know. She ain't fifty-three."

"And she has 'expectations.'"

"She sure do."

Ray picked up the gun, pointed it straight ahead, and pretended to pull the trigger. "She's my last chance."

"Why don't you put that away."

"Like father, like son?"

That rocked me a little. "You want to talk?"

"Nope."

He smiled and put the gun in his jacket pocket.

"Isn't that dangerous?"

He pulled it out again. "This little old thing?" He dangled it by the trigger guard. "Not even loaded," he said.

XV

The sky was flat gray. "Snow in the air," Ray said. I could smell it, a brassy taste of water, a stillness among the birds. Forces were gathering. Courtney came by the house about four, dressed for work. Through the kitchen window I saw her silver Honda pull into the drive; she left the engine running, the door open, and walked toward Ray, who was working on the garage. She looked nervous. Under her open coat she wore a short black taffeta skirt that swelled below the waistband, a white shirt with a black bow tie. The penguin, Ray called her when she was dressed for work.

Ray was replacing some damaged siding on the west side of the garage, fitting it in up under the eaves, and didn't come down off the ladder to talk. He didn't even turn to face her. I slipped the kitchen window open to listen.

"Hell, I don't know," I heard him say.

She circled underneath him, looking up. The rungs of the ladder formed a grid that separated them. Her words were muffled.

"I guess," he said. "I just . . ."

She said something more.

"Do whatever you want to do," he said.

"There's a woman with problems." Bill had come in the front way and joined me at the kitchen window.

"What's under discussion?"

"I don't know. I can't hear."

"Probably the baby."

"What do you think she'll do?"

He shrugged. "The obvious."

I stared at him.

"Well, you asked me."

We were giving the kitchen what my mother would call "a lick and a promise," painting fast, a sunny yellow that covered well. I handed Bill a brush.

"I'm not very good at this," he said.

"It's only a hobby."

"Hey," he said, "that's my material."

Bill sometimes told a Myron Cohen story about two old guys, one of them retired.

"So, tell me," his friend says, *"now that you're retired. How do you keep busy all day long?"*

"Me?" the other guy says. *"Me, I got a hobby."*

His hobby is bees. He catches them in his back yard and puts them in an empty mayonnaise jar.

"And then I bet you punch some holes in the lid of the jar," the other guy says.

"No, I don't do that."

"What?"

"I don't do that," he says.

"Crazy, you gotta do that. You don't' punch those air holes, the bees gonna die."

"So, they die," the guy says. *"It's only a hobby."*

"The hospital offered me a job," Bill said.

"Doing what?"

"Writing a newsletter. It's an in-house thing. Goes to all the staff and some of the doctors."

"And?"

"And, I'm not going to do it."

"Why?"

"Exactly."

"Bill."

"It's not *instead* of what I'm doing now," he said. "It's *in addition to*. They know I can write and they don't want to hire a full-time guy. Screw 'em."

"Would they pay you?"

"I don't know. I suppose. A little."

I stopped abruptly—my mother's trick—and walked briskly into the living room, forcing Bill to put down his brush and follow me out of the kitchen.

"What?" he said.

"It's none of my business."

"But?"

"I think you know."

"I'm too good to be an orderly."

"Well, you are."

"It's only a hobby."

"What is it with you? You didn't start the war, you know. There would have still been casualties even if you had gone."

"I know that."

I began to wash windows, fast, spraying Windex and wiping in quick, hard circles.

"If you wanted wealth, you should have gone after it," he said. "Like Chris did."

"Chris didn't have much choice."

"All I'm saying . . ."

"And what is this shit about wealth? I don't want wealth. I want . . ."

"What?" he said. "What, Maggie?"

"I don't know."

He sat at my feet. "I'm happy where I am," he said.

"And that's all there is to it."

"No, . . ."

"Everything's falling apart," I said. "The house, Chris, Ray. Jesus, Bill."

"Ray's not going to do anything," he said.

"How do you know that?" I said. I put down the Windex and rag. "You always talk as though you have some kind of personal pipeline to God."

"I have my own kind of faith."

"Well, that don't feed the bulldog," I said.

I pressed my forehead against the cold windowpane and closed my eyes. "I don't know; we're just not *getting* anywhere. And then there's Mom."

"What about her?"

"Well, there're going to be bills," I said. "Therapy, medication. Everything isn't covered by Medicare."

"We'll handle it."

"How?"

Ray walked in.

"It's a lie, Maggie," Bill said. "All this American Dream crap."

Ray ducked out again. "Sorry, folks."

Bill looked up at me. "Really, kid."

XVI

My father did not come home for supper on the night my mother planned to put up the tree. He came in late, and I can remember lying in bed, listening to their fighting and staring at the pink rose wallpaper, my eyes weaving in and out of the network of lace.

"Damn it, Ruthie," my father shouted, "I'm doing this for you."

"Oh, no," my mother said. "Oh, no."

In the morning my mother gathered me into her grief. She may not have known she did this, but she babied and coddled me outrageously and turned a purely efficient manner on Ray and my father. She decided that I was ill—the sniffles, she said—and kept me home from school. Then, when my father and Ray were out of the house, she let the tears slide silently down her face, and the two of us sat on the sofa for hours, it seemed, in front of the barren tree, just letting the tears come.

My father came home on time that night, and I could tell that she was glad. When she heard his car in the drive, she ran to the hall mirror. She never wore any makeup around the house, but that night she put on a little lipstick. He seemed glad to see her, too, but he was distant.

"I can't stay," he said.

"Oh, Ray."

"Cappelli wants all the countertops in by Monday so he can get the painters started." He looked away.

"What about the tree?" she said.

"You go ahead." He gave her a weak smile. "You and the kids do most of it anyhow."

I think if my mother had not been so tired by then, carrying Donna, other things, she might have stopped him from going. Or, if she could have stormed and thrown plates, she at least might have made herself feel better. But she was not that way. Instead, she sat down at the table and served us our supper, and it was, I remember, the longest and most silent meal we ever ate together.

My father had finished eating and stood awkwardly at the door. Mother always kissed him, always, lightly on the cheek and patted his back before he left, even if he were only going to the grocery store. This time she stood rigidly at the sink, pretending to wash the dishes.

"Ruthie?" my father said. She wouldn't answer.

The air seemed to be charged between them, but my mother's anger would not flare.

"Well," my father said. "Hold the fort." He put on his cap and backed into the night.

My father worked late the next night, a Thursday, and then it was Friday, four days before Christmas, and school was out and our tree was still dark and barren.

"All right," I heard my mother say into the telephone when my father called from the job about suppertime. "All right."

We ate without him, and after supper my mother dragged the Christmas box down from the attic and, silent, began mechanically to hang ornaments on the tree.

"The lights," Ray said. "The lights go first." He had them strung in a tangle across the living room floor.

"All right," my mother said.

"We'd better test them." Ray plugged the lights in, and they burst into a fiery nest on the floor. One or two were out.

"Dad always likes the red ones," Ray said, screwing in new bulbs. He draped the string of lights on the tree and began to arrange them.

"The old World War II bulbs are still burning," he said. "One or two anyway."

"Our first Christmas," Mother said dreamily, "that's all we had, your father and I."

"I'm getting a basketball this year," Ray said. "Dad said. Regulation. I'm getting a hoop, too. Dad's putting a hoop up on the garage."

My mother and I watched him work, hardly listening.

"You're not gettin' nothin'," he said to me. "You're gettin' that yucky Christmas candy in your sock, and that's all."

My mother flicked on the radio and fiddled with the dial until choral music, "Silent Night," came in, and then she turned the sound way up.

When "Silent Night" was over, the choir sang "O Holy Night," then "Little Town of Bethlehem," "Away in a Manger," "Joy to the World." My mother sat, watching Ray struggle with the lights, humming beneath her breath. By that time I had begun to help him.

I suppose at some point she got up from her chair to join us because I remember clearly that she was standing with a silver tinsel rope dripping from her left hand and the pale blue ball with the wise men on it cradled in her right and that she half-turned toward the door when my father came in. I would not have needed to look at him at all to know that something was wrong. I knew from her face and the quick way she turned back to her work and lowered her head.

"Well, well, well," my father said. "Looky here."

We didn't know how to speak to him.

"Ray?" he said. "I got something for you."

He was weaving a little, holding a paper sack out at arm's length. "They're new," he said. "They're the latest thing, I got them at the hardware store when I was picking up some screws."

Inside the bag were three small glass cylinders shaped like candles with red plastic bases and metal screwthreads at the bottom. The cylinders were full of liquid.

"Now, watch," my father said.

He removed one of the old Christmas tree light bulbs and replaced it with one of these "bubble lights," as he called them.

"Watch."

The liquid in the cylinder glowed with light from the base, and after about twenty seconds or so, it began to bubble.

"It's the heat from the base," my father said. "It makes the stuff boil or something."

We watched, fascinated, as the bubbles rose in the glass cylinder.

"See? Ruth?"

"They're very nice," my mother said.

"Ah, Ruthie," he said. "You like them. Admit it." He took the pale blue ornament from her hand, grabbed her waist and waltzed her across the hardwood floor. "They bubble, just like you."

She broke away from him. "I said they were nice."

My father tossed the ornament in the air and caught it behind his back. "Ever see my juggling act?" he said.

He tossed the ornament again, caught it, then balanced it in the crook of his elbow. "Watch this," he said.

"Ray, please." My mother tried to stop him.

"Watch out, Ruth." He was weaving back and forth.

"Don't, Dad," I said.

"A drum roll, please."

The pale blue ball rolled inevitably down my father's forearm, crossed his palm, and glided down his ring finger, hung there forever, then fell, and my mother dropped with it, sank to her knees, her arms outstretched, seeking to gather the fragments back into unity as they skittered across the floor.

"Oops." My father smiled a crooked, wet smile. He fell on one knee and made clumsy scrabbling motions to help her.

"Oh, leave it," she said. "Just leave it."

My father sat down heavily on the floor. "You have to have something new," he said. He ran his hands through his hair. "You have to want something, that's what keeps you going." His voice was thin. "No matter what happens," he said, "you have to keep going."

My mother turned her back on him.

My father drew a rumpled sack from inside his coat and held it out to me. "I bought this for you, Pumpkin," he said.

It was a picture book of horses—Morgans and Arabians, all breeds, with simple one-line captions, a child's book. I had already read through the "Billy and Blaze" series and all of Marguerite Henry. The book was designed for someone much younger than I.

"When you really love something," my father said, "you should try to learn all you can about it." Then he began to cry.

"Oh, for Pete's sake," my mother said. She circled behind my father, scooped her arms under his, and tried to lift him.

"I guess you didn't hear," he said.

"What?"

"I said, you didn't hear." My father had tears running down his face. His hands were limp and useless in his lap.

"Ruthie," he said. "It's burning." He looked up at my mother, empty-eyed.

❧

The apartment house where Mickey Tanner's family lived caught fire about six o'clock that night, probably from defective wiring, the newspaper said. Tanner was working with my father six blocks away. They saw the smoke, but by the time they got there, the building was completely engulfed in flames.

"Involved," Mickey Tanner said, telling my mother the story later in the same mechanical if not quite accurate way he had heard it reported on the radio. "The house was involved in flames."

Tanner's wife and his daughter, Peggy, were dead. Apparently, they had smelled the smoke and tried to escape down a back staircase but had gotten lost in the smoke and the maze of flimsy partitions and narrow, dead-end hallways. Firemen found the bodies heaped together in a corner, the mother's body on top. They surmised she had tried to shield her child.

XVII

"Are you a relative?" The woman behind the desk was dressed in white and had a navy blue cardigan sweater tossed over her shoulders. She had a small silver Christmas wreath pinned to her uniform with a bell in the center that swung back and forth soundlessly.

"I'm her daughter."

"She may not recognize you."

"That's all right."

"She may not even be awake."

"I want to see her," I said.

The nurse looked me over. "This way."

She led me, shivering, down a dark hallway and opened a door to more darkness and air as heavy and close as a wool blanket. On the far wall dingy slits of light struggled through the blinds. The nurse retreated, leaving me alone in the gloom.

My mother lay on the bed, a single merciless lamp bolted onto the headboard bleaching her face with light. Her hair appeared white under the lamplight and stood up in wiry, surprised shocks all over her head. Her hands on the blanket were curled the way poodles curl their paws to beg and so thin they seemed almost transparent.

She stirred a little. "Who is it?" she said.

"Nobody," I whispered. "Go back to sleep."

I paced the room, picking up objects at random. "Ray's getting worse," I said. "I don't know what to do."

He'll find his way.

"We're losing him."

My mother sighed in her sleep.

"He won't talk. He's drinking a lot. He has a gun. Courtney doesn't know what to do either, and Bill's useless."

I sat down beside her bed. "I don't mean useless," I said. I leaned over and whispered, "I'm afraid."

We fought constantly, my brother and I, whenever we were together. A man who, literally, couldn't get his story straight, Ray told version after version of our lives, the same story over and over, each time with a slightly different slant. No scholar, he would patch together some half-baked theory, according to which Dad was society's victim, and I would counter with an equally phony "psychological" explanation or maybe just a brutal accusation like the one I advanced last Thanksgiving, just before Mother's stroke, when Ray was once again drunk and we were once again hammering out an acceptable life story for ourselves, side-stepping, for Mother's sake, what had really happened.

"He was selfish, Ray," I told him. "He never thought about us."

"You're crazy."

Bill was pouring wine, pretending not to hear but with his head cocked at an angle. Mother stood beside the dining room table with her shoulders straight and her arms limp at her sides, a tired soldier. Neither one of them wanted trouble again.

"And he drank."

That was not true, but it wasn't a total invention either. My father did not "drink" in the melodramatic, lost weekend sense. But there was a sentimental sorrow about him that emerged sometimes when he drank, and then he would shed those crocodile tears that run down the comic faces of cartoon drunks.

"You got it backwards," Ray said. "I'm the one."

The American family, ours included, collapsed of its own weight; that's Bill's explanation. An excess of feeling, unexpressed, ideals and expectations far too grand. He called that Ozzie and Harriet nuclear family "a brief phantom blip on the cosmic radar screen of history," something we though was there and really wasn't.

"The war scared everyone into domesticity; that's what happened," he said.

"Nothing *happened*," Mother said. "We were a family. We lived our lives."

"Those flimsy firetraps Cappelli built. Dad knew."

Bill sat down at the table. "Why would a man nurse a tragedy like that for forty years?" he said. "It doesn't make sense."

"It wasn't just that, just Peggy, just Donna," I said. "It was everything."

"What's *everything?*" my mother said. "What are you talking about?"

"He didn't drink," Ray said. "Maybe a beer or two."

"Ray, I saw him."

"You want to open the whole thing up again," my mother said, suddenly turning on me. "Well, I won't have it. He had an *accident,*" she said. "He had an automobile *accident.* They happen all the time. And just because that young policeman . . ."

"Let's tell the truth for once."

"Was *speculating,*" she went on. "That was all just pure conjecture."

She dabbed at her eyes. "I don't know why you do this," she said to me. "He simply did not"—her voice faltered—"do . . . that," she said. "And I won't have you saying any such thing."

❦

My mother did not stir. I had an impulse to wake her. "Everything's falling apart," I whispered. "Tell me what to do."

She sighed in her sleep, and a faint smile played upon her lips, as if her spirit were roaming free within the fragile sculpture of her bones. She was beyond the house on Delaware, beyond the past with all of us forgotten. *Do? What to do?* she seemed to say. The smile again. *I've forgotten, Dear.*

XVIII

"So," Bill said, "are we ready to do this?" He had the apple box and two bushel baskets full of papers.

"I don't know." I said.

"It's just old paper. I've looked through everything."

"Not the stuff in the apple box. I have to sort that out."

We had returned for the last time to strip the hangers from the closets and scoop the sliver of soap from the bathroom sink, erasing every trace of ourselves. We roamed the attic, searched the basement, and found a few more papers, some of Mother's old magazines. What we found was worthless, and yet I hesitated.

"What are you looking for?" Bill asked me.

The baskets contained receipts for items long ago consumed, bills paid, notes read and acted upon, junk. My father's doodles appeared on some of the papers, and there were some of his drawings—he was always drawing—plans for houses never built, projects never completed.

"Do you want to look through everything again?"

❧

After the fire, my father got old fast. Donna, the dream daughter for whom he had planned so savagely, was born in the new year, but almost as though this, too, were a part of the plan, she died in less than three months of sudden infant death. My father lost interest in the family room project. It was never finished, and we never moved again, and the house on Delaware settled into a routine that, under better circumstances, my mother might have almost described as normal.

Dad replaced the siding he and Mickey Tanner had torn away the previous summer and gave the house a new coat of paint, and no one driving down Delaware could have guessed that the house had ever been any different than it appeared. In the summer of 1959, Joe Nordell took up the trumpet, and the air was filled with halting military tattoos and a painful, rapid-fire screeching that Joe maintained was "Trumpeter's Lullaby." This was his musical year, and he and I danced to Little Richard and Buddy Holly on the screened-in porch of our house and waltzed on roller skates at the Tromar Skating Rink, circling endlessly on the hard maple floor while a sphere of broken mirrors overhead sprinkled light down on our shoulders.

It was only with Joe that I was outgoing and talkative. In fact, I was so silent at school that my teachers began to wonder about my shyness and to send notes home to my mother in which they worried that I might not be working up to my "potential."

"Margaret is intelligent and cooperative," one wrote, "but does not seem to push herself to achieve."

I was given a series of hearing tests, eye tests, IQ tests by scientific specialists to determine what was wrong. The tests showed nothing. The reason for my withdrawal lay beyond their probing, and, because it did, their probing became relentless.

"It's not anything anyone can notice," Mrs. Luther told me. She was my fifth-grade teacher. "It's just something we're going to have to work on."

"Working" meant instruction from Miss Pitts, the visiting therapist. Miss Pitts was very young, with severely crimped, obedient dark hair that jumped back from her pale high forehead in an outraged wave. She wore thick, black-rimmed glasses and had a sign on the wall behind her desk. "Children are the hope of the future," it read.

Through circumstances I don't now quite remember, I had been found—along with a ragged, undersized black boy named James—to have a speech impediment that needed Miss Pitts's attention. Every Thursday morning James and I were pulled from the security of the classroom and sent down a shadowy hallway to Miss Pitts's makeshift office where, guilty and self-conscious, we would sit on the worn wooden chairs in front of her desk, listen to her slow, relentless voice, and, when we failed in "precision of expression," promise to try much, much harder next time.

My problem was S's, and I was made to keep a scrapbook in which I collected magazine photographs of troublesome S words: snow, sausage, snakes, suspenders, smiles. It was a disorienting experience, one that turned me around about who I was. The whole world was suddenly unpronounceable for me, rainbows and sunlight beyond my linguistic reach, and it was best, I decided, to hide and remain silent rather than to speak and be ridiculed.

I was diagnosed as having a "lazy tongue"—children with defects were always "lazy" in some way. David Crowell, the boy who sat next to me, had a "lazy eye" that wandered shyly inward. Perhaps as a consequence his whole body seem to curl and follow that wayward eye. His left shoulder rising and pushing forward, he seemed to be constantly huddled against the cold.

Laziness was a child's worst sin, and to correct this fault, I was given a bundle of wooden tongue depressors, with which I was to practice every night, pressing down on the center of my tongue to make it curl in an acceptably energetic way while I repeated, ten times each, all of the S words in my book.

James, on the other hand, had trouble with L's, and his book was filled with lions and ladders and leaves. Short and perfectly round-eyed,

James had a shy grin and a flat, button nose, which ran continually from October to May. He was poor, even by my family's standards, and probably no genius, but his response to everything was "okay." His Charlie Chaplin trousers were okay with him, as were his flap-soled shoes, which gaped open at the toes and made a hollow slapping sound as he walked along the hallways. His coat was pinned together with safety pins, and that was okay. It was okay that his grubby lunch sack never contained more than bread and peanut butter.

Sitting next to James in the glare of Miss Pitts's tiny office, listening to the rolling mumble of his speech, I heard many wonderful, improbable tales. Once, at Miss Pitts's urging, James told us about a stone he had found on the playground, an oval ruby that glowed in the dark and revealed, when you held it up to the light, a miniature circus within itself. Another time, there was a golden cloud that swooped down to our broken asphalt playground and lifted him above the school. I loved his stories; I loved James, simply, as a child, unaware of how complicated some kinds of love could be.

Miss Pitts took an instant dislike to James, however, and feigned elaborate offense at the way he looked and the way he smelled and the stories he told. I was never certain how to act, whether to copy Miss Pitts and raise my station or side with James, who, it seemed to me then, had succeeded in shutting out all social judgments, creating an inner world for himself that functioned like my mother's poetry, an abstract structure of language so beautiful that he need not trouble himself with reality.

"I'm afraid I find what you're saying hard to believe," Miss Pitts would say.

And James would say, "Okay."

James, it seemed, had made a separate peace and, free of Miss Pitts's standards, his mind roamed happily beyond Longfellow School, which he could not pronounce and to which it could not really be said that he belonged. It was nothing to learn from James that he had traveled overnight to California.

"California, Iowa?" Miss Pitts asked him slowly, drawing the question out in her painfully earnest way in order to give the child every chance to confess his lie.

"Okay."

Miss Pitts liked to expose "little fibbers" like James by asking leading questions that looped back on themselves. It was discovered in this way that the cartoon lion in James's book was, in fact, real, that he lived with James and his mother and wore a red bow tie.

"And what does the lion do?" Miss Pitts asked, shooting me a pointed look that said, *We are not fooled, are we, we better-bred people?*

"Does he growl and eat up all your enemies?"

"Okay."

James's stories were not so much told as tricked out of him, question by question. The lion and the trips to California were tokens of a hopeless and inappropriate love, but Miss Pitts, far from rejecting these gifts, never even saw they were being offered.

"Why, James," she would say, her eyes innocent, "is that really the truth?"

Miss Pitts seemed to enjoy humiliating—not James, she didn't see James, but a little black boy who, in her eyes, was expendable, and, by a series of winks and knowing glances, implicating me in the destruction.

"Conversation is part of our work," she said. But, at some point, Miss Pitts would tire of the game. And then she would clap her hands and say sharply, "Very well, James. That's quite enough."

One day in Mrs. Luther's class we had a visitor, a Mr. Michaelson from the school board. Mr. Michaelson wore a rich blue suit, a white shirt, shiny wing-tip shoes. Clearly, he was not from our neighborhood. Mrs. Luther showed him the model pueblo, complete with clothespin Indians and cardboard adobe, and Christine and another girl sang "Whispering Hope" as a duet. Neither entertainment seemed to amuse Mr. Michaelson, however, who was introduced to us as a highly trained specialist in the modern science of education. The visit was not going well, and just as Mr. Michaelson seemed about to leave, Mrs. Luther, perhaps to assure him that she, too, was scientific, snatched me from my desk and told me to stand on top of the work table near the blackboard in front of the room and show the class my book.

I was terror-stricken. I imagined all the eyes, Mr. Michaelson's sea blue eyes especially, riveted on me, piercing me through. I heard my own lisping recital of scissors and shadows and stars hiss through my head, and underneath it all, I heard a defining and never-ending laughter.

"Hurry please," Mrs. Luther said.

Slowly I walked to the front. I climbed up on a chair, and Mr. Michaelson, very gallantly, offered his hand to help me up on the table.

"Just start anywhere," Mrs. Luther said.

I stared out over the upturned faces. No one was laughing. Instead, they looked at that girl as though they had never seen her before. *I'm Margaret Gerhardt, Maggie. That's what I wanted to tell them. Not some strange, mute bird. Maggie. See me.*

"Sparrow," I said, pointing to a picture.

"Louder, please."

I turned the page. "Silverware."

"We can't hear you," Mrs. Luther crooned.

The book was endless. Anxious to please, I had filled page after page. "Sky," I said. "Smoke, spade, spaghetti."

I suddenly knew the value of stories. I knew I was going to cry, and that that was the worst possible thing I could let myself do because, in our school, crybabies were taunted mercilessly. Classmates would follow me home, jeering, pass notes about me, and make up funny names.

"Spur."

The tears were almost there, and I couldn't stop them. My voice had faded to a faint, helpless squeak.

"Sorcerer."

"Is something wrong?" Mrs. Luther came forward and lifted my chin with her hand. "Maggie? Is something wrong?"

"I think I've seen enough to get the idea." Mr. Michaelson reached for his leather briefcase.

"I'll just walk you out," Mrs. Luther said. "Maggie, you may resume your seat."

"You know, I think this would be a positive thing to present at Open House," Mr. Michaelson said. His voice faded as they walked out the door. "It's in line with our goals for the future and makes a very graphic presentation."

"I'm sure you're right," Mrs. Luther said.

"But not that girl."

The door closed behind them. I climbed down and walked to my place at the back of the room, feeling the eyes follow me as I went.

"Oooooo, the creek is rising," Donnie Wilson said.

"How do you spell Mississippi?"

"Hey, Maggie, cry me a river. Boo hoo hoo."

I walked stiffly down the aisle and took my seat. I held my head up, the way my mother had taught me, and stared straight ahead and vowed never, ever to speak in public again.

As things turned out, my refusal made little difference. My performance had been so unacceptable that James was substituted at Open House. *He* was made to stand on the desktop and display *his* book, chanting "lemons and lions and leaves" in order to demonstrate Miss Pitt's scientific methods.

"Longfellow is a leader in this field," Mrs. Luther announced to the audience. "A trained therapist comes to us once a week."

It was comic, of course, people laughed. They laughed kindly, my mother explained to me, and not in order to hurt him, but they laughed.

"Is that your little boyfriend?" my father asked me.

"That's her boyfriend," my brother said.

As James's parents were not present, I felt obliged to witness his performance. It was quietly savage. James stood on the desk in his rags, which were suddenly not okay, and hung his head while Mrs. Luther explained the method. He would not or could not look at me, and once, when Mrs. Luther had turned her back, he made a half-hearted effort to escape, but Mr. Hughes, the principal, caught him, laughed, and set him up on the table again.

His recital was endless.

"Keep turning the pages, James."

"Lumonsh, luionsh, lueavsh."

"Hold your book up high."

On the way home in the car, my brother imitated James—"lumonsh, luionsh"—and my father laughed.

"Ray, really," my mother said.

"You didn't tell us your boyfriend was a shine."

We rode through the darkened streets and I thought about James. And I remembered that, once, when I was five or six years old, and my brother and I were visiting Grandma and Grandpa Gerhardt down on the farm near Albion, we went for a walk in the woods behind their house. It was a very hot day, July or August, and the air above our heads swirled with iridescent dragonflies. The humidity was visible, shimmering low over the watery grasses, and the rocks beside the creek were slimy with bright green moss.

The woods were shadowy, but just at the spot where we stopped to rest, a beam of sunlight fell through the trees, creating a patch of intensely white light. Our bodies glowed, and I remember my brother's face was like a luminous skull, the eyes dark in shadow. He kicked over a flat rock, exposing a sad, white-bellied slug to the light, and I remember that Ray had a stick in his hand and that he kept jabbing at the thing with short, hard thrusts. And I remember that, instead of burrowing down, which is what I would have expected, the slug, blind, helpless, clung to the stick.

On the Thursday morning following Open House, Miss Pitts did not appear. It was a snowy day, and I thought at first that perhaps she had just been delayed. This sometimes happened. While Mrs. Luther traced the outlines of nations on a pastel wall map, I sat at the back of the classroom and wished for James. He often came late. Sometimes it was nine-thirty or ten before I would see him from the window—a small, dark flutter of rags crossing the broad white playground.

But that day, like Miss Pitts, he did not appear, and I learned during the noon hour that it was over.

"I'm afraid there's been a change," Mrs. Luther said. She paged through my scrapbook and smiled. Then she handed it back to me. "This isn't anything that you need to worry about."

My therapy had ended as suddenly as it began. Funding had been cut, perhaps, or Miss Pitts—this was unlikely—had run away to get married and live happily ever after in California, Iowa, with a man as scientific as she was herself.

At recess I ran outside to look for James, who often haunted the far end of the playground; but he was nowhere in sight. I searched the narrow grassy space between the two red brick arms of the school, the shelter of the doorway. He was not there. Back inside, I ran down the long, dim hallways where the soft gleam of the hardwood floors formed puddles of pure light, finally slowing down to a walk, finally stopping.

꧁꧂

Bill had lit a fire in the bare patch of soft dirt that was Mother's garden. Newspapers and magazines smoldered, their pages curling up at the corners and turning a silver black. A light breeze played in the ashes, and, occasionally, a small flame leapt up, wavering.

He lifted one basket and pushed the other at Ray, but Ray backed away. "Why don't you do it?" he said.

꧁꧂

My mother's diagnosis of my silence and solitude, which, after several conferences, she eventually forced my teachers to accept, was that "girls simply mature faster than boys," and I was, according to Mother, even faster at maturation than other girls. Having at last an explanation for me, teachers came to see my silent compliance and lack of effort as female maturity, and after that, except for an occasional comment on my good manners and grown-up common sense, I was left alone.

꧁꧂

Bill danced in and out of the smoke, advancing to toss on more papers, retreating, waving his arms.

"One at a time," I yelled. "Don't pile on so much or it won't burn."

Ray watched the fire from the back porch, leaning against the door frame. He called out nonsense advice from time to time, which Bill ignored. He seemed disinterested, but I understood from his posture, from the way he smiled, not really smiling, that ancient fear of fire that he and I shared.

Bill tipped a basket upside down and tapped the bottom. Fragments of old, forgotten paper floated down. He crushed the basket and threw it onto the flames, then did the same with the other basket.

Smoke curled up and drifted west over Nordell's driveway. Light danced in my mind on the sky blue ceiling of the porch. I remembered lying on my cot, thinking how the sparks from the bonfire I'd tended—Grandma's pictures and magazines and clippings—would find their way to the tree house, thinking I should tell someone what I knew. But how could I tell? I could not speak. I was the watcher; I was the audience.

And then the light, dancing on the ceiling, sky blue at midnight, and my father . . . *Call the fire department.* My mother a statue. *I'll do it,* he said.

I learned later that James had done something "foolish," my mother said, and that his mother, on the advice of Miss Pitts, had taken him out of Longfellow School and enrolled him instead in a special school—for dumb-dumbs, my brother said.

XIX

The three of us stopped at a restaurant.

"Authentic greasy spoon," Bill said. "Meatloaf, pork roast."

"Bring it on," Ray said. He shucked out of his jacket.

"Still wearing your star?"

He nodded, pulled his shirt front forward, displaying the medal still pinned to the pocket flap.

"Well, I'm impressed," Bill said.

"My bad luck piece."

"Did you call Bethie yet?" I said.

"Ever tell you how I got this?"

"Ray?"

"Will you get off me?" he said.

"You should go to Chicago and meet him."

"Who?"

"Alex," I said. "The groom?"

"Oh, him."

"You're gaining a son."

"Christ, I can't even handle what I got."

Ray looked around him.

"So?"

"I'm gonna call her, don't worry."

"When?"

"I don't know. Whenever I get ready."

❧

The smoke rose high in the humid air and curled through the limbs of the horse chestnut tree, which was still there, which had not yet burned. The air above the fire shimmered, wavering like water, and my father, an El Greco monk, floated behind the flames, entering the house over and over, carrying out the past like a man in a dream.

Don't you think, . . .

I know what's here.

❧

Ray lit a cigarette. "This'd be a good place to open a restaurant." He looked around for a waitress.

"I believe that you would be received with open arms," I told him.

"Think so?"

"Blood's thicker than water."

"Yeah," he said. "She is my daughter."

"Right."

"Only kid I'm ever gonna have."

I glanced up, and Ray pretended he didn't know what he'd said.

"So."

"Yeah. Old Courtney give up on me." He shrugged. "Probably the best thing."

❧

My father took me by the hand and led me away. *Is that everything then?* The fires connected.

❧

The waitress came to take our order. As she wrote, Ray ran his eyes over her ample hips and smiled, gave her his Groucho Marx eyebrows. "In your dreams," she said and walked away.

"You're going to get us thrown out of here," Bill said. The waitress was talking to the fry cook, a big guy who had come out from behind the counter and looked our way.

"Fuck 'em," Ray said.

The fry cook continued to stare. Bill and I gazed out the window with studied innocence. Finally, the cook went back behind the counter.

"It's a pretty simple operation," Ray said.

"So I've heard."

"She don't want me to go with her."

A breeze lifted glowing shreds of paper from the bonfire, carried them to the tree house; fires connect. Past and future. My father's hands on the wheel. Donna. Steady, steady. Crazy Nordell's irrational impulse teasing. Steady. Something clean and final. The white lines pulse on the highway. A way to untangle everything. So perfectly simple. Steady, now. The bridge comes up and the impulse is irresistible.

The waitress brought Ray's beer. "Your order'll be right up," she said.

"Wonderful." Ray puffed his chest out so she could see his medal. "I'm a veteran," he said. She walked away.

"Ever tell you how I got this?"

"Gee, I don't know. You might have mentioned something."

"It was a dark and stormy night," Ray said, making his voice go spooky. "But, as you know, I was known in Nam as the cat man."

"Uh huh."

"It was a desperate mission," he said, "against desperate odds."

"But somebody had to do it," Bill said.

Ray scowled. "Let me tell it, okay?"

"Sure."

"They needed a brave and fairly stupid man to infiltrate the VC camps, a man who did not know the meaning of fear. Naturally, they thought of me."

"Naturally," I said.

Ray had ordered a hamburger, rare—he never ate anything else—and Bill and I had asked for vegetable soup, which arrived steaming in the bowl, hot, smoke rising. The waitress set it down and walked away.

"Looks good."

"You want a taste?"

Ray shook his head. "I'm a . . . what's the word? You know, a meat eater, like a wolf."

"A carnivore."

He smiled, howled softly. "Carnivore."

"The lone wolf."

Ray whispered the word under his breath.

"Remember that picture Grandma had in her room? The Lone Wolf ?"

Sunlight crept across the oriental rug, the colors blossoming. A summer breeze drifted through the windows.

"Wonder what ever happened to it," I said.

"Who cares?"

"I thought it was neat. Valuable, too, I bet."

Ray set his beer bottle down. "Maggie, stop remembering," he said.

"What?"

"Just quit it."

"What am I doing?"

Ray refused to answer me.

"What?" I said "What? Ray?"

Bill rubbed my shoulder, smiled. "You do sort of live in the past."

The cook stood at the grill, half turned toward us and listening, it seemed to me, a toothpick in the corner of his mouth. His thick fore-arms were speckled with tiny scars, burn marks from the spattering grease. He flipped a row of patties, and the flames beneath the grill leapt up, the only spot of color in the place.

"I don't want to remember anything," Ray said.

"Silence is golden."

"Somethin' like that."

Bill picked up his spoon. "Let's just eat."

❦

My father was not wearing his seat belt. My father always wore his
seat belt. My mother mentioned this at the time of the accident, and
the older policeman first said that he didn't know what to make of it.

"But he always wore his seatbelt," Mother said.

So, he gave her a story.

❦

"I guess it's all in how you tell it."

"Leave it alone," Ray said.

❦

Floating, inside the car, spinning, slowly, his pale blue eyes wide
open. He bumps gently against the roof, his thin hair lifting. His arms,
crooked at the elbows, beat like wings. Gliding, turning—not wearing
a seatbelt. The light is a pale blue. My father, like a bird in a watery
cage.

❦

"Ah-oooo," Bill howled softly. "Come on, you guys. Eat."

"Maggie?" Ray said.

"I'm ignoring you."

"Be friends, you guys."

"Maggie?"

"What? What, Ray?"

"What *is* the meaning of fear?"

❦

It was late at night. My brother and I were sleeping on army cots
on the screened-in front porch to catch what little breeze there was,
and my mother and father were talking earnestly in low voices at the
dining room table. I drifted in and out of dreams, aware at one point
that my mother had come out to check on us and then aware suddenly of light.

❀

"Why do you bring it to me?"

"Bring it?"

I saw Ray in my mind, in a dream, walking toward us, my mother and me and Chris. The ground was clay, uneven, scarred, a battlefield at night. Firelight and weird, persistent crying. His arms were outstretched and, draped between them, he carried his bloody uniform like a gift.

"I didn't tell you to go. You didn't do it for me or Chris or Dad or anyone else."

"What the hell are you talking about?" Ray said.

"Your sorrow, your pain. Well, you chose it. You made it. You men."

They looked at one another, Ray and Bill. "Too deep for me," Bill said.

"My father killed himself."

Bill almost dropped his spoon.

"Killed *himself*," I said.

Ray put down his beer and stared at me. The fire was high and wavering like a torch.

"What are you telling me?"

The platform fell in a flaming square of light.

"Now it's said."

XX

Ray called, drunk, crying, and told me, to hide it, that he had a cold. "Can't shake it," he said. I knew he was lying.

"Courtney's looking for you," I said. "She called and said she was going to sue you. What's going on?"

Ray chuckled. "She ain't a bad old girl."

I could hear music in the background, a jukebox playing "Rockin' Around the Christmas Tree," laughter.

"Ray?"

"Hey, I got one for you," he said. "You're always remembering shit. 'Member that old dog Dad had, old Duke?"

"Yeah."

"'Member he used to chase the car every morning when Dad went to work, runnin' like hell down the alley, trying to go with Dad, and Dad was always scared he'd get run over?"

"What are you talking about?"

"And, Dad'd try to reason with the dog, remember that? Tell him to go on home and old Duke whinin', wantin' in the car with Dad?"

"Where are you, Ray?"

"Dad knew he'd get hurt. He knew it. And 'member that old dog just wouldn't go home and wouldn't go home, and one day Dad stopped the car and got out and rolled up the paper and beat the holy shit out of that dog to help him see the light?"

"Ray, . . ."

"Just beat the crap right out of the god-damned dog. Jesus. I never seen anything like it. Dog limped home and didn't come out the dog house for three days."

"Do you still have the gun?"

Ray chuckled. "God, the old man really loved that dog."

The music in the background grew softer. "I'll Be Home for Christmas." Ray began to hum along.

"Ray?" I said. "Why don't you go home?"

"No can do, Little Sister."

"You're not doing anyone any good."

"I was supposed to hold everything together."

"Where are you?"

"Maggie," he said. There was some kind of fumbling at his end; maybe he shifted the phone. I heard a crash, like glass breaking, and the line went dead.

XXI

There were difficult days in late winter, but by March my mother could walk, haltingly with a four-pronged cane, could dress and feed herself.

"She's made wonderful progress," the doctor said. "She's been lucky, too, of course."

There was some memory loss. My mother stumbled over the most common words, sometimes falling into a fit of frustration when a name or concept eluded her, but I knew she was all right one day in February, when I brought her a purple hyacinth and she said, out of nowhere, "for my soul."

"Do you remember that?"

"Sort of."

"'If of thy mortal goods thou art bereft,'" I quoted. "'And from thy slender store two loaves alone to thee are left.'"

"Wait, don't tell me." She raised her weak right hand a little, the index finger extended, as though she were leading a sing-along. "'Sell one, . . .'"

"'And with the dole,'" we said together, "'buy hyacinths to feed thy soul.'"

She smiled. "I remember."

"And the poet is?"

"I don't remember."

"Neither do I," I said. "Who cares?"

It was always clear from her tone of voice that she knew what she meant to say, but the words were sometimes scattered, and she would make sweeping, corralling motions with her hands as though she were trying to gather them up again.

To help her recapture language, we talked for hours, working jig-saw puzzles at the table by the window, and we sang. Surprisingly, although at first she could not remember my name or the names of common objects, she could remember every song she'd ever heard. In the long afternoons, we sang our way though the scores of *Oklahoma, Guys and Dolls, My Fair Lady.* We sang "Home on the Range" and "Chattanooga Choo-Choo," anything we could think of until the woman in the next bed and her family begged us to be quiet for a while.

We whispered poetry, taking turns reciting:

Does the road wind up-hill all the way?
Yes, to the very end.
Will the day's journey take the whole long day?
From morn to night, my friend.

A part of her therapy was reading from the newspaper, and during the late winter I spent many hours listening as she plowed through the Home and Family section, using her index finger to trail the words. She read me Ann Landers, features on fashion and child rearing, a dreary and seemingly endless account of the nutritional value and culinary uses of the avocado, and a story on how to select the perfect diamond.

"I don't understand a word I'm reading," she said once. "It's not like reading at all."

"Well, you have to give it time."

Bill was on the night shift at Vets, so he was able on most afternoons to stop by and see her before he went to work.

"Your husband," Mother said—she'd forgotten his name—"is very kind."

She knew me, or knew that she knew me, but she could not remember Ray at all, and when he visited her she was cordial but distant. "Who is that man?" she would ask me after he left. "I know he's not a doctor."

Yet she could remember in detail stories from the past. "It was a Thursday," she would say, "and I was wearing that plum-colored wool coat I used to have with the oval jet buttons and my black pillbox hat and black gloves. I was quite . . . What, Maggie?"

"Fetching."

"What does it mean?"

"It means you were very lovely," I said. "And your husband . . ."

"Ray."

"Yes. Your husband adored you."

Those afternoons were like my childhood again, the two of us having soup and sandwich lunches, chanting our poetry to fill the hours, all the while waiting for the man, for Bill or Ray or the ghost of my father to come back into our lives and give them a focus.

She told me about how, when Donna died—"that baby," she called her—my father sat in the dark in the nursery for hours. "Bethie," she said, searching my eyes. "Was that her name?"

He only agreed to come down when the man from the funeral home arrived. "He was so . . . broken," she said. I couldn't imagine my father being broken.

"But he didn't drive away then," she said. "That was later."

"Why . . ."

"Funny. You'd think that would be it. Bethie dying."

"Donna."

"But the driving was later."

She told me that he used to play the harmonica, something I never knew and couldn't imagine. She said he played "mourning music," by which I assume she meant the blues, and lush, romantic dance tunes like "Deep Purple" and "Stardust."

"The mind is selective," Dr. Hayes said. "Or, rather, compartmental. A patient may have perfect recall of one person or one event or one point in time, and know absolutely nothing of another."

"When you were born your father wanted to name you Victoria," Mother told me. "But I thought that was too high and mighty somehow. He was just so happy to have a girl because that was his ideal family, a boy and a girl."

"I don't think I turned out quite girlish enough to suit him," I said.

My mother looked puzzled. "You were the apple of his eye," she said. "You and the boy."

"Tell me about him."

My mother said nothing for a while, just looked into my eyes. Her eyes were a soft amber, flat and without emotion. I tried to hold her gaze, will her to tell me something about him, drop some clue that would make what he did make sense. Then she said, "You know, I always used to lose my handbag. I'd lay it down somewhere, and the first thing you know, it would be gone."

It was common, apparently, to forget, misplace the past or rearrange it, and that was what Mother did. All in all, however, she was fortunate. Her stroke had been comparatively mild and had not been followed, as is often the case, by additional strokes. There had been one major aneurysm, which had been patched like an inner tube, and the patch had held.

XXII

"The funniest Christmas we ever had," my mother said—she told me this story just before her stroke—"was the time your father came home from the war and I was living with Ginny Farley in Winterset over Mendel's grocery store."

My father was wounded in World War II and sent home just before Christmas. It was a leg wound—not too bad, I guess.

"There wasn't anything funny about it really," my mother said. "We were poor as church mice."

She and I were wrapping Christmas presents; Christmas carols played on Bill's stereo. He had kept all his old LPs: Johnny Mathis, Andy Williams. "For those sentimental times," he said.

"I don't think I'll do much this year," my mother had said. But she said that every year, and every year Ray and Bill and I ended up loaded down with sweaters and scarves and chocolates. Last year, she finally meant it.

"Something's gone out of it," she said. "Without him."

When Ray and I were kids, my mother always put up the tree exactly a week before Christmas, and, no matter how much we tried to persuade her to buy some new bauble, she always used the same old ornaments, the ones her mother had left her, antique glass.

"When your father and I were first married," my mother said, "it was wartime, and there wasn't a thing to be had. It was all just, you know, necessities."

There was nothing in the stores, my mother said—she'd told us this story every Christmas—no colored lights, no ornaments, nothing pretty. She and my father scrounged up an old string of Christmas tree lights, but they couldn't find colored bulbs for it anywhere.

"And Dad used your nail polish," I said. Somehow, with him gone, I wanted to recall that story, hoped, I guess, that she would take it over and tell it for me the way she used to.

"Well, we had to make do," she said.

"Necessity is the mother of invention."

"I suppose."

My father found some small, clear glass light bulbs—the kind they use in refrigerators—and secured them in a vise in his workshop. He used my mother's fingernail polish—"the very last I had," she said— to paint them. Red and pink and coral.

"They weren't handsome," my mother said. "They were downright ugly, in fact."

I sometimes imagined my parents' first Christmas tree, how it must have glowed a soft rose from the pink and red and coral lights my father had improvised. Did my mother, who was always so vain about her hands, think the sacrifice of her nail polish worth the effect? I see her cutting snowflakes from plain white paper like a girl and imagine the intricacies of the folds and the mystery of cutting, how she made secret patterns that could be known only in the unfolding. She pasted some of the snowflakes to the windows, she had told me, and watched the way the sunlight filtered in, reproducing the patterns on the floor. And at night, she said, when the house was lit, the windows from outside were laces of yellow light, each one cut by hand and each one different. Behind those windows, she and my father embraced, snug, happy, before I was even a thought to them. And years later the pink and red and coral lights still burned, long after the need for their make-do beauty had passed.

My mother strung popcorn that first Christmas. It was all they had, until the second year when my father had just come home from overseas and Grandma Carlson gave them ornaments of fragile blown glass and the cherrywood dining room table and matching hutch, my mother's pride and joy.

"I think that was Mother's way of saying it was all right," my mother said. "That she didn't blame me anymore for marrying Ray. And after that, Father came around. We talk in things sometimes," she added, "when we can't find the words."

"Remember that pale blue ornament? With the three kings," I said.

"Which one was that?"

"You know, . . . It was Grandma Carlson's favorite."

"Oh, I don't think she had a favorite," my mother said.

It seemed impossible that she didn't remember.

"Anyway, your father was just home," my mother told me, "and we wanted to make a feast, and, of course, we had no money, absolutely none—not that there was anything to buy."

My mother and Ginny Farley lived in a one-bedroom flat above a little grocery store called Mendel's, and Ginny made it a habit to mock the grocer, Isadore Mendel, talking in his Yiddish accent and doing imitations of the way he fussed around the store and dusted the teetering pyramids of tinned vegetables.

"There was never anyone like Ginny Farley," Mother said.

"'Vell, Missus, I tell you, . . .'" My mother laughed. "He started every sentence that way, and Ginny could do him exactly."

"Mendel was the guy who used to tear the pages out of his books as he read them," I said.

"No, no. That was somebody else, somebody your father knew in the army. Tore out each and every page as he finished it."

"He didn't want to carry around all those used-up pages," I said.

"Yes, and he said, 'why should I let some other s.o.b. read my story for nuthin'?'" My mother was laughing. She had an outrageous laugh, and it embarrassed her terribly. It was hard to get her to laugh, and then, when you did, it was hard to get her to stop. I loved her laugh.

"Anyway, Mendel had some Christmas trees," Mother said. He hung them upside down from the ceiling to save floor space, apparently, and to keep the customers from rubbing the needles off, admiring them. They were hard to get, and Mendel had only half a dozen or so. And, they were expensive. "But Ginny was determined to have one," Mother said.

The morning of the feast, Ginny visited Mendel's wearing a huge tweed coat. "It was that tent style," my mother said, "with a wide swing to the hem. It had those enormous, wide sleeves."

While my father watched, on crutches, my mother distracted Mendel, and Ginny Farley stuffed the coat with groceries, including a raw egg tucked under her right armpit. She held her arm close to her side to protect the egg.

"And, we want a tree," Ginny said as Mendel totaled the order.

"'Vell, Missus, I have many nice trees,'" my mother said.

"That one." Ginny Farley lifted her right arm to point.

"She'd forgotten, you see, and the egg . . ." released, rolled down the inside of her coat, and splattered at her feet in the pine-scented sweeping compound on Mendel's wooden floor.

"Well, there was raw egg all over the place," my mother said, and she was laughing. "Your father remembers this, too. He . . ."

She stopped.

"It's okay."

"I mean, he always *remembered* it," she said. "He liked to tell this story." She lifted her head, a deliberate gesture. "I'm not going to cry," she said.

"I know you're not."

"I could, though," she said.

"So, what happened?"

"You know, I can't remember. Isn't that funny?"

I smiled at her.

"Your father called Ginny Farley the Queen of Sheba," she said. "He paid for the groceries, of course. He was so embarrassed. Your father said he'd never met anyone, much less any woman, like Ginny Farley." She paused. "He always said that somebody should put her in her place."

I cut a yard of paper and wrapped a book I'd bought for Bill. "What happened to her?" I said.

"Oh, she got married." Mother smiled again. "That's all any of us could think to do back then."

"That put her in her place," I said.

"I suppose it did."

Ginny Farley married an army buddy of my father's named Arthur Hewitt, and they had a baby, "a little too quickly," my mother said. "That's when your father decided that *we* should have children."

I glanced at her.

"I mean, he *wanted* children."

My mother was still lean, almost scrawny. Her arms suggested a strength she had never used. Her hair was not so much gray as tarnished seeming; her skin was faded to ivory, and deep copper freckles dotted her hands.

"Are you sorry you never got to teach?"

"Oh, I don't know. *Sorry* isn't the word."

Art was a great kidder, my mother said. "We used to play canasta every Saturday night, and Art Hewitt kept us all in stitches."

Hewitt had a temper. "I think sometimes Ginny just pushed him too far," Mother said. "She was so . . . restless."

Often the Hewitts seemed silent and cautious with one another, my mother said, as though something had just happened or was about to happen between them.

"Everything changed after the war," she said. "The men were so determined to succeed."

My mother had finished her wrapping. A neat stack of boxes sat before her. "I always think of Ginny," she said, "this time of year. I always wonder where she is, if she is . . ."

"Why don't you write to her?" I said.

"I wouldn't know where to send it."

She put down the scissors. "You know, a good friend, a girl-friend, . . . I thought I could do anything in the world when I was living with Ginny Farley."

"Why did she marry him?" I said.

"I don't know."

"I mean she chose him, and he had this temper."

"We don't always choose," my mother said. She was holding a yard of crimson ribbon that flowed over her pale, freckled hands. "We were lonely, I suppose. And there was the war. And that made everything different, of course, the war."

The war never ended for Arthur Hewitt. One day Ginny arrived at my parents' door with blood dripping from her nose and fingertip bruises darkening on her arm. Her left eye was swollen shut. She had a pathetic little suitcase with her, which contained, my mother said, nothing but lingerie and cosmetics.

What happened to restless women? "What happened to her?"

"She drifted away. She wasn't the marrying kind," my mother said. "I think she went out to California to live. Arthur Hewitt divorced her, of course." My mother looked away. "I mean, he had to."

XXIII

By late March Mother was ready to come home. I stopped by the hospital one last time to pack her things. Ray called and volunteered to drive us, but, as it turned out, it was Bill who took us home.

"Ray had a little accident."

"Who?"

"Ray. Your son, the man in the plaid shirt who visits you some-times."

She seemed to know who I meant.

"He's very sad," she said.

"Well, he's more sad now," I said. "He had a little fender bender."

"What's that?"

"A car wreck, an accident. So he won't be driving you home."

"I was wrong about him."

"How so?"

"What?"

"How were you wrong about him?"

She stared at me, puzzled.

"Never mind," I said.

Ray called the room about half an hour later.

"I want to be there when Mom goes home," he said. "I wanted to drive her, but the doctor says no."

"Courtney's been trying to get you," I said. "She even called Bill. What happened?"

"We got into it a little bit."

"She says you beat her up. What happened?"

"I rolled up a newspaper and bopped her on the nose."

"Okay, don't tell me."

"I won't."

I hung up and sat on the bed. Mother was sitting in the armchair, dressed and ready to go, her powder blue overnight case at her feet.

"Your father went out and bought a bassinet," she said.

"What?"

"When you were born. The most elaborate thing you ever saw. White wicker. And it had a pink gingham lining with little ribbons on the side. It was so expensive. And I said, 'Ray, we can't afford a thing like that.' And, of course, we had a baby bed, still perfectly good, that the boy had used. But he said, no, he wanted the best for you."

"When was that?"

"When you were born."

"No, I mean, where, where is it?"

"What, Dear?"

"The bassinet. The wicker bassinet that Daddy bought."

She was confused. "What bassinet?"

Bill arrived and Ray came in just behind him, wearing a comic white bandage around his head. "Is that Arthur?" Mother said.

"No, this is Ray."

She shook her head. "I thought it was Ginny's husband."

Ray had been drunk enough the night before to plow his Monte Carlo into a stop sign and had spent most of the night in the emergency room, having his skull X-rayed and fifteen stitches put into his forehead.

"What in the world happened to you?" she said.

"Had a little dispute with the old immovable object," Ray said. "I *am* the irresistible force, you know."

This completely baffled her.

"Ray had a little accident," Bill said. "He's fine now."

Mother's brow knotted in concern.

"He's fine," Bill said. "Really."

Had she been herself, the Ruth Louise Carlson Gerhardt who was the mother of Ray's and my childhood, she would have scolded Ray, attempting to impress upon him a sense of the world's dangers and the need for constant vigilance. But now, instead, she said simply, "Will you help me?"

Bill took one arm; Ray took the other, and together they lifted her gently to her feet. As her eyes came level with mine, she smiled. Happy in the arms of two solicitous men and obviously the center of attention, she recaptured some of that old regal bearing she used to have, and as though I were a casual acquaintance, she said, "Why, Maggie, you're here, too."

XXIV

"What ever happened to that young woman," Mother said to Ray as we walked to the car. "Chutney." Bill laughed out loud. "She was having a baby," Mother said.

Ray tried to dodge her. "What woman?" he said. "I don't remember."

"You remember that girl," she said. "And she was pregnant."

"Oh, *that* girl," Ray said. "Change of plans."

Bill and I said nothing.

"You mean she's not having a baby?" Mother said.

"Not any more."

"She was mistaken then."

"Something like that."

We drove home through the raw, watery green of early spring with no one talking and pulled up in front of our building. Barbara Stanwyck was peering down from a window.

Bill named Stanwyck for her relentless, sultry stare and the way she had of flipping her tail when she was angry. "I always think that's such a funny name for a cat," my mother used to say. "Imagine a cat with two names." But when I introduced them again, after Mother's stroke, she said simply, "What a beautiful name."

My brother was one of Stanwyck's favorites, and we had no more than settled in around the dining room table when she sailed gracefully into his lap, curled twice, and sat, facing him, staring into his eyes.

"Why, Stanwyck," Bill said, "you're here, too."

Stanwyck leaned into Ray's chest, purring. "Puss, puss, puss," Ray crooned. He scratched her ears until her eyes dropped shut.

The cat remained in Ray's lap all through lunch, during which Ray drank three beers, pulling them off a six-pack resting on the floor by his chair. He poured them down one after another, barely touching his sandwich, and asked for the phone. "Can't disturb my partner here," he said.

I dragged the phone over to Ray's chair, and we all sat suspended, listening.

"Not home," Ray said, hanging up.

"Who is he calling?" Mother asked.

"I knew she wouldn't be." Ray opened another beer.

"That really isn't smart," Bill said, "on top of medication."

"I done her wrong."

Bill marshaled all his medical evidence: liver damage, brain damage, chemical interactions. Ray didn't bother to listen.

"You look like something out of an old Errol Flynn movie," I said. Ray smiled and adjusted his bandage at a more rakish angle.

"We're both wounded in the head," Mother said.

The room grew silent. She smiled, flustered. "It's just a joke."

"Anybody want dessert? Ice cream?"

Bill shook his head. Ray wasn't listening.

"I don't think so, Honey," my mother said. "I had so much ice cream in the hospital. It's all they ever served. That and Jell-O."

Stanwyck woke and stretched, and I could see by her eyes that she was looking for trouble. A moment later she found the medal pinned to Ray's shirt pocket and gave it a few exploratory taps with her paw. Finally she hooked it and began to tug.

"Hey, hey," Ray said. He disengaged her claws and settled her back on his lap.

"Ever tell you how I got this?" Ray said.

"Uh, oh, war stories."

Ray got that mocking twinkle in his eye. "I was all alone in a dingy bar in Saigon. Just me and my trusty rifle, which had not been fired in many days."

"Poor baby," I said.

"A lonely soldier far from home." He stopped.

"Is this that Arab war?" Mother said.

"Go on," Bill said. "This sounds like the best one yet."

Ray looked away.

"What happened?" I said. "We're all dying to know."

Ray glanced at Mom. "It's real stupid," he said.

There was silence. Stanwyck had lost interest and curled herself in Ray's lap to sleep.

"I'll tell you if you really want me to."

More silence. Bill cleared his throat, toyed with his coffee cup. My mother and Ray stared into each other's eyes.

"Tell it," my mother said suddenly. "Tell it, . . . Raymond."

Ray smiled. "Well, good morning," he said. She smiled back.

"Do you know who this is?" I said.

"Ray's son."

"That's right. Raymond Gerhardt, Junior," Ray said.

He looked at me, and his eyes were wide open and incredibly round, glistening, with the white and amber brown contrasted sharply. It seemed as though I could see straight into him.

Bill settled back in his chair. "Tell it," he said quietly.

"Tell it," I said.

Ray leaned forward and crossed his arms on the table. "I was the only guy in my squad that wasn't wounded. Did I ever tell you that?"

"I don't know," Mother said.

"It's the truth. Guys were getting zapped in front of me, in back of me. I never got a scratch on me. Cut my hand one time on a casing, that's it. Twelve months and just that one lousy cut. I didn't even bandage it," he said.

"You were . . ." My mother stopped. She motioned to me, her hands churning, as though she were trying to pull the right word out of me.

"Lucky," I said. She nodded.

"Then I come back home and I'm fucking accident prone," he said. "Runnin' into stop signs. How dumb can you get."

"Maybe somebody wants you to stop," I said.

Mother sipped her coffee. "You were going to tell us," she said. "About that." She pointed to Ray's star.

"Oh, yeah." He shifted his weight. "Well, see, there was this guy in our squad we called the Boss," Ray said. "God, he was a mountain, great big guy."

"The Boss," she said.

"Nothing bothered Boss, he was so god-damned big. The rest of us are dyin' under our packs, and old Boss is dancin' up the trail."

"I think you wrote me about him," my mother said.

"From Georgia."

"That's right. Merritsville, Georgia," she said. "I even remember the name, now isn't that funny? I can hardly remember my own name." She laughed.

"This little bitty town, and they lost about eight or nine guys from there," Ray said.

I lifted the coffee pot, but Bill and Mother both shook their heads.

"I'm good," Ray said.

I poured a little into my own cup.

"So, this one day, we're headed for the LZ," Ray said, "where there isn't supposed to be any gooks, except the thing is, of course, that there are gooks, hundreds of 'em, seemed like, and we get to this little clearing, and just as we get there all hell breaks loose. And we're firing away, and we don't know where the hell they are exactly.

"Anyway, me and the Boss had this signal."

Ray stopped, confused. "Wait a minute. Something before . . ."

"Go back," I said.

"Oh, yeah. The day before." He took a deep breath. "We're on patrol, and Valdez gets hit from behind—snipers, right? So we bunch up—stupid thing to do—and we wait, and we're waiting, and this mortar round comes in and takes out half our guys, we got three or four KIA I can see right away.

"And we call in, right, and we wait. And guys are dyin' and we're waitin' and waitin' and the choppers can't get in. And it's like seven hours before they take us out, and by that time, two more guys are dead."

"You were pinned down," my mother said, interpreting. We looked at her in surprise.

"Right."

"You can't be blamed for that."

"What?"

She looked around, confused. "Well, isn't that what he means?"

"Sure," I said.

Now Ray was confused. He had forgotten his story.

"So, what about the medal?" Bill said.

Ray leaned back in his chair. "Oh, yeah. So, this did not sit well with the Boss," he said. "Old Boss did not take shit."

My mother frowned.

"He's pissed off at the war and the gooks and our guys all at once, and he figures next contact he's gonna kick some butt."

Ray stopped. "Where was I?"

"You had a signal," Bill said.

"Oh, yeah. Me and the Boss. We had this signal that if anything happened, anything, I'd drop and roll one way and Boss would drop and roll in the other direction. Or if one of us got ahead of the other one, you know, and something went down, we'd drop and roll, same thing, stay out of the line of fire, and that way . . ."

"You could watch out for one another," Bill said.

Ray flared. "Will you let me fucking tell this?"

There was silence. Bill shifted in his chair. "Sorry," he said.

More silence, oppressive.

"Well, *tell* it," I said.

"He wasn't even fucking there."

"Just say what you have to say."

Ray glared at me and went on with the story, telling it now like a punishment, relentlessly, making us pay for it.

"Except that this time, near the LZ, Boss is way out in front. Looking for gooks, way, way out ahead. It's too far, and I can't cover him, and this time when he drops, he rolls right into a god-damned ambush and they open up, and it's like in slow motion, you know, I can see the flash from the AKs."

The story was turning on him. "I can almost see the god-damned rounds," he said, "going through the air, you know, like Superman, X-ray vision and stuff." He stopped.

"You don't have to tell any more," I said.

"The Boss is hit, and I'm yelling, 'corpsman, corpsman,' and I turn the old Boss over and his chest is just like lace, and blood is bubbling out about a million holes and I'm trying to stop the blood with my hands, cover the wounds, but my hands are too damned small, and I can't control it."

He started to cry, silently, and turned to my mother. Huge tears were rolling down his face. He wiped them on his shirtsleeve and went on.

"And then this corpsman comes up, and he just looks, real fast, and he doesn't even kneel down, Mom. He doesn't even kneel down to get a good look."

"Ray, . . ."

"So I grab my .16 and I'm just blasting, you know, Mom? I'm kinda crazy, just blasting away." His voice died. "And I guess I got a few," he said.

"Ray, . . ."

"Let him tell it through," my mother said.

Ray looked at her; their eyes locked. She nodded so slightly I could barely detect it, and Ray waded in again.

"So there's a big body count, right? And this colonel—Phillips or Fillmore or something—comes around and he's talking up what happened, and he doesn't even know what the fuck he's talking about."

"Ray, . . ."

"Oh, Christ," Ray said. "And then this guy—the man's a full colonel. You know what he does?"

Bill shook his head.

"He takes a watch off this dead Viet Cong."

"What?"

"Strips the body, man, I ain't shittin' you."

"Unbelievable," Bill said.

"And then the captain says to me that they're putting me in for a star. For valor, he says, that's a joke. I'm in there winning watches for this asshole."

He stopped. The room grew so quiet we could hear the minute hand drag itself up the face of the kitchen clock; we could hear Barbara Stanwyck, with her eyes squeezed shut, purring in Ray's lap.

"Everyone who went there was brave," Bill said. "I know that's a laugh," he said, "coming from me."

Ray said nothing, just fingered the star pinned to his shirt and stared out the dining room window. Finally he tipped the medal up and read the inscription, as though he'd never seen the thing before.

"So, two months later, my star comes through," he said. "That's how I got it. For extreme valor." He removed the medal from his shirt and flipped it into the center of the table.

XXV

April again, the cruelest month, the month when my father died. The morning was hazy; thin sunlight filtered through a blanket of clouds, and the grass was pale along the parking strip in front of our building. Ray's Monte Carlo sat at the curb, packed with Mother's luggage. The powder blue Samsonite contrasted sharply with the rusted-out, surly look of Ray's car, the red cellophane taped over the broken-out tail light, the new crease in the grill, the black and white bumper sticker that read, "POW/MIA: You Are Not Forgotten."

The car bulged with boxes and bundles, each one labeled—so like my mother—with a list of contents. A hanging rod stretched over the back seat, crowded with neatly pressed blouses and slacks, and the only sign of Ray's presence was the little aromatic cardboard skunk that hung from the rearview mirror and a small duffel bag on the back seat.

Mother had left the apple box of papers at the house, and I had promised to retrieve it, store it in the wire cage in the basement of our building.

"There's just not an inch of space left in the car," she told me.

This was not true. There was a spot on the floor behind the driver's seat that would have nicely accommodated the box, but Mother said, "No. You keep it. For now."

Someday, perhaps, we would sort through it all, the way we used to sort through her satin-lined jewelry box on rainy days, heaping our arms with bangles, looping our necks with pearls. My mother had a brooch with a big blue stone the color of sea water, and I used to stare into it until I fell through the silver mounting, the complex ring of facets, and felt myself free-floating, enveloped in blue. My mother said I would make myself dizzy, staring so intently.

Seated on the bed, perhaps, in her condo down in Florida, we would sort through the letters and photographs, gingerly touch the bruises of memory and discover that they were fading, and that we were rich in treasures lost and found again, that all along we had the love we pined for.

"You'll check on the house," my mother said. I told her I would.

"The Realtor has the . . ." Her hands churned. "That little gold thing."

"The key."

"The key." She smiled shyly, turned her head away.

"It's okay," I said.

"I *am* going to beat this," she said. "Estelle's going to help me."

I put my arms around her, and Bill put his arms around both of us. Finally Ray joined in, and we stood in the raw spring sunlight, a cluster of people, sticking and stuck together, a raveled love knot of contradictions, unresolved.

Then we broke apart.

"You'll check," she said.

"Yes, yes."

"Pick up that box. And go through it," she said. "Carefully. I don't want anything left behind."

"Don't worry."

"Well, then," she said, "that's everything."

She gave me a twisted smile. Things are confused, rushed, it seemed to say, I can't help it. She hugged me again, throwing herself off balance; she hugged Bill. For a minute she seemed about to say something, something that should have been said. Her hand fluttered around her mouth in confusion, and I caught the glint of her diamond in its worn old-fashioned mounting.

"I'll phone you when we get to Estelle's," she said. She stepped back, an act of finality, and hid herself by fussing through her handbag.

Ray, too, gave me an awkward hug. He was wearing a bright yellow T-shirt with a cartoon of a wild-eyed carpenter on the front. The little guy was waving an oversized hammer and a saw, and underneath the shirt read:

It Takes
STUDS
To Build Houses

"Love your shirt."

"Present from my daughter," he said.

"No kidding. You called her."

He nodded. "Belated birthday present."

"Your birthday's in September."

"She don't know."

"So," I said, "you're giving away the bride."

Ray shrugged. "They're rentin' me a suit. Regular soup and fish. Can you see me in somethin' like that?"

"Sure."

"I figure to wear it without no underwear. Get their money's worth for 'em." He smiled.

"I'm glad you told us," I said.

"What's that?"

"The Vietnam stuff."

He opened the car door, climbed in behind the wheel. "I don't know where you're comin' from," he said.

"Your Vietnam story." I whispered. "I think it cleared up a lot of things for Mom."

"Oh, goody." He slammed the car door.

He lit a cigarette, threw the match at my feet. "You know what they say about Vietnam?" Mother raised her head.

"Keep your voice down."

Bill opened the car door on the passenger side for my mother, but she refused to get in the car until Ray had buckled his seat belt. They had a running argument about this. Ray said if they hadn't gotten him by this time, they weren't going to get him now. But after a few moments of willfulness, he buckled up. She got in, leaning her cane precisely on the seat beside her, and gave us the synthetic mother's smile that I had known since childhood, her official seal of approval.

"Well," Ray told her, "I'm driving you home after all."

She looked at him and smiled again, her real smile, and almost gave us her old-time outrageous laugh. She stopped herself, self-conscious, but it was enough. Bill leaned through the window to kiss her goodbye.

"What is it with you?" I whispered to Ray.

"You want it easy," he said.

"I thought . . ."

"Uh huh." He smiled to himself, smug, rolled his eyes toward me. "My best yet."

He turned the key in the ignition. The car cranked up and died. He tried it again, and that time it caught.

"So it's not true," I said.

"Some of it's true."

"Which part?"

He pulled his cap down low to shield his eyes. "Never look a gift horse in the mouth."

"Neither a lender nor a borrower be," I said. "A stitch in time saves nine."

"Now you got it."

Bill came around to the driver's-side window and shook Ray's hand.

"Don't do anything I wouldn't do," Ray said.

"That's an old one."

"Hey, I'm an old guy."

The car pulled away from the curb, choking a little, sputtering. Ray pumped it and it caught solidly and began to hum. They drove to the end of the block and disappeared around the corner.

"I wouldn't drive that car to the grocery store," Bill said, "let alone Florida."

"They'll make it," I said.

XXVI

A warm breeze played through the budding trees and nudged the grass, so soft and teasing it seemed almost alive. It was the wrong day, perhaps, to go back to the house, but we had promised to pick up the apple box and give the place a final going-over before the Realtor began to show it.

We let ourselves in with my mother's key and prowled through the empty rooms. Our footsteps whispered up the stairs, down the narrow hallway to my old room, painted now a discreet pastel somewhere between blue and green, a color so pale and noncommittal it was hardly worth noting.

"There used to be a really gaudy wallpaper in this room," I said.

"Yeah?'

"Roses. Little girl pink. Endless rows of them. God, I hated that paper."

"Who picked it out?" he said.

I talked about my father, his expectations, how I never felt I measured up.

"Maybe you're reading too much into it," Bill said. "You do tend to do that."

I shrugged.

"Maybe he just thought it was pretty. Maybe it was just wallpaper."

❧

In the kitchen, we gave the faucets an extra final turn. The cupboards were all lined with fresh paper. Ray insisted on doing that while Mother was in the hospital. He spent the better part of an afternoon cutting shelf paper, lining even the linen and silverware drawers.

The apple box was where my mother had left it, just to the right of the sink. *Pick up that box. And go through it.*

"I don't want this stuff," I said.

"What?"

"Let's just toss it."

"I don't believe you," Bill said.

"Why?"

"This is the family jewel box, the archives. You've been dancing around this stuff for months."

"I changed my mind."

He looked at me. "Just dump it?"

"Yes."

"No." He shook his head. "No, this is your mother's stuff. We need to look through it, at least, to see what's here."

"I know what's here."

Nevertheless, we opened the box—Bill insisted—and sat cross-legged on the floor to sort through it. Photographs, letters, mostly from Dad. Most addressed to my mother, but some to me.

Bud sent me a few letters. Everyone always imagined we'd get together some day. It seemed natural, my brother's best friend, the boy next door.

Dear Folks, he wrote. *Made contact with beaucoup gooks today, my first real firefight. What a trip.*

"He was really in his element," Bill said.

"See what you missed?"

"I did," he said.

"Bull."

Bill lifted Ray's American flag out of the box and held it in his lap. "It's an identity," he said. "A fraternity. The guys who went. They were part of something, still are."

He ran his right hand over the field of stars, picked at a flaw in the stitching. "I don't have that," he said. "I'm just me. It's like I don't have any past."

The flag was still folded in a tight wedge, the way Ray folded it on the day that Mother brought it down to him. He and Chris were divorced. Ray had come home again. This was the late seventies; my father was still alive. Ray took the sleeping porch at the end of the upstairs hall, the room where Grandma died.

The porch was sparsely furnished; just a day bed and a card table covered with an old, flower-print cloth, a calendar on the wall, a spindly rubber tree plant that Mother was nursing along. Ray moved in his stereo and his tapes and very little else. Instead of curtains, which he said were not necessary, he hung an American flag over the east windows to block out the morning light.

This, in its seeming disrespect, enraged Harry Leech next door, who complained to Dad.

"Here we are, three vets," Ray said, meaning himself, and Leech, who had fought in the Philippines, and my father, "fighting over the flag. That's weird to me."

Leech turned to my father, towering over him. Leech was a big man, well-muscled, even then—he must have been in his sixties. He had his fists up. "I want that down," he said. I think my father believed he would really hit him.

Then Leech's anger fell apart; he dropped his hands, and he was just an old man, hurting. "For Christ's sake, Ray," he said.

"I fought for that flag," Ray said. "Just like you, and Bud."

Leech pulled out a handkerchief and blew his nose. He was crying. Fat tears ran down his face and dripped off his big, red nose. I don't think it ever occurred to any of us that, despite everything, all the drunken fighting, he loved Bud. Something that simple, and we missed it. Then Leech turned around and walked back into his own yard and never spoke to any of us again.

The flag stayed up for a day or two, and then my mother removed it and carried it downstairs in her outstretched arms, the way she might have carried a delicate ball gown. She brought it to Ray, who was watching television with me and Bill in the living room. "Fold this," she said. "I don't know how to fold it."

The papers were there. I knew they would be. The paid-up receipts Estelle told me about.

"Mom knows," I said.

Bill shrugged. "Yes and no."

"Now she's telling us."

His whole life was there: his discharge papers, his Social Security card, his union card. His life insurance policy with the name and home phone number of his agent neatly penciled in the top right-hand corner.

"An orderly man," Bill said. This made me smile.

I shuffled through the photographs until I found one I wanted: my father in his gracefully sloping hat.

"This is it," I said.

I studied it, as though some secret communication might seep into my fingertips from the photo, travel through my blood, and nestle in my brain, some final stamp of approval.

"He was really young then," Bill said, "younger than we ever were."

There were other pictures of my father, a dozen or so, including a later one—'93?, '94?—in which he stands, frozen, old, holding open the door of the rusty bronze Bonneville, in which he died.

"And who have we here?" Bill said. "It is herself."

He held up a picture, very familiar: me, age five or six, in a short

plaid dress, the black patent leather Mary Jane shoes I begged my
mother to buy, my hair long, the color of new pennies, not the dingy
amber it was now. Me, new, whole, before everything, sitting on my
father's lap and smiling unafraid into the camera.

"Pretty cute," Bill said.

"I was never cute."

"You lie," he said. "You were adorable. Look at your father's expression. He worships you."

I looked. I saw it. Something in the eyes. The way he had his hand
cupped under mine, as though, when the camera were through with
us, we would begin to dance.

"Why . . ."

"Why is a word from which we make fiction. What you have here
is just history," Bill said.

He handed over the picture, and in the background I noticed my
mother, smiling. She was leaning into the frame, and her hands were
outstretched, as if to protect the delicate balance, me on my father's
knee. Her image was faint, but unmistakable. She was there all along. I
never noticed her.

Dad's letters were yellow with age and had, some of them, a lacelike quality. Army censors scanned the mail before it was sent home,
my mother told me, cutting out single words or lines or sometimes
whole blocks of information. The pages unfolded like the fragile wings
of butterflies, like my mother's Christmas snowflakes, and as gently as
I handled them, I knew that every reading would hasten their eventu-
al disintegration.

My dearest Ruth, I read. *I am writing this from the back of a truck. Seems
like all we do over here is wait. Or march. Some war hero I am. I am not even
sure where we are. It has been raining for three days now with no let-up in
sight, and we have not had any hot food.*

My mother had carefully arranged the letters by date and bundled
them, tying them up with red, white, and blue ribbon, the crinkly paper kind that can be curled with a knife edge, and she had, in fact,
curled the ribbon.

"They're almost gift-wrapped," Bill said.

Each letter was filed in the packet in sequence—my mother's rage for order—and she had noted on the backs of some of the envelopes what she was doing at home when the letter arrived and how the weather was: *cloudy, washing whites, mail came early.*

I read them at random: the weather, the food, some joke a buddy told him. *The socks you sent for my birthday were just the ticket. All the other guys . . .*

"What are you looking for?"

Dear Ruth, Nothing much to report. Harris, the guy I wrote you about, took sick—not very bad—anyway, he was sent back. He was the joker of the bunch, and we all miss him.

"They're just old letters," Bill said.

Weather is still cold. My sergeant says . . .

There was nothing, no trace of him. Certain phrases jumped out at me as typical, but for the most part, the voice in the letters could have been anyone's.

"Maybe you shouldn't read any more," Bill said.

He tried to take the letter from my hand, but I pulled back, reluctant to let it go. He scooped up the others and dropped them into a big tan envelope. "When your mother gets settled in Florida, we'll send these on to her," he said. "They're her letters."

I sat on the floor, staring down the long tunnel of our house, a view unobstructed from where we sat, our backs to the garage. We could see all the way to the front door, which stood open.

I was still holding the letter. "Maggie, let go." Bill took it from me, stuffed it into the tan envelope and sealed it.

"I guess I always felt I cheated him."

A whisper of air floated through the open door and stirred the shades, half drawn, at the living room windows; and it was almost as though I could hear the wind like a flame, fluttering at the base of the staircase, uncertain, then twining around the banister, spiraling up.

"Listen," I said.

After the fire on Montrose Street where Peggy Tanner died, my father became obsessed with the image of fire. Perhaps as he sat at the kitchen table, the rest of the family asleep, he heard a sudden spark ig-

nite in the walls. Perhaps he imagined Ray, like Crazy Nordell, lighting candles or smoking in his room, stubbing out the butts on the windowsill. Ray and I received lectures on playing with fire. Even my
mother was cautioned about the stove. The number of the fire department was taped to the telephone, and there were even fire drills, in
which the four of us practiced marching calmly out of the house.

"Or, he cheated me."

"Let go of it."

I closed the box, folding the flaps in. "Know what my mother used
to say? 'Whatever doesn't kill us makes us strong.' "

"Well, they haven't killed us yet," Bill said. "Though they have
tried."

I smiled and discovered that I had been crying.

"You really got the blubbers today, Kid."

"I'm stopping," I said. I wiped my tears on his shoulder.

I leaned against my husband and he held me, held me and the house
faded away. Not just the color and scent went out of it, but the life itself, the pulse. The wind retreated. The blinds ceased to stir and fell
back in place. The rooms shed their unique associations, and the house
reassumed the neutrality it had when my father found it. It grew quiet
and was just a house again.

Epilogue

Courtney called yesterday, asking for Ray. I told her the truth: I
don't know where he is. Ray disappears in summer, drifts west. He
picks up odd jobs on construction crews, works as a laborer, lays sod.
His route seems almost inborn, like the patterns of migrating birds:
Nebraska, Wyoming, Idaho. Stomping out forest fires in northern
Montana, driving a truck down the California coast. He never calls—
brothers don't call their sisters—he seldom writes, usually only postcards and not many of those. He fades from our lives, and we almost
forget about him for a while. But when the year begins to wane, he
comes home. Something in the air, too subtle to analyze, alerts me. I
look up from my life and he is there.

Ray knows only one poem: a John Crowe Ransom ballad about a

knight called "Captain Carpenter," which Bill taught him and which he sometimes recites, drunk, swaying to the meter like our mother used to do. Poor Captain Carpenter. Rogues and villains of all stripes have hacked away his arms and legs, piece by piece reduced him until at last only his heart is left, and a tongue to taunt his enemies. It's an odd poem, bittersweet, and Captain Carpenter, the veteran of many battles, is an ironic knight. "The only good man left in a decadent world," according to Bill.

The last real letter I got from Ray was written on motel stationery, mailed from some place in Texas. It was a long, rambling account of some magazine piece he had read, something about "generations" and pendular swings and recurring patterns. "This guy's got it all figured out," he wrote. "But the thing I still don't know is, was it me?"

There are only two facts, birth and death, Bill says, "and in between some necessary fictions." In the last analysis, our story exists in the tales we do not tell.

Mother says Ray changed right after Dad's "accident."

"Don't you think so?" she asked me. This was a few weeks back. She calls me every Sunday now from Florida.

"You mean when Dad *accidentally* ran his car off the bridge?"

There was a pause. "Yes," she said uncertainly.

At first I didn't know what to say.

"Maggie?"

Bill was sitting next to me on the sofa, reading a novel, with Stanwyck curled in his lap. The silence lasted so long that it penetrated and he glanced up. We looked at each other, two aging students of literature, and smiled.

"Yes," I said. "Yes, the accident changed him. I mean, it was so unexpected. Well, you know what a wonderful driver Dad was."

Warmth flooded back into Mother's voice. "Well, we just can't worry about him, can we?" she said. "I'm sure that Ray will find his way."

I said nothing.

"Is Bill all right?"

I hesitated. Ray would not find his way. Or, on second thought, perhaps, he had. It was possible, after all, that my brother was wiser than

I. He had made the compromise with defeat that Dad never could, and maybe he was okay, as much as he could be, settled into a story he couldn't tell. Maybe I'd been wrong.

"Maggie?"

"I'll let you talk to him."

I handed the phone to Bill and relaxed against the rhythms of his voice.

"Mom? Hi, how's Florida? Oh? No, nothing special."

He fell silent. She had launched into one of her stories, I guessed. Next to me, Bill was her favorite listener. I could hear the rise and fall of her voice, laughter. Now and then he would make some comment to keep her going.

"Uh huh."

"Oh?"

"Really?"

Almost Home

Chris is propped up in bed, and I am trying to line her eyes in a frosted turquoise color that only brings out the red in them and gives her face a pinched, unhappy expression.

She studies her face in the mirror I hold for her. "Not helping much, is it?" she says.

"I smudged it," I say. "I never was very good at this makeup thing."

It's been more than four months since she called me: *Hi, Merry Christmas. I have cancer.* All of her lovers were jumping out of hotel windows, she told me. *Chicago mourns.* The biopsy was positive. Still she delayed it. Sought a second opinion and a third. *The near north side is devastated.* "Couldn't face it," she told me. "You know me."

She wears a loose, white hospital gown that conceals most of the bandages. It is so large that it billows away from her body and makes her seem like a severed head, floating on a cloud of pure white cotton.

"I'm glad you came, Maggie," she says. "I know it's expensive to fly."

"No problem," I say. Of course, it is.

Chris has her own business, House of Fashion. Since she divorced my brother she's done well for herself. "I'm a late bloomer," she likes to say.

Christine Leech Gerhardt Davis, the little blue-collar girl from Iowa. In high school it was Chris who taught me how to make a mock apple pie out of margarine and Ritz crackers, how to mend sheets on the Singer by stitching back and forth across a worn spot, how to make the dresses we saw in the windows of the J. C. Penny store downtown. Her mom died young; Chris ran the house for her dad, raised herself and her brother, Bud, on nothing. Ray had a hard time talking her into marriage.

"Bethie can't handle things like this," Chris says. Beth is their daughter, my brother's only child. "Besides, why should she? She's young. She's getting married. She got a promotion, did I tell you?"

I nod.

"Ray says Beth gets her ambition from him," I tell Chris. "You've noticed, of course, how many business tycoons there are on our side of the family."

She smiles, motions for water. I bring the glass and hold the straw to her mouth.

"You're not going to ask about him, are you?" I say.

"Nope."

"He's better, " I say. "Not drinking so much, just off and on."

My brother has a "substance abuse" problem. A common drunk, my mother once called him. My husband, Bill, agreed. "Not that that isn't a viable option," he added.

"He tried to call me two weeks ago," Chris says. "He's still on my machine, in fact. I guess I just don't have the heart to erase him."

"Do you want to?"

"No."

The nurse comes in, flutters around the room. She is young and seems unduly impressed with her own efficiency.

"How are we today?" she says.

"Not worth a shit."

The nurse doesn't bat an eye, doesn't seem to hear. She fills the water carafe and plumps the pillows; she reads the chart and fiddles with the blinds, then leaves the room, completely professional.

"Unconscious," I say.

"Lucky her."

Chris closes her eyes.

"Want me to go?"

She shakes her head.

"Want the TV?"

"Not unless the Chippendales are on Jenny Jones."

I say nothing.

"Course, what good is lust going to do me now?" She starts to cry.

I try to hold her and realize that I can't; she's in too much pain. I take her hand instead, then let go. It doesn't seem like the right gesture between us.

"Nothing's changed," I say. "You're the same person."

"You don't believe that."

We sit in silence, me perched on the side of the bed and Chris propped up on three fat pillows.

"When I was a kid in Missouri," she says, "we rented a farm. This old run-down place, and my dad—he tried, I guess, said he did anyway, but he was no farmer. And Mom was sick, and he had Bud and me to worry about. In the afternoons sometimes my mother and I would walk out into the pasture, looking for dandelion greens. She looked for herbs, too. She knew how to use them.

"Anyway. She used to hold the hem of her dress out like this." Chris lifts the hem of the bedsheet a little to form a shallow basket. "And I'd run back and forth to her with greens—you know, she'd cook them. We lived on them, practically. Ever have dandelion greens?"

I shake my head.

"You're lucky. They're for shit. Anyway. When her skirt was full of greens, I'd start picking wild flowers. There were these little purple ones that grew along the fence—I don't know what they were called—and yellow black-eyed Susans, real tall ones." She makes a weak fist, holding a phantom bouquet. "I can still smell them sometimes.

"And when I'd bring them to her she would wrap her arms around my shoulders and hold me, hold me against her breasts."

She says nothing for a while.

"I don't know why I told you that," she says.

There's an old woman in the next bed—terminal, Chris says. She wears her dingy white hair in two long braids and keeps her pink and white teeth in a glass of water on the nightstand beside her bed. She has been sleeping, but now she stirs; her frail arms motion away some danger or distraction.

"Want anything?" I ask Chris.

"Yeah, I want my tit back," she says.

❀

I was the only one waiting for Chris through the surgery; I was there the whole time—with nothing to read but *People* magazine. I thought about Chris's lovers, conspicuous in their absence, the ones she claimed would be jumping out of windows.

And, of course, I thought some more about Bill.

Things are not going well between us. Nothing dramatic, just a kind of quiet defeat seeping into our marriage. Half my life—more than that—is over.

When I called the apartment back in Des Moines, Bill was reading. I imagined him stretched out on the couch, with Stanwyck, his cat, curled like a cashew beside him.

"Any news?"

"She's still in there," I said.

He didn't want to talk about it. "Got anything to read?"

Bill always has a good paperback tucked in his pocket for just such emergencies. Catastrophic illness, Armageddon—my husband is ready, able to flee the world and return at will.

"Nothing bothers you, does it?" I said to him once.

"Hey, it's the old horse-shit joke," he said. "With so much horse shit around, there just has to be a pony here somewhere."

⁂

"Want to hear a joke?" I ask Chris.

She squints, frowns.

"Pain?"

She nods.

"I'll get somebody."

"No. I can handle it."

She closes her eyes and tips her head back. Her mouth opens, as though she is going to scream, but there is no sound. The room is so silent it almost seems to be moving, beginning to swirl with Chris and me hanging on.

"Harlan!" The old woman in the next bed cries out suddenly and as though in total terror, "Harlan, watch out!"

The room jerks to a stop, and the nurse comes running—"Har-

lan!"—settles the old woman down with something, maybe an injec-
tion; we can't see. The woman must be ninety years old. Her family
rarely visits her, Chris says.

"Close the door," she hollers. "Harlan? Close the door."

The nurse pulls the curtain, sealing off the old woman's bed.

"That's what's waiting," Chris says. "That's the joke."

We hear a low moan, something mumbled, maybe the same name
again, a long-dead love. The nurse emerges from behind the curtain,
still brisk, still efficient. "She'll sleep now," she says triumphantly and
leaves the room.

"Being alone's a bitch," Chris says. "I can feel for that old doll." She
tosses back a loose strand of hair. "It's different when you're young. You
don't even know you're alone, you're just yourself. And anyway there's
always somebody new coming along."

"For you," I say. "You were the pretty one."

She thinks about that; she knows that it is true. That was always her
special blessing, her ace in the hole. She made the most of it, too.

"I was so damn dumb when I was young," she says. "God, it was
great."

"Haven't changed all that much, have we?"

"I still love him." She looks up at me. Tears have dissolved her eye
makeup, and streaks of frosted turquoise slide down her cheeks.

"I know."

"They were always our heroes, weren't they? Ray and Bill."

I smile.

"What?"

"I don't know. Just funny to think of Bill as a hero, I guess."

She settles back into the pillow and closes her eyes loosely for sleep.

"I'm thinking about moving here," I say. "Remember you always
said I should move to Chicago?"

"Without Bill?"

"Just for a while," I say. "You and me. The old dynamic duo, remember that?"

"There isn't much work here," she says. "Course, there isn't much
work anywhere. Everything's part-time."

"It wouldn't be permanent. I mean, I wouldn't plan on it being permanent."

"You got troubles?"

"I don't even know."

"Bill's a good guy," she says.

"I know."

"They aren't that common." She opens her eyes and motions for the mirror. "I got to take this makeup off."

She wipes her eyes with a damp Kleenex. "Ray's a good guy, too," she says. "Just a little messed up. A lot messed up. Hand me a towel."

"I don't know, I just thought we'd be further along by now."

"Along?"

"Bill and me. We'd have a house or kids or something, some kind of permanence. And I'd be happy, you know, the way Mom was, the way women are in all the magazines."

"Harriet Nelson?"

"Everything's so . . . ordinary."

Chris says nothing.

"I keep reading about how privileged we all were, how we had everything. This doesn't feel like everything to me."

"I see it more in Beth," Chris says. "She thinks it's always been like this. I want to take her back to Missouri sometimes and show her that farm. She's seen pictures, but she doesn't really believe it."

"Maybe I'm just getting old," I say. "Mental pause."

She smiles. "Being old sucks."

"You can say that again."

She whispers: "Sucks."

She slathers on cold cream, sweeps it up from the base of her neck in long slow strokes, and dabs it gently around her eyes.

"Once when I was a kid," I say, "we were all going somewhere—my dad was driving the Buick—and I lipped off. I don't even know what I said. And my dad stopped the car and told me to get out. I didn't know where the hell I was."

"You mean he just left you?"

"Drove around the block, I guess. Picked me up. I was still standing right where he dropped me."

"Made his point."

"He sure did."

"My father used to beat the shit out of me," Chris says. "That's how I learned to love men."

She begins to wipe off her makeup, leaving black and turquoise streaks on the towel.

"You always wanted a happy ending," she says. "Expected it, in fact. What did you call it?"

"Resolution," I say.

"That's the difference between us."

"Maybe."

"Absolutely," she says. "When Ray and I broke up? I thought I'd just go back to being myself. You know?"

She puts down the towel and looks at me. "But you don't. They mess up your life, but . . ."

"Why is it always them?"

She shrugs. "They're it."

"Sometimes I really do want to leave," I say, "but then I think, 'What the hell would I do?'"

"What do you want to do?" she says. A perfectly logical question.

A rattling cart goes by outside the open door; a doctor is paged on the intercom. The old woman sighs in her sleep, dreaming of something, someone, maybe, way in the past.

"I do love him," I say.

"Keep telling yourself."

She closes her eyes again and nestles down in her pillows. The pain eases out of her face as she drifts into sleep, and, for a moment, watching, I remember the way we were: Chris in her mini skirt and her go-go boots, bossing us—Ray and Bill and me—into a line and teaching us all that quick hop-step the Temptations used to do, the elegant lifted half-twist of the wrist when they seemed to pluck something magical out of the air.

For once there is no waiting on the runway. We take off with the kind of efficiency airlines show us in television commercials. A sharp white web of highways forms below us, and everything hums along just the way it's supposed to. We spiral up in wide, slow loops and level out, launched into formless blue. The setting sun glows on the edge of the wings, and we fly straight into it, blazed with copper.

"Take care of yourself." That was the last thing she said to me. I held her hand for a moment and then let go.

"I'll call you when I get home," I said.

The plane ascends through ragged layers of clouds until we reach a sort of celestial desert, an endless platform of white. It stretches out underneath an infinite sky, and the light is so intense it burns my eyes and shapes my pale reflection on the window. A ghost face, transparent, stares back at me.

❀

My mother called it "female troubles"—this was a few years back. "Well, after all, dear, you're thirty-eight," she told me. "And you and Bill have decided . . . I mean about children."

"We haven't *decided*."

"Well, whatever."

I cut my hair; I cut my fingernails short. I figured I might as well cut away everything.

Bill put his arms around me and gave me a self-conscious hug. "You're the same person," he said. "Nothing has changed."

"I don't believe that."

"Frankly, I don't see what the fuss is about," my doctor said, stripping off his gloves. "It's perfectly routine."

A hysterectomy was indicated, he said, by the presence of large uterine fibroids. At the time, I believed him. He removed my ovaries, too. Just "to be on the safe side," the surgeon took everything.

"It's not going to change anything," Bill said. "Might even make things better."

"How?"

"I don't know. No more periods. No more wondering: Are we, aren't we? Things settled, finally."

"I like my periods."

"You could always adopt," my mother said.

"That's not the point."

The flow of my blood had persuaded me I was strong. Even child-less—"barren," my mother said—I felt myself in synch with the ancient clockwork of the moon. There was a future, possibilities.

"Think it over," Chris advised me. "Once they start cutting, they don't quit. They'll hack you down to nothing, piece by piece."

She said it again in Chicago, and I agreed. She patted the emptiness where her breast had been. "I told you," she said.

❧

I doze. In a dream, Bill is building a house out of odds and ends, and it keeps collapsing. He scrounges up more material: magazines and tin cans, old inner tubes.

"There's no lumber because of the war," he says.

I understand that. "We'll have to make do," I say.

I wake with a start. We have begun our descent through thick clouds, burrowing deeper down until only the wings are visible through the small, square windows.

"Ladies and gentlemen"—a sterile feminine voice comes out of the air—"the captain has turned on the seatbelt sign."

Clouds rush the windows and swallow us up. The cabin becomes an airless coffin. I hold my breath.

"Are you visiting?"

"What?"

"Are you visiting in Des Moines?"

"No," I say. "No. I'm going home."

The woman sitting next to me is smiling, the polished certain smile of a grade-school teacher; I would have known that confidence anywhere. She is tall, straight, silver-haired, and wears a smart gray suit with a gold pin positioned on the left lapel: a small circle with a single pearl perched on the rim.

"You seem a little nervous." She smiles on. "Would you like a peppermint?"

"Oh, no," I say. "Thank you."

"I'm visiting," she says. "I went to school in Des Moines." She smiles. "It's changed a lot, I imagine."

The pilot cuts back the engines, banks, and I catch my breath, a child-woman, drowning in a cloud. The teacher takes my hand quite suddenly, with authority.

"I don't like it much either," she says, still holding my hand. "Especially the takeoffs."

"It's when the clouds close in."

"And the landings."

She wears a worn gold wedding ring, a watch with a large face and a sweep second hand that glides around the dial like a swift dancer. "I just endure it," she says. "My granddaughter thinks I'm a real baby. Of course, she loves to fly."

We hold hands. The flight attendant notices, but barely cracks a smile.

And the irony is, it is unbelievably smooth, so smooth coming down that my body seems to float out from under me. The landing gear descends and locks in position. We are still smothered in clouds.

"There're the wheels," the woman says brightly, trying to cheer me. I can barely smile.

"Stupid," I say.

"What?"

"Nothing. I was just thinking of something."

What did the Zen Buddhist say to the hot dog vendor? I can see Bill grinning in my mind, the way he leans forward, moving into the punch line.

I give up, I say. I'm expected to.

Make me one with everything, he says.

The plane slips into a soundless glide. The engine whines. The flaps move into position. I look around me, strain to see, but the clouds are still too dense against the windows. I will myself and my stately companion, the airplane itself, to come through.

Mother Earth, Mother Earth, I chant. I do not pray. I know only two prayers by heart, and neither one seems appropriate.

"What did you say?" the woman asks me.

"Nothing."

And then, in an instant, bright light floods the cabin; sunshine falls in my lap, and we are through, in robin's egg blue with a firm horizon, settling down and suddenly moving fast.

"There it is," the woman says, pointing.

Only a few scattered clouds remain below us, casting shadows like giant wings on the land. I know this patchwork of fields and fences like the back of my hand: the bulky white farm houses, the hunched red barns. I have wandered through that stand of pines. It is possible here to be discontent and restless, to feel passed by and provincial; lonely, bored; but it is impossible ever to be lost. Narrow, straight highways order the land, and cows stand stolid in the feedlots up to their knees in rich brown mud.

Des Moines appears below us, a faint pastel checkerboard; we dip down and streak along the runway. *Bill.* The shock of contact, brakes against our speed. "We're down," the woman says. A gentle pulling back.

Everyone breathes again, smiles again, thinks of husbands, children, friends who are waiting.

The woman releases my hand.

"Thank you," I say.

She hands down my raincoat from the overhead compartment. "Any time."

⚜

"Maggie!"

I am one of the first people off the plane, walking a pace or two behind the teacher, who veers away from me and is lost in the crowd. Bill grabs my arm, kisses me.

"Hey, Kid, you look a little green."

He walks me, weaving, past the numbered gates in descending order; at the bar he pulls me quickly inside.

"Scotch," he tells the barman. "A little water."

He settles me in a booth. "You don't look so good."

"I hate flying."

"It's all over now."

The drinks come. They are light amber, marbled with ice, in heavy, octagonal glasses. I have never been so glad to have a drink.

"Bad flight?"

"No, it was really smooth. Perfect," I say.

He stares at me, innocent of my complications.

Bill is compact and well-muscled, not much taller than I am. But where I am—more so every day—thick and clumsy in motion, Bill still has a delicate grace about him, a lightness. In high school he had wanted to be an actor, and sometimes I still catch him posturing in the bathroom mirror, practicing his voice exercises in the shower. "Ha, ha, ha, ha, ha," he chants. "Ho, ho, ho, ho, ho."

He has aged. It is something I don't notice day to day. A melon of fat rides on his belt buckle. His hair, a light chestnut brown, has gone gray at the temples; his mustache is almost white, and his eyes, like mine, have a fan of creases at the corners. There is a certain slackness about him, an ease, a worn comfort in the way he slouches in the booth, his fawn-colored corduroy jacket bunching at the shoulders, cowling the nape of his neck.

He folds and unfolds a matchbook, shifts his glass and the ashtray as though executing intricate chess moves. Likewise, his eyes are restless, the relentless prowl of intellect.

Muzak filters down from an overhead speaker, and Bill points up. "I have a new theory," he says. "In the whole history of music, there are only three actual tunes."

"Tell me."

He counts them off on his fingers: "'Take Me Out to the Ball Game,' 'Greensleeves,' 'Yes, We Have No Bananas.'"

"You're probably right."

"Of course," he says. "There's a limited supply of everything; that's my theory. Just endless variations."

He talks on, the news he has heard, the book he is reading—not very good, he tells me. He tells me why.

I don't really listen. I don't respond. Except to announce to myself that I am home. This is the house I live in, myself and Bill, a house of flesh and bone and memory. A cat, a wall of paperbacks. This is all there is, old wounds and little jokes, imperfect understanding of a less than perfect life, someone at the airport, waiting. Nothing more, but amazingly, almost enough.

I reach across the table and take his hand.

"What?" he says, looking up, surprised.

Previous Winners of the Drue Heinz Literature Prize

The Death of Descartes, David Bosworth, 1981

Dancing for Men, Robley Wilson, 1982

Private Parties, Jonathan Penner, 1983

The Luckiest Man in the World, Randall Silvis, 1984

The Man Who Loved Levittown, W. D. Wetherell, 1985

Under the Wheat, Rick DeMarinis, 1986

In the Music Library, Ellen Hunnicutt, 1987

Moustapha's Eclipse, Reginald McKnight, 1988

Cartographies, Maya Sonenberg, 1989

Limbo River, Rick Hillis, 1990

Have You Seen Me? Elizabeth Graver, 1991

Director of the World and Other Stories, Jane McCafferty, 1992

In the Walled City, Stewart O'Nan, 1993

Departures, Jennifer C Cornell, 1994

Dangerous Men, Geoffrey Becker, 1995

Vaquita and Other Stories, Edith Pearlman, 1996

Fado and Other Stories, Katherine Vaz, 1997

LIBRARY OF CONGRESS CATALOGING-IN-PUBLICATION DATA
Croft, Barbara.
    Necessary fictions / Barbara Croft.
    p.   cm.
    ISBN 0-8229-4078-7 (acid-free paper)
    I. Title.
    PS3553.R5367 N43   1998
    813'.54—ddc21   98-9033
                                               CIP